The F

Amanda James

Also By Amanda James

Another Mother
RIP Current
The Cornish Retribution

Women's Fiction
The Calico Cat

Praise For Amanda James

Amanda's writing flows brilliantly, and the characters and story are highly believable. **MillyMollyMandyDB – Amazon Review**

Not only does Amanda tell a thrilling story, she paints her settings in Cornwall so brilliantly you can picture yourself there, walking the streets of St Ives, looking out across the sparkling ocean, or walking the beach with the sand between your toes. **Sue Curran – Amazon Review**

Well done for keeping the reader just wanting to read more and more. Great plots. Great characters. Just Great! **Katiematie – Amazon Review**

I loved the build up through the story as we crept along to the end at a steady pace that suited the book perfectly. This books has some fascinating characters and I loved the writing style - it is a very good psychological thriller. **Donna Maguire – Goodreads Review**

High praise to Amanda James for her writing skills in character development and sense of place, and chilling edgy read. **Alexina Golding – Goodreads Review**

For Christine who has always had such lovely things to say about my stories. Thank you for your support.

Chapter one
1818

Smoke snakes into his nostrils, an insidious herald of destruction. Kenver Penhallow paws at his face as he slowly drifts from the depths of sleep. Fire… he's dreaming of fire. Ferocious tongues of yellow and red lick high along tinder-dry wood, leaping after stars sharp against a navy night sky. Smoke wraps itself around his lungs and squeezes until he wakes fully with a jolt. He's up and out of bed retching, choking, gagging. The room's glowing red.

This is no dream!

His wife wakes too, coughing and clutching at her chest. Her eyes are wide and fearful, her face amber-lit from the inferno outside.

'Oh my Lord! Ken… what's ado?' She joins him at the window.

'Fire, Wenna. Fire! Look, the barn is almost lost to it, and the outhouse too!'

Kenver runs to the bedroom door, pulling Wenna behind him. 'Get the children. Run to the well, form a line! We need to vanquish this devilry before it consumes the house!'

In his nightshirt, Kenver runs to the paddock, a scarf around his mouth to protect against the thick acrid smoke. It proves no barrier and soon he's on his knees by the well, coughing so hard he feels his lungs will collapse. Somehow, he pulls up a bucket of water and runs at the barn, hurls the water at the wall of fire and staggers back a few paces as the flames force a retreat. A bucket of water against this? It's like a teardrop. There is no hope.

He raises his arm to shield his eyes and watches his family of six mustering by the well to form a human chain. They pass hand over hand – bucket to hand to bucket to fire and back. The fire mocks them. It's too little too late. Kenver hurries to his wife and children. 'It's no good. We are beaten. Come, we must take the horses and flee. The farmhouse will burn, and us along with it if we stay much longer!'

Wenna shakes her head. 'I can't go until we've found Jago. He's nowhere in the house!' His wife kneels on the ground, sending a wail from her throat keening up to the sky. Kenver is reminded of a wounded animal he once heard caught in a trap. She must be deranged given the calamity, because no one is missing. His children are all here. He sweeps her up into his arms and yells at his children to follow him to the hill at the top of the field behind the house.

Once safe from danger, he set his wife down on the grass. Then he looks at his clinging huddle of children and counts only four… not five. Wenna's right! He must have been mistaken when he watched them form a chain! But where is their youngest son? Where is Jago? He flings his arms to the side, demands of his brood, 'When did you last see your brother?'

His next youngest, Tilda, rubs streaks of soot from her eyes with the back of her hand and sobs, 'Father, I am sorry to tell 'ee that my brother went to the barn to be with the ailing pup. He said not to tell 'ee in case 'ee were mad at him for sleeping all night out.'

All eyes fix on the barn just as the last blackened wall collapses with an ear-splitting groan. Sparks chase each other to the heavens and then race along the ground to the farmhouse. Wenna sends up another wail more heart-rending than the first and the children join in, hugging each other in despair.

Bewildered, Kenver asks, 'He went to be with that sickly scrap of a sheepdog pup that I said wouldn't see daylight? The one I forbade him to fret over?'

Tilda's mouth forms a square of anguish. She nods and collapses next to her mother, wailing at the sky like a banshee.

Kenver forces his legs to carry him a few feet away. He can't let the children see him weep. They would lose all sensibility. His legs do their duty then refuse to do more and he finds himself on his knees in the grass. The roar of the fire deafens him as it takes possession of the farmhouse and right now, Kenver can't care less if he ever hears anything again – sees anything again. He would rather be deaf, dumb and blind than to be here and witness such carnage. His little five-year-old son is gone. Taken, burnt, consumed in hellfire.

'Father, how can this be? It is too much to bear,' George, his eldest, says, as he kneels next to him, puts a hand on his shoulder.

Kenver shakes his head and wipes moisture from his eyes. 'I know not, lad. But I swear I'll find out and avenge my youngest son. Fires don't start by themselves.'

George gasps, takes his father's arm, a horrified expression on his face. 'But who would do us such evil?'

Kenver hawks smoke-filled phlegm from his throat and spits it out in disgust. 'I have just the evil devil in mind, lad. And he'll be sorry for what he's done. I swear by almighty God, he'll be sorry – and so will his sons and his line ever after. Mark my words.'

Chapter two

From behind the windscreen of his car, Matt Trevelyar looks at the grey austere Victorian school appearing and disappearing. The school isn't performing a magic trick, it just seems that way, due to the back and forth of the windscreen wipers as they battle against the deluge. It's been raining on and off for six hours since he left his flat in London for the last time, and journeyed south to Cornwall. For the last hour since he crossed the border into the county, the rain hasn't been off at all. It's been on. Full on. A lot like the feeling he's got in his gut that he's making a big mistake leaving his teaching job in the capital to take an assistant headship in a 'God forsaken backwater at the arsehole of the world', as his former girlfriend Kay had described St Agnes.

Matt links his fingers and stretches his arms above his head until the knuckles click and tilts his head from side to side to try and undo the crick in his neck. He reminds himself that Kay has no sway in his life any more and to stop listening to the memory of her vicious little tongue. What a mistake he made taking up with her. She's his former girlfriend for a reason – more than one, actually. He goes through them in his head: controlling, self-centred, manipulative… Then he tells himself off. She's the past. London's the past. This is his new start, a new life.

It had been so hard to say goodbye to his previous school, friends and old haunts, but if he were honest, the only people he was breaking his heart over were his parents, grandparents and the memory of his darling wife, Beth. Matt's heart twists as it always does when he thinks of Beth. Then he smiles. The good thing about memories is that you can take them with you wherever you go. An image of her beautiful smile surfaces, melancholy floods through him and he asks no one in particular why she'd been taken so young for what feels like the millionth time. What he needs is to get out, stretch his legs and have a brisk walk along the cliff path, but of course doing that in this weather would be a really bad idea.

The school continues its magic act and Matt remembers how different it looked in the sunshine last time he was here. It was still grey and Victorian, but it felt part of the village, a stalwart of comfort to many who'd passed through its doors over the years. Many older villagers would have attended it and their children and now grandchildren. It was as much a part of the landscape as the Cornish slate stone walls and the rock under which St Agnes stood. Penhallow Primary School – strong, steadfast, unchanging, no matter what the elements threw at it. A bit like his grandparents, who were born here, and attended this school.

Matt switches off the wipers and grabs some books and his brolly before rushing from the car to the front door of the school. He grabs the brass knocker handle, twists and pushes. Nothing. Shit – it's locked. Hammering on the door, he yells, 'Hello! Anyone here?'

The head, Deborah Ginty, said she'd meet him here at four, and it's now ten past. As he's trying the handle again, a gust of wind pulls the brolly from his grasp, turns it inside out and hurls it across the playground into a hedge. It's stuck there like some alien species of spider, buffeted and broken. As if it senses he's unprotected, the rain doubles its efforts and drenches every inch of him in seconds as he pounds on the door, yelling.

Suddenly it's yanked open and Matt's catapulted inside, and almost goes flat on his face in the corridor. He grabs at a wooden strut of intricate lattice work around the door and saves himself at the last minute.

'Afternoon, Matthew,' Deborah says through a tight mouth, her twinkly dark eyes telling Matt she's trying her best not to burst out laughing at his unorthodox entrance and drowned-rat appearance. He'd warmed to her as soon as he met her. She was friendly, yet very professional, and her no-nonsense approach was refreshing and let everyone know where they stood.

'Afternoon, Deborah.' Matt pushes his dark shoulder-length hair back from his forehead and wonders if it's time to get it cut. It is getting a bit unruly. Though it'd been tied back at interview, he remembered that Deborah had looked askance at it once or twice. Or perhaps he'd imagined it. But as he follows her matronly figure down the corridor, he decides he's not getting it cut just to satisfy some outdated idea about what was acceptable.

In Deborah's office they talk about the six-week break and what they'd both done, his journey up and – obligatory for the British – the weather. Once the small talk dries up, there's a comfortable silence as they wait for Jessica Blake, the deputy head, to join them. Deborah flicks on the kettle and makes coffee, setting it down on the desk just as there's a tap on the door and Jessica walks in.

She's a tall, striking woman with a voluptuous figure, and upon seeing her for the first time, Matt was reminded a little of the actress in *Pulp Fiction*. Jessica has the same raven hair, cut in a sharp bob with a severe fringe. Her bright green eyes miss nothing and on the three occasions they've met, her wide pouty lips have always been covered with a sheen of red lipstick. She's very attractive, but Matt's not remotely interested. There's something about the way she looks at him. At interview she never took her eyes away from his, even though she only had a couple of questions. There she goes again now as he shakes her hand. It's a predatory stare. He feels like a gazelle under the watchful eye of the pride's finest hunter.

Deborah pats her short grey hair and asks if Jessica would like coffee. Matt has the impression that Deborah feels intimidated by her deputy's beauty. She's only forty-five, but Deborah's hair colour makes her look older. But then if she was worried, she'd have dyed it wouldn't she? Matt reminds himself not to judge on appearances and certainly not to imagine what others are feeling

– especially women. He isn't much good at understanding his own feelings at the moment, never mind anyone else's.

For the next half-hour, they talk about the upcoming term and go through arrangements for the first week back. Jessica explains the background of one of the pupils in Matt's class. The boy had a difficult upbringing and has a few special needs. Try as he might Matt can't picture Jessica in front of a class of eight-year-olds. He'd have been terrified of her at that age. Perhaps that's how she maintains authority around the place. Fear of being eaten by Ms Blake.

'Something amusing, Matthew?' Jessica asks, one thick dark eyebrow arching towards her hairline.

He realises he's smiling at the image his brain's presented of her red lips peeling back from sharp white fangs, her mouth opening to swallow a child, and forces his lips into a line. 'No, sorry. Just thinking about how much I'm looking forward to working here.'

Jessica gives him a warm smile. 'We're so looking forward to having you here. We've not had a male teacher in this school for ages, have we, Deborah?'

He expects she ate the last one.

'No,' Deborah says. 'There's still far more women than men in the primary sector. A shame, as some of our young lads need a positive male role model.' Deborah's gaze settles on his hair and then she frowns and changes the subject.

Business over, a few hours later Matt's dismayed to see the rain still sheeting down as he opens the door. Pulling his jacket up over his head he prepares to make a dash to his car. With one foot outside, he's stopped by:

'Wait up, Matt. Do you fancy a bite to eat and a drink at the local pub later?'

His heart sinks as he steps back inside and turns to face Jessica. There's the look in her eye again, a pouty red smile on her lips, and Matt feels like he'll be the bite to eat if he's not very careful. He needs an excuse and fast. 'Um, that's really kind of you, Jessica–'

'Call me Jess. All my friends do.' She does the pouty smile again.

'Right, Jess. But the thing is, I've not been to my cottage yet and I need to unpack, settle in and stuff. It's been a knackering drive and–'

Jessica shrugs and removes the smile. 'No probs. Another time, hm?'

Matt thinks that sounds more like a threat than a request. 'Oh yes, definitely.' He looks at his feet and then quickly up at her face. Her eyes have narrowed, and she seems to be weighing him up to search for signs of a lie. Matt clears his throat and puts a hand on the door handle.

'I'll hold you to that, Mr Trevelyar,' she says, as if he's an eight-year-old who's disappointed her, and walks quickly away up the corridor.

'I bet you will,' he mutters under his breath, and then pulls his jacket back over his head and hurries to his car. Badger's Holt, the rented cottage he'll be living in until he decides if he's going to stay long-term, is only a mile out of St Agnes. Matt's already got ideas of setting off a bit early on sunny mornings so he can feel the sea breeze on his face and get a bit of exercise. Badger's Holt is old, small, but perfectly formed. He smiles as he remembers the white stone walls, colourful cottage garden and cosy wood burner in the living room for those long winter nights.

Matt pulls his car onto the tiny scrap of a drive and switches off the engine. The rain is easing now, and he can see a patch of blue in the afternoon sky. Is it a sign that things are on the up now? He doesn't know, but he expects that if he's looking for signs in the sky he must be tired and the best thing to do is get inside, unpack, have some food and relax a bit.

***

Opening the bedroom curtains the next morning, he can see the patch of blue from yesterday has spread across most of the sky and the sun is bathing the landscape of hills and fields in a warm golden glow. A few jackdaws sit having a chat on the shed and a cow or two graze in the pastureland to the right of his garden.

Matt opens the window and inhales a mixture of wet grass and cow pat. He feels so much better than he did yesterday and thinks the move down here was unquestionably the right one. It's amazing what a can of soup, a hunk of fresh bread and a long sleep will do for your spirits.

After a quick breakfast of what remained of the bread, he's ready to go to the local supermarket to stock up, then he'll have a bit of an explore. There's almost a week before term starts and he's got that giddy holiday feeling in his stomach. A new house, new job and a beautiful new place to explore. A return to his Cornish roots. What more could he ask for?

Whistling, Matt steps outside onto the gravel path and points his keys at the car. As he turns to lock the door the whistle sticks in his throat and his stomach comes up. Right in front of him there's a rustic plant barrel in the recess by the front door; inside it there's a wooden pole with… He swallows hard and forces himself to look. To look and make sure he's not hallucinating. No. No, it's real. There's a badger's head stuck on the top of a pole stained red with the poor creature's blood. Like its eyes, the mouth is open, showing a row of bloodstained teeth. Secured with twine further down the pole, there's a white sign with red writing that Matt assumes is also blood. It reads:

FUCK OFF BACK TO LONDON!

Shaking, Matt releases a slow breath, leans against the wall and wonders what the hell to do next.

Chapter three

Two hours later Matt's still wondering what the hell to do next. He's gazing out over the fields from the patio doors in his living room and drinking a can of beer, despite it being only eleven o'clock in the morning. He needs it after such a brutal start to his day. The police have been, taken the badger, asked lots of questions and said they will be in touch, if and when they have any information regarding the perpetrator. He thinks there's as much chance of that as bringing the badger back to life and sending it scampering across the fields.

PC David Cross had chewed the end of his pen and sighed a lot. Matt thought he could have been the stereotypical village bobby in an episode of *Miss Marple*. He didn't ask very many pertinent questions but cut across the nameless female officer when she did. Old school. Slow brain. Perhaps that was uncharitable, but right now he didn't feel particularly generous towards his fellow man. Cross had in his infinite wisdom concluded that someone in the village wanted him gone. Matt had been tempted to say, 'No shit Sherlock', but managed to stop himself. Cross further divulged that some older villagers in particular resented those from up country coming down and stealing the jobs that should have gone to locals. The fact that Matt told him his roots were Cornish had no bearing. Cross said that people wouldn't know that – they just saw a city lad coming into their school. However, the officer had also said that if he had to bet on it, that would be the end of the matter. Whoever had stuck the badger head on that pole had made their point with the hope that Matt would take the hint, because people round here were more bark than bite, didn't he know? The female officer raised an eyebrow but kept her own counsel.

Matt takes a deep pull from his beer and sits down on the sofa. He has two options as far as he can see. Keep calm and carry on, or fuck off back to London. What would his gran do? Matt had always gone to her rather than his parents for advice. She and him were always very close – he was her 'beautiful boy' and could do no wrong in her eyes. She understood him completely and she'd always had a knack of making him feel better. Elowen grew up here in this village along with his grandad, Terry. They met as teenagers and had been inseparable ever since. They hadn't wanted to leave Cornwall, but Terry was bright and ambitious, and when a job came up in a London bank, he'd seen it as too good an opportunity to miss. Elowen had taken some convincing, but in the end agreed it would be a good move for their unborn son, Matt's dad. He was born in Cornwall, but moved to London not long after. Elowen in particular had never forgotten her roots though, and they had holidayed in Cornwall as a family as often as they could when Matt was growing up.

Reaching for his mobile phone, he scrolls down the list for her number. She'll know what to do as she'd have a better idea of what the whole badger thing was all about, and what the local feeling might be. Okay, she'd not lived here for over fifty-odd years, but she kept her ear to the ground and what she didn't know about Cornish folklore wasn't worth knowing. Perhaps the badger had a particular significance? Matt remembers that she told him lots about country ways, herbs and nature and animals, when he was a boy. His finger hovers over the phone, about to dial her number, but he stops. What's the point in worrying her? Because she would, wouldn't she? Her 'beautiful boy' under threat as soon as he sets foot in her old home. No, he'll have to sort this out himself. He's thirty years old, hardly a boy any more.

Matt crushes the can in his hand and decides it will take more than a badger head and a nasty warning to change his plans. He has a right to be here as much as the next person; more really, given his heritage. He'll stick to his guns, go down to the supermarket and act as if nothing has happened. As his gran was fond of telling him when he was unsure of something as a kid, 'You're a Trevelyar, my lad, remember that. Cornish and proud, afraid of nothing.'

***

The supermarket has no dead badgers or torch-wielding villagers storming up the aisles towards him, so his spirits start to rise a little. Once he's got the shopping home and had a quick bite, he will set off on the cliff path for the afternoon. A brisk walk in the sea air will do him the world of good. He always feels better next to the ocean; it's good for the soul. The last bag of shopping in the boot, Matt's just about to slam the lid shut when his eye's taken by a young woman walking past. She looks like she's just walked off the set of *The Lord of the Rings*. Long flowing white-blonde hair, threaded through with wild flowers, blue and turquoise boho dress and shawl, a basket over her arm, her features sharp, yet delicate. Elfin is the word that springs to mind. That and beautiful. Stunningly so, because he's never seen eyes like hers. If Matt had to describe them, he'd say they were violet.

The woman catches him staring and a furrow knits her brow. She bows her head and hurries into the supermarket. *Great. Another villager who hates me.* What does he expect standing there with one hand on the boot, gawping at her with his tongue hanging out? Must have looked like a right perv. He's torn between going back into the shop to apologise and just leaving. After a quick scenario plays through his mind of him rocking up to her, trying to explain that he was only staring because he thought she was incredibly beautiful, and her backing away into the baked bean shelf, he decides to leave. Time to head for the hills.

The walk on the cliff path has done him good, as he knew it would and as he turns into the lane leading up to his cottage, Matt decides to go to one of the village pubs for dinner later. He'd much rather stay skulking at home, but instinct tells him that whoever wants rid of him would expect that. He needs to show no fear and get to know the locals. Once they know that his grandparents grew up here, it might change things too. Thankfully no more dead creatures are stuck on poles by the door and he goes inside feeling much more positive than he had that morning.

The Driftwood Spars is just the kind of pub Matt was hoping for. A seventeenth-century white stone building next to the sea with good beer, food and a jovial atmosphere. He's got a snug table in the corner and from it he people-watches the locals, but surreptitiously. He doesn't want to get a reputation for staring at folk. Putting down his knife and fork, he thinks the oven-baked cod wrapped in ham and creamy mushroom sauce is as good as any meal he's had in a swanky London bistro and the beer is real Cornish ale on draft. They've even got a little microbrewery across the road where it's made. Heaven. Matt thanks the waitress as she takes his plate and picks up the pudding menu. He shouldn't really after such a big meal, but what the hell. The walk on the cliff path has given him an appetite and he'd only had a sausage roll for lunch.

Matt decides on the ice-cream and is about to order it when another woman catches his eye. She's very different from the ethereal beauty he saw earlier. She's sitting at the bar nursing half a pint of beer and glaring at him from under bushy black brows. She looks to be in her late seventies, has long grey curls, lined walnut-brown skin, sharp hazel eyes and a mean mouth. Oddly, she looks to be wearing similar clothes to the woman he saw earlier. The colours are different however – browns, blacks and oranges like autumn leaves. The woman sees him looking at her and turns down both sides of her mouth in a clown grimace, then slowly looks him up and down as if he's shit on her shoe before shifting her gaze away across the room. Nice. What the hell has he done now?

Taking a deep breath, he walks to the bar to order the ice-cream and feels her eyes on him again. She's just a few feet away to his right and after he orders he turns to face her. 'Good evening,' he says with a smile.

'It was until you got here.' The old woman crosses her arms and fixes him with that stare again. What the hell?

'Excuse me?' Matt says and finds himself mirroring her body language.

'You heard right enough.' The old woman takes a swallow of ale and wipes her mouth on the back of her hand. 'You're that new teacher, aren't you? Mr Trevelyar?'

'Yes, that's right. How do you know—'

A snort cuts him off. 'I know everything that goes on round about. Born and bred here, unlike some.'

Matt bristles. What the hell is wrong with the old crone? 'Actually, my grandparents were born and bred here. My dad was born here too. That makes me Cornish.'

She makes a sound like a concertina being thrown to the ground and begins to wheeze. Matt realises she's laughing, or what passes for laughter from such a twisted old root. 'You, Cornish? Well that's the best I've heard in a long time.'

Matt's about to repeat that his grandparents are from here, but she raises a twiggy finger and stabs it through the air at him, hatred burning cold behind her eyes. 'And I know your grandparents were born and bred here. Don't mean nothing. Your dad was only here a matter of weeks. Then they buggered of quick enough to bloody London, didn't 'um? Main thing is you weren't born here. Nobody wants you teaching our kids.'

A chill creeps along Matt's spine. The air between them seems to crackle with malevolent energy and the short hairs on his forearms are raised. This woman is vile. Was she the one who put the badger head outside his door, wrote the warning in blood? She's weird and nasty enough by the sound of her. 'How very welcoming,' he says, the ice in his voice unmistakable.

'Just sayin' truths. Nobody wants interlopers, especially not a Trevelyar.'

Interlopers? Has she just walked out of a nineteenth-century novel? He sighs. 'Sounds like you knew my grandparents? What did they ever do to you?'

The woman snorts, drains her drink and bangs it down on the bar top. 'What didn't they do, you mean, lad. They're evil, and all the Trevelyars afore 'em.' She gives him a nasty sneer. 'And all those who come after, I shouldn't wonder.'

Matt's had enough of being polite and raises his voice a little, although his nerves are taut as piano wires. 'Now wait a minute, you can't bad-mouth my family without an explanation—'

'I can do whatever I like!' she spits, her hazel eyes darkening with fury. Then she slips from the bar stool with surprising agility for her years. She takes a few steps towards the door and then turns, points a twiggy finger at him again. 'I suggest you go back to London, before it's too late.' The woman glares at a couple who have clearly overheard and then back at Matt before sweeping out of the pub in a tumble of autumn leaves, like a villain in a play.

There's a tap on Matt's arm and he turns to face the bar. The barman who'd greeted Matt when he'd first come in leans across and says in a low voice, 'Don't mind her. She's crackers. There's only a handful of older ones who think like her. Everyone else in the village is happy we have a male teacher for once.' The barman's green eyes twinkle and he strokes his dark beard. 'Mind you, some say you need a haircut.'

Despite the shock of dealing with the nasty old woman, Matt feels a smile play over his lips. 'Well, I'm happy with it as it is, thanks.' Self-conscious, Matt pushes his hair back. Even if it needs a cut, there's no way he'd do it now. He nods as the barman questioningly raises his empty glass. 'So what's that woman's name?'

'People call her lots of things,' he says with a laugh as he pulls Matt's pint. But her name's Morvoren Penhallow.'

Chapter four

Two weeks into the new term Matt has almost forgotten the anxiety and worry of those first few days after he'd moved. The staff at Penhallow School are great, the villagers welcoming, and the pupils are just wonderful. There have been no more badger incidents and he's not seen Morvoren Penhallow since the night in the pub. Betty in the newsagents was a mine of information thankfully, and explained that her family had lived here for generations. Her great-grandfather built the school, hence the name, and she ruled the roost in her small family unit. Even when she married, she kept her surname, unheard of back then. Her husband died a few years ago, but her son, daughter-in-law and family dance to her tune, by all accounts. She never has a kind word for anyone and wanders the countryside collecting herbs, and some say casting spells. At this point in the tale, Betty had lowered her voice and said, 'A bit of a white witch on the quiet, some say.'

Matt had wanted to ask Betty if she thought Morvoren was the one behind the badger, but thought better of it. She might have been, or she might not. He just wants to put it all behind him now and get on with his new life. When he'd spoken to his gran on the phone the other night he'd been tempted to tell her in a jokey manner what had happened and about Morvoren, but decided not to at the last minute. His gran might not have found it amusing, and he didn't want to cause her worry. Since he'd come to St Agnes, his mum had told him that his gran and granddad were contemplating moving back to Cornwall, and he didn't want to put them off. His mum also said that if his grandparents moved, so might they in a few years, when his dad retired.

In the classroom, Kirsty Clark is drawing a picture of the Kremlin. They have been looking at major cities of the world and Kirsty is particularly taken by Moscow and the grand buildings. She says the domes on the Kremlin look like onions and turbans and Matt has to agree.

'Sir, why do they call this building the gremlin? Can it change into a monster and kill people?'

He hides a smile. 'Kremlin, not gremlin, Kirsty.'

She stops drawing, raises her freckled face to him, and wrinkles her brow. 'Oh. So what's Kremlin mean?'

Matt has no clue, but he says, 'It's where the Russian government business takes place and has lots of important offices. It has a palace and a museum too, I think.'

'But what does the *word* mean?'

'Well, it's Russian, so I don't know. I'll find out for you if you like.'

Kirsty raises an eyebrow and turns back to her drawing. 'Thought teachers were supposed to know everything,' she says quietly.

Matt smiles. 'We are always learning, Kirsty. The main thing is that we never stop asking questions, because if we do, our mind gets smaller and closed off. I'll find out for you at breaktime, okay?'

Kirsty shrugs and doesn't look up.'

Matt walks on to the next pupil, feeling like he's failed some important test. At breaktime he's in the staffroom googling the Kremlin on his phone, when a whiff of expensive perfume and a cool hand on his shoulder tells him that Jessica Blake is standing behind him. Close behind him. He can practically feel her breath on his neck.

'Nice that some of us have the time to play on our phones, Mr Trevelyar,' she says with a giggle.

He turns round quickly, forcing her to take a step back. 'Just finding out what Kremlin means for Kirsty Clark.' He forces a smile and looks back at his phone.

'There's dedication for you.' Jessica touches his arm lightly. 'And may I say I think your hair looks great tied back. You remind me of that artist, can't remember his name now.'

To his annoyance her unexpected compliment and direct gaze brings colour to his cheeks. He mumbles, 'Oh, right. Thanks.'

Her red mouth stretches into a wide smile over perfect white teeth and mischief twinkles in her eyes. 'I do believe you're blushing, Matt.'

He gives a self-conscious laugh and swallows hard. 'I believe you're right. Now, you'll have to excuse me, I need a quick coffee before class begins again–'

'You're working too hard.' Jessica's face has assumed a look of concern and she reaches out, squeezes his shoulder. 'All work and no play, eh?'

Matt shakes his head. 'No. I'm good, actually. I have been walking a lot, exploring the area. There's a great pub I found–'

'Oh, which one?' Jessica's eyes light up. 'Perhaps we could have a drink or a bite tonight? I'd love to have a chat – get to know you better.'

Shit. I walked into that one. 'Um, it's the Driftwood Spars… But tonight?' Matt looks up to the ceiling, pretending to think about it. 'Er, I think I have some marking to do.'

'You can do that tomorrow. Come on, it will be fun.' She makes it sound more like an order than a request. The twinkle has gone out of her eyes and the smile looks fixed.

He feels backed into a corner. Why can't he think of a decent excuse? Resignedly he says, 'Okay, but just for an hour or so. I really have got marking to catch up on.'

'Excellent, see you there at six?'

As he's about to leave the staffroom Jane Gregson, the jolly and gossipy tea lady, whispers in his ear. 'Go careful with that Miss Blake. By all accounts her husband divorced her cos she was insanely jealous of anyone he was friendly with. Bunny boiler comes to mind.' Jane does her trademark belly laugh and wheels the trolley out.

Marvellous.

After break, once again in the classroom, Matt's not happy. Jane's words keep repeating in his mind. Why couldn't he have been more forthright and just said no to Jessica? Going out for a drink with the woman is not sending a back-off message, is it? He absently twiddles a pencil as he watches Kirsty finish her picture. But at least he's shown willing, been friendly to a colleague. That has to count for something. Tonight will be a drink with a colleague and nothing more. Nothing in the future, unless it's with other staff too.

'You look miles away, Mr Trevelyar,' Kirsty says, looking up.

'I am, Kirsty… Just thinking, you know.'

'Thinking is good for you, isn't it?'

'It is, Kirsty.'

'Did you find out about the gremlin? You know, what it means?'

'Kremlin. Yes. It means a fortress. Like a big castle with soldiers inside to protect the city. That's what it was in the distant past anyway.'

'Oh good. I like castles. We don't need protection like in the old days in our cities now, do we, sir?'

'No, thank goodness,' Matt says and wanders off. *We just need protection from certain members of staff with the capacity to eat me for breakfast, or dinner as the case may be.*

***

After school, Matt's looking in a shop window, lost in thought. He's contemplating buying a new shirt to go out in tonight, but that might send more wrong signals to Jessica. The trouble is, he does need a new shirt. His other two smart-ish ones are in the wash and it's been a long time since he's gone clothes shopping. Just as he's about to go inside the shop, he catches a glimpse of a turquoise-clad figure in the window's reflection, walking past on the other side of the street behind him. He turns and sees the elfin woman from the other week go into the greengrocers, her pale hair lifting on the breeze.

The sensible thing to do would be to just carry on, go about his business, but he's drawn to her. There's a weird feeling in his gut and it's telling him to wait outside the shop and casually bump into her as she comes out. But why? What the hell is his gut playing at? He has no wish to start a relationship, but still, he knows he must follow his instinct. Matt looks at his own reflection in the window and makes sure his hair is tidy, then before he can change his mind, he hurries across the street and waits just along from the greengrocers, on the cobbled pavement, his heart thumping.

A few moments later she comes out, her basket heavy with vegetables, but turns right not left and walks away from him up the street. *Shit.* Now what? The panic of missing her drives action. Matt's feet seem to have a mind of their own as they rush him down a side alley, round a corner and then back onto the high street a few steps from where the woman is heading towards him. Matt ducks his head, whips his phone out of his trouser pocket and pretends to look at it, but as he passes her he bumps into her shoulder and drops the phone.

She stops, bends to pick up his phone at the same time as Matt does and they narrowly avoid banging heads. 'Oops, here you go,' she says as she hands it to him. Her face is flushed from bending over and dodging his head and her eyes are even more unusual close up than they were the first time he saw her. Bluey-violet. Her voice has a soft Cornish lilt and a half-smile plays over her lips. She is exquisite.

Matt gapes at her, his hand half on the phone, half on her hand. He's aware he's opening and closing his mouth, but his words stick in his throat and she's looking at him as if he's deranged. *Is there any wonder, Matt?* He feels pressure in his palm as she shoves the phone into his hand and retrieves her own. He says, 'Oh, thanks. I'm sorry for staring, it's just that I've seen you somewhere before, I think.' *Lame, but better than nothing.*

'Really? Not sure I've seen you.' As she says this, Matt can see she's struggling to place him. Her eyebrows knit together, and he hopes she can't place the last time, when he stood with his hand on the boot of his car gawping at her just like he is now.

'Yeah, must have been around the village.'

'Right. Well I must get on.' She gives him a quick smile and makes to leave, so he says the first thing that comes into his head.

'Do you know where the nearest bank is? I've not lived here long, and I haven't got cash out yet, so I don't know where it is. I've been paying for everything with my credit card, which isn't ideal when you only want one or two bits from the greengrocers.' It all comes out in a rush and Matt cringes. *One or two bits?* And why doesn't he just go to an ATM? Why does he need a bank?

Thankfully, she doesn't ask this, but nods and points back down the street. 'Yeah, it's down there to the lights and then across the crossing. Can't really miss it.'

'Thanks. What's your name?' Another cringe. That came out a bit blunt.

The woman shifts her basket to her other arm, pulls her turquoise shawl tighter round her shoulders. 'Lavender.'

Of course it is. Because of her eyes. They aren't violet, they're lavender. Matt smiles. 'What an unusual name. Your eyes are the same colour as your name.'

Lavender blushes. 'Funny enough, that's why my parents chose it.'

'Yes, I can see that. Do you live here in the village, Lavender?'

'On the edge, really. I have a cottage near the sea and a little shop down there not far from the bank. I'm an artist and sell my paintings and art supplies from there.'

'That sounds fascinating!' Matt notices her slight frown at his gushy words and cringes for the third time. He sounds overenthusiastic to say the least.

'Not sure if it's fascinating, but it's what I do, and I love it.' Lavender shifts the basket again. 'Anyway,' she nods at the vegetables. 'I must get these home before my arm drops off.'

'I could carry them home for you.' The look on her face tells him he's gone too far. What is he thinking?

'No. Really, I'm fine.' Lavender quickly steps around him and waves a hand. 'Okay, see you... er?'

'Matt. Matt Trevelyar. I'm the new teacher at Penhallow School.'

Lavender's face drains of colour and her mouth falls open. Without another word she hurries away down the street as if he's just turned into an axe murderer. Not quite the reaction he was hoping for. What on earth has he said? Okay, he was a bit forward offering to take her shopping home, but it was more than that. Matt's caught between running after her to ask what had offended her and going to look at her shop for more clues. He opts for the latter. Much safer.

Okay, so here's the bank... next shop is hardware. Matt stops, raises his hand to his brow and squints against the sun. The last shop on the street has a colourful lintel and some words written in entwined painted flowers which he can't read from this angle. He hurries along and stands square to the shop. In the window there's a range of canvases – stunning seascapes and country scenes, and the sign in flowers reads:

Lavender Blue
Original Artworks by Lavender Nancarrow

Chapter five

The cottage feels cold today, or perhaps it's just because of the chill of learning that a Trevelyar is back in the village – and a teacher too. How much worse could it be? Lavender puts her shopping away and rubs the goosepimples on her arms. It's only mid-September – too early to light the fire? Through the window a huddle of bruised clouds gathers over the ocean and a gull hovers above the garden wall, struggling against the wind. Lavender pulls a cardigan on, walks into the living room and picks up some logs.

Curled up on the sofa with a mug of tea, Lavender yawns. The warm glow from the open fire and the walk in the fresh air over the fields and lanes from St Agnes are not conducive to making a start on the next painting. She's not in the mood at all. Her mind is too taken by thoughts of the Trevelyar man. Is he one of *the* Trevelyars, or is it just a coincidence? It might well be, and if so, she overreacted big time. He must have wondered what the hell was wrong with her as she scuttled away down the high street. Mind you, he was a bit odd. All that staring and offering to take her shopping home. What is very annoying and extremely disconcerting, however, is she's attracted to him. Probably something to do with the fact he's stereotypically tall, dark and handsome with turquoise eyes and a tumble of ebony curls. Nothing will come of it though, so no harm done.

As Lavender takes her mug through to the kitchen determined to at least have a go at picking up her paintbrush, the back door opens and in walks her gran. Much as she loves her, she knows the painting won't get started this evening if she stays for long. Gran's got that determined look on her face and she's already reaching for the kettle.

'Want a cuppa, Lavender?'

Anyone would think her gran lived here. Lavender holds up her empty mug. 'No thanks. I was just about to start a new p–'

'Because you might need one when I've finished telling you my news.'

Lavender's heart sinks. 'Good or bad?'

Gran rolls her eyes. 'Bad, I'm afraid. To be honest, it's the worst for some time.'

Lavender takes the biscuit tin out of the cupboard; she's going to need sugar to help keep her eyes open. The news is probably a long tale about one of the village elders who just looked sideways at Gran or something. She does tend to over-exaggerate nowadays. The older she gets the worse she gets, Lavender's found. 'I'll take these in the living room, you bring the tea.'

Gran sits opposite on the armchair and dips a biscuit in her cup. She holds it up but doesn't eat it, just stares across at Lavender, a faraway look in her eye, and Lavender watches the biscuit wobble, heavy with liquid. Why doesn't she just put it in her mouth before it plops onto her chest? Gran focuses, gobbles the biscuit down in one and fixes her keen hazel eyes on her granddaughter. 'There's a Trevelyar in the village. He's a teacher at the school. How *dare* they employ an outsider to educate our children?' Gran's voice is quiet but shakes with fury.

For once this isn't one of Gran's long-winded stories then. Lavender nods. 'Yeah, I ran into him today.'

Gran chokes on her tea and wipes her chin with the back of her hand. 'What do you mean, ran into him?'

Lavender tells her.

'What? He actually had the bloody cheek to offer to walk you back home? A young woman living alone? Bastard! We all know what he was after.'

Lavender sighs inwardly. 'I think he was just trying to be nice–'

'Nice! Nice? Trevelyars aren't nice. They pretend to be, but they're all out for themselves – for what they can get.'

Lavender puts her mug down and sits back. 'Hmm. How do we know that this guy is one of *the* Trevelyars? There are other Trevelyars in Cornwall and–'

'Because he's got a look of his rat of a grandfather…' Gran turns her mouth down at the corners. 'And anyway, he told me his grandparents lived here the other week when I saw him in the pub.'

'You chatted to him?' Lavender thinks it's a wonder she didn't strangle him.

Gran snorts. 'Well, chat is a bit soft. I gave him short shrift. I knew who he was before then though. Knew as soon as I heard they'd employed a new teacher and that his name was Trevelyar. Warned him off soon as he arrived, but he didn't take the hint. I saw the cheeky swine looking in your shop window today. *That's* when I knew we had to do something. We have to act before it's too late.'

A nest of vipers writhe in Lavender's belly. She'd seen what her gran had done to those who crossed her over the years. None of it was pleasant. She doesn't like the *we* bit either. *We* have to act before it's too late. Lavender swallows and asks, 'You warned him off. How?'

'Same way as I drove that homosexual pair away a few years ago. Scum.' Gran settles back in her chair, a self-satisfied smile on her face.

Oh God. Lavender closes her eyes and pinches the bridge of her nose. She hadn't spoken to her gran because of that for weeks. Lavender had told her that there was nothing wrong with being gay, and she certainly didn't hold with the dead-animal-head warnings and God knew what else. But Gran told her that she didn't want their kind round here and – 'It ain't right and it ain't proper.'

'What exactly did you do?'

'I found an old brock by the roadside and beheaded it. Stuck it on a pole and told him to fuck off back to London on a sign below.

Wrote it in blood.' Gran nods her head, pride shining in her eyes. 'Said a few country words over it – made it potent.'

Before she can stop herself, Lavender says, 'He's still here. Can't have been too potent.'

Gran narrows her eyes, leans forward in her seat and spits, 'No. And that means you and me have to put our heads together. Our hands too. 'T'aint no mistake we both have the webbing. You're a guardian of old ways, a protector of our lands.' Gran splays the middle and index fingers of both hands, holds them up to the light as if seeing them for the first time. 'You'll take over when I'm gone.'

Lavender looks away and down at her own fingers – flexes the extra skin between both thumbs and index fingers. She'd been bullied mercilessly at school for having webbed fingers. The other kids said she was a freak and a mutant or a witch. Others said she had mermaid ancestors, because her surname, Nancarrow, meant mermaid in Cornish. This was stupid, because her gran was a Penhallow and she had the webbing too. The witch part might be nearer the mark on Gran's part. Whatever the truth, it meant that Lavender had been a lonely child, singled out and shunned. Sadly, not much has changed and she's almost twenty-six.

'What are you thinking about? Why aren't you saying anything?' Gran purses her lips, frustration furrowing her bushy brows.

'I'm wondering what you propose to do next.'

'We.' Gran wags a bony finger at her. 'We, Lavender.'

They lock eyes for a few seconds. Lavender wants no part of the old woman's plans. Yes, she'll be furious when she says no to her, and in the past Lavender has just gone along with everything she's been told to do. Her dad is the same and mum too – Gran's the matriarch. Morvoren Penhallow is a hard woman to say no to, but Lavender will draw the line at terrorism. Because that's what it is, plain and simple. 'I don't want to do anything bad to him. I don't know him and whatever the Trevelyars did to our ancestors years ago, he won't be the same. He probably doesn't even know about–'

'Whether he knows or not is neither here nor there. What he's done nowadays is enough, the filthy bastard.' Gran does a mock shudder and folds her arms.

'What? What do you mean, nowadays?'

A flicker of gleeful excitement in her eyes, Gran leans forward. 'The same person as told me there were a Trevelyar coming to the school, told me his wife died in mysterious circumstances – overdose. Couldn't cope with living any more. He was handy with his fists, apparently. Never proved anything though. But more disgusting was his *interest*, shall we say, in young maids at his previous school. I thought *you'd* be particularly concerned about that one.'

The pit of vipers in Lavender's belly starts spitting as she takes in this information. Her gran's watching her face carefully and instinct drives a reaction. 'He molested girls in London? How the fuck did he get a job here, then!'

'Beats me. Might have said it was just rumours. Trevelyars have silver tongues. Evil as they come.'

'Who told you all this?'

'I keep my sources secret, even from you.' Gran's eyes dance away and she pretends to pick at a thread on her shawl.

'Oh, for goodness sake.' Lavender jumps up and, with a shaking hand, takes her cup into the kitchen. In her head, memories of a little girl cowering against the wall in a school classroom set her stomach churning. She feels dizzy and her heart thuds in her chest.

'It's all true, Lavender. My source isn't one to lie and they know about the Trevelyars. They suffered at their hands too, many years ago.' Gran's beside her at the sink, her face flushed with anger. 'We have to drive him out... by any means necessary. Are you with me?'

Lavender glances at her grandmother's earnest expression and lets out a long sigh. What choice does she have? Men like Matthew Trevelyar are the scum of the earth and have no place in her part of it. She nods. 'I'm with you.'

Chapter six

Why are his hands clammy? Matt wipes his palms along his jean-clad thighs just before he steps up to the door of the pub. His heart's thudding and his brain's giving the old fight or flight messages. He should have to do neither. It's just a drink and a bite with a colleague. Turning people down has never come easy to him, but as he checks his reflection in the glass panel of the door, he kicks himself for being too accommodating. He would rather be anywhere else but here, wearing his new shirt and his hair scraped back within an inch of its life into a ponytail. Why couldn't he have made some excuse, and why had he bought a new shirt? It felt too perfect, smelt new as well.

The door opens and a man comes out, affording Matt a glimpse into the bar. Is it too late to turn and run? The flight message is winning…

'Hey, Matt! Over here!' Jessica half stands from a bar stool and waves her arms, windmill-like. Yep. Too late to run.

Matt swallows, takes a deep breath and strides over to Jessica in what he hopes is a confident yet nonchalant manner. 'Hi, sorry I'm a bit late. I decided to walk, and it was further than I thought.'

Jessica touches his knee as he settles himself on the high bar stool. 'Don't worry. I haven't been here very long myself.'

Matt eyes her almost empty wine glass. She's either a fast drinker or a liar. 'Can I get you another?'

'Go on then. A large Pinot please, I'll take these menus over to that table over there, yes?'

Matt watches her go, her bottom in a tight red skirt swaying as she struts in high stilettos. God knows how she managed to walk down the hill in those. Other eyes are watching too. Exclusively male. One man practically has his tongue out and notices Matt watching him. The man nods in a respectful way at Matt and turns back to his pint. Matt shakes his head and orders the drinks. *You can have her, mate. I have no interest whatsoever.*

At the table he takes a sip of his pint and looks at the menu. He's thus engaged, but he knows her eyes are all over him, scrutinising, appraising. Matt flicks his gaze up and catches hers lingering over his chest. His shirt's open a few buttons and his chest hair seems to hold particular fascination for Jessica. He shifts in his seat and folds his arms. 'I think I fancy the chicken.'

Jessica flutters her lashes and gives a too-high and tinkly laugh. 'That's mad. I fancy the same. We must have similar tastes, eh?' She puts her head on one side and gives him a slow smile.

Please. Matt pushes his chair back. 'I'll go order them. My treat.' The more time he has away from her the better. This was such a big mistake.

After a one-woman self-appreciation society talk lasting fifteen minutes, Jessica does the head-on-one-side slow smile again. 'Anyway… as they say, enough about me – tell me about your life, Matt.'

'It's not very interesting. Besides, I can't let this chicken go cold.' Matt shovels a huge mouthful into his mouth and chews noisily. That should put her off.

'You do like your food. Nice to see a man with an appetite.' Jessica does the tinkly laugh again and pats his hand. *Great.*

'Yeah, I'm always hungry and anything will do. Can't be bothered with all this cheffy stuff. Bangers and mash, chicken and chips, beans on toast. Fart for Britain afterward though.' He gives her a wink, grins and wipes his mouth on the back of his hand.

'Ew, too much information.' Jessica flaps her hand and wrinkles her nose. 'So, you were brought up in London, but have relatives here?' She takes a dainty mouthful of her food and looks at him expectantly.

'Not now. My grandparents were born right here in St Agnes. They left when my dad was a baby, but my gran especially misses Cornwall, even now.'

'Hmm. It is rather quaint. I'm from the other side of the Tamar. Much prefer Devon, but a job came up here and…'

Matt notices Jessica's eyes grow moist. He's tempted to ignore it, but he's been brought up to care about others. Even red-lipped man-eating ones. 'You okay?'

The hand flap again. 'Don't mind me. I came here because of the breakup of my marriage. I needed to put some distance between all our old haunts and my poor battered heart.' Jessica sniffs and dabs at her nose with a napkin.

'Oh, I'm sorry to hear that.' Matt looks away and concentrates on his food.

'Yes. He said I was too controlling. Went off with a little mouse of a woman who worked in the office – he was a walking cliché, my Harry.' She draws her fingers down the stem of her glass, looks into the middle distance. Then she snorts. 'Controlling, my arse. Some men can't cope with successful women, that's all.' She takes a sip of wine and looks at him. 'Your wife passed away, didn't she?'

Jeez, is she for real? Matt nods. 'Yes, leukaemia.'

'That's terrible. How are you coping with it?'

How do you think, you mad woman? 'It gets easier with time.' Matt puts his fork down and leans back in his chair. 'To be honest I'd rather not talk about it.'

Jessica leans forward, her face a mask of concern. 'Oh, of course. I'm *so* sorry for bringing it up. I can be far too blunt at times without realising it.'

Matt takes a large pull on his pint and finishes his food. Ten minutes and he's making an excuse to leave. She's more than he can bear.

'Are you getting to know the village and the locals?' Jessica does a stretchy smile in an obvious attempt to lighten the mood.

'Kind of. I chat to Betty in the newsagents and the guy behind the bar here – the landlady too. Not had a chance to make many friends so far.'

'They can be a bit reserved where strangers are concerned. I've been here two years and only have one or two people who I'd call friends.'

I wonder why?

'I heard that you had a nasty incident at your house the first day you were here. Any more news on that?'

'The badger head?'

She nods and pushes her plate to the side.

'No. But I have a feeling I've not heard the last.' Matt tells her about his encounter in the pub with Morvoren Penhallow and that he wouldn't be surprised if she was the culprit.

'I wouldn't put anything past her. She's a right old witch by all accounts. She's not well liked in the village. Her granddaughter's a bit odd too.'

'Really. Why?'

'She has a little art shop in town – a great artist, but weird.'

Matt's very interested all of a sudden. 'Lavender Nancarrow? I looked in the shop window this afternoon.'

'Yeah, that's right.'

Matt's heart sinks. There's no way he'll ever get to know Lavender now if Morvoren's her gran.

Jessica pats her hair. 'Pretty girl, if you like that boho kind of look, but no man can get near her, apparently.'

Matt can see the barely disguised jealousy in Jessica's face and says, 'Yes, she is stunning. I saw her locking up the shop.' A lie, but he won't go into the embarrassing truth of his meeting with Lavender.

Jessica twists her mouth to one side. 'Hmm. Well, one of the local men I was seeing for a while told me she was strange. He went out with her a few times and she raked his cheek with her nails when he tried to go further than a kiss. He's still got the scar.'

Irritation flares. 'And that makes her odd? Perhaps he was too full on.'

Jessica's perfectly plucked eyebrows arch. 'Enough to get a scarred face?'

'Maybe. I don't know the guy.'

'Paul?' She laughs. 'Paul's a teddy bear.'

'Maybe he was a grizzly bear that time.' Matt fakes a yawn. 'Anyway, it's been fun, but I'm going to call it a night, Jessica.'

Her face falls. 'Have I offended you somehow?'

Yes. You're here, breathing in and out, aren't you? 'Of course not. I'm just tired.' Matt forces a smile.

Jessica's catlike eyes slide to her watch. 'It's only just gone eight.'

Matt spreads his hands. 'What can I say? I'm boring.'

'Don't be daft. It would have been nice to have chatted for a while longer, that's all.'

Matt pushes back his chair and stands up. 'Another time perhaps. See you at school tomorrow.'

Jessica opens her mouth, but before she can say anything, he turns and hurries out into the September air, thick with woodsmoke. By the time he's reached the cottage he's feeling much better. The brisk walk up the hill in the damp air, pungent with autumn leaves crushed underfoot has lifted his spirits. Just because Lavender is related to the old witch doesn't mean he won't be able get to know her. But then again, why does he want to? Yes, she's gorgeous, but oughtn't he be concentrating on his job, fitting into the village? A relationship in the future might be something he'd want, but not now. Too much at once always ends in tears, he's found.

As he approaches his front door, the security lights come on and he notices his car parked by the fence looks… odd. It's lower on one side than the other… Matt hurries over and sees the reason for the listing vehicle. The driver's side tyres have been slashed to buggery. On closer inspection, the entire side panels of the car from nose to tip have been keyed, or worse. There's so much damage he'll have to have a total respray. Oh shit. The headlights have been smashed in too. Why the fuck does Morvoren Penhallow hate him so much? Mind you, he wouldn't have thought she'd be strong enough to smash the headlights. Unless she had a crowbar. Yeah, that would fit.

Inside, he pours a generous whisky and picks up his mobile. Then he throws it down on the sofa and knocks back the Scotch in one, coughing as it leaves a burning path behind in his throat. What's the point in contacting the local plod? They'd only send out PC Cross again. He was as much use as a chocolate fireguard. There'd be no clues left worth having. The nearest neighbour is a quarter of a mile away, so nobody will have seen anything. And the whole thing would be futile. He'll just pay up for a respray and new tyres. It will cost a bit, but it's better than getting a crime number, insurance involved and all that malarkey.

Matt pours another drink and sticks the TV on. He needs mind-numbing crap to wash through his troubled mind. He doesn't want to think, just to forget about it all until the morning. Helpless is something he doesn't do, but at this present moment, he's no choice. He's sure as hell not leaving the village, so he'll just have to put up with it and keep vigilant. Matt closes his eyes and then quickly opens them again as an idea occurs. There *is* something he can do. He'll get a CCTV camera fixed. It will have to be well hidden though if he wants to catch the old boot in the act. Having some semblance of a plan, at last he feels more positive. If old Penhallow wants a fight, she's got one.

Chapter seven

Lavender looks at the crimson liquid swirling down the plughole and shudders. The gash on her forefinger could be much worse, but she's never been able to cope with the sight of blood. Her gran laughed at her when she'd come running in earlier from 'her mission' at Trevelyar's. Lavender, when she'd seen the cut on her finger in the light, had apparently turned the colour of snow. She'd had to be led to a chair before she'd fainted. Gran wrapped up her finger and told her to rest a while. She'd also scolded her for getting clumsy with the knife when she'd slashed the tyres. If the blade had gone any deeper there'd have to be hospitals involved, and then Trevelyar might have heard somehow, got suspicious. *Yeah, Gran, don't worry about my finger, will you?* Gran had said to leave it wrapped in an old towel for an hour and then clean and dress it. She couldn't stay to help as she had to meet her friend for a drink. Charming.

Lavender takes her hand from the running tap and dabs at the wound with a handful of kitchen roll. This seems to stem the blood a bit and she quickly slaps on a bit of gauze and wraps a bandage tight round her finger. It's feeling less throbby already. Unbidden, an image of Matt Trevelyar's smile and the damage she wrought on his car surfaces. Guilt looks back at her from the bathroom mirror, so she walks out and into her bedroom. No point in having second thoughts now, is there? He's a pervert and a wife beater. Why should the children in their village school suffer at his hands? He has to go, and there's no way he will unless she and Gran drive him out. It's a pity Lavender didn't have someone looking out for her when she was ten years old. She squashes that thought and goes downstairs.

She has a painting to flesh out, and one-handed or not, she's doing it.

***

Morvoren curses her creaking legs as she struggles through the field – a shortcut to the pub. There was a time that she'd scoot across it like a hare in spring but no longer. She should expect nothing less, now she's in her eightieth year, but her mind is still as sharp and active as it was when she was a girl. If only there was a cure for old age. Still, Lavender would carry on the old ways after she was gone. The girl took on today's task without question. She was loyal, brave and true. Three qualities that had been passed down the Penhallow line from time out of mind.

Morvoren stops to rest by a wall, leaning her bottom against it, and thinks of the past and future. She sees it like a plume of woodsmoke. The future drifting up and off, unseen, the past smouldering beneath, fuelling its existence. She looks out at the landscape of fields, dales and ocean, feels it wrap around her like a comforting blanket. This is her land, her village, her reason for being. She's lived, laughed and loved here all her life and given a good chunk of it over to the protection of this land – this haven.

Lavender would be the next matriarch, the next protector of her haven. Because there is no way Morvoren can trust her own son to step up. He'd always been a bit wet, happy to be blown by the wind – going with the flow, despite Morvoren's nagging. Tony was too placid; took after his father, God rest his soul. There were times Morvoren willed her son to bite back, refuse to do her bidding and show some spirit. But he'd always done as she'd asked, like a little lamb, whether he'd agreed with her or not. And that wife of his. Dear, oh dear. That was the only time Tony had gone against her wishes: when he'd married her. She is like a little mouse, scared to death of her mother-in-law. God only knows how she produced such a wonderful daughter.

In the pub, she sees her best and oldest friend, Annie, is already here. She's at a corner table near the open fire reading a book – a pint of beer at her elbow. Morvoren hopes this meeting won't prove to be more difficult than it should be.

'Nippy for September, Annie,' Morvoren says, and warms her hands at the fire for a few seconds before sitting opposite her.

''Tis, Mor. I have me long johns on!' Annie laughs and puts her book to one side, marking the place with a beer mat. She pats her grey curls and leans across the table, her dark eyes searching Morvoren's face. 'Right. What's so bloody urgent you had to drag me away from my front room? I'll have to watch Corrie on catch up now.'

Morvoren smiles. 'That programme is getting dafter as it goes on.' She stops to thank young Gary as he sets a pint down in front of her. Nice that he doesn't have to be asked. She takes a sip and wonders how to start. 'Thing is... we're going to have to put our matchmaking to one side for a week or so.' She holds a finger up to silence Annie's protest. 'It will all be back on, don't you worry. It's just I have a plan that needs executing and our Lavender is going to do it.'

'What plan's this? Because our Jamie is getting wilder by the day. I reckon he'll up and off before too long if we don't give him a reason to stay.' Annie pulls her neck back and rubs her nose. 'There was a scare a few months back when me and his mum thought he'd got some tourist pr–'

'Pregnant. Yes, you said, *about a thousand times*, and once this thing's over the marriage will be back on track. I think April next year at the latest.'

'But they've not even been on a date yet. Our Jamie keeps asking if I'll put in a word for him with you – you know, seeing as how your Lavender won't have anything to do–'

'With men, yes. I know. But she'll come around, with the right coaxing. It's time she had a husband and a purpose. She's twenty-six next birthday and–'

Annie holds up her hand. '"Gran," he says, "will you put a word in with Morvoren, cos I really like Lavender and–"'

'Yes, you said.' Morvoren's fed up of this. 'Look, it will only be for a week or so, but I'm trying to match her up with that bastard Trevelyan…'

Annie's shriek turns a few heads in their direction. 'What? Are you mental?'

'No. Because Lavender's the one that will get rid.'

Annie sits back, folds her arms, pulls a sour face. 'Will she? I think you're playing with fire, Mor. After all that you went through with his granddad, not to say what happened all those years ago when–'

'Trust me. I know what I'm doing. You just need to tell your Jamie that there's nothing to worry about and that she really likes him. Tell him that she's only going out with this Trevelyar because she's scared of showing her feelings to Jamie. Tell him to bide his time and that I'm working on it. Obviously, Annie, she's not actually going out with the useless bag of rubbish – it's just part of the plan.'

Annie sighs and takes a big swallow of her drink. 'Hmm. Well I don't like it.'

For God's sake, give me strength! 'No, neither do I,' Morvoren barks. 'But I don't like that disgusting pile of shit teaching the cream of Cornwall either. He'll be gone inside three weeks, mark my words.' She takes a gulp of beer and bangs it down on the tabletop, spilling some of its contents across the surface.

Annie eyes the puddle and her expression changes from sour to one of apprehension. 'Hey, don't upset yourself. I'm sure you know what you're doing. Always have.'

Morvoren nods. Annie knows when to back down. Morvoren has always looked after her since primary school. She was like the little sister she never had – bullies ran a mile if Morvoren was around. There was another girl in her teens who'd meant even more to her than Annie, but she'd betrayed her. The thought of what she did, even now, makes Morvoren's blood boil. In later life, Annie had done whatever she could for Morvoren and her kin. She'd owned a bakery and confectionery with her husband,

and Morvoren had never had to pay for a loaf or cake in her life. Annie's daughter and husband ran it now, and eventually it'd be Jamie's. A local business run by local people. Jamie is perfect for Lavender. Handsome, smart and a man of means.

She mops up the spilt beer with a tissue and says less harshly to her friend, 'Yes, I *do* know what I'm doing. You just have to do your bit. Put young Jamie's mind at rest.'

*****

Lavender can hear ringing in her ears. Is she falling, sinking? Her eyes snap open and she realises she's been dozing in her chair and the phone's ringing on the table. Hauling herself up, she winces, forgetting about the cut on her finger, and grabs the phone with her good hand. 'Gran?'

'Yeah. You sound like you're half asleep. It's only half nine.'

'Hmm, fell asleep in front of the fire.'

'Well listen. I have a plan to get rid of Trevelyar and you need to be very brave because it's only you as can do it, maid.'

Lavender's suddenly wide awake. Brave? She doesn't like the sound of this. 'I don't want to do anything else, Gran. Let's just see if what I did today has any effect.'

'Oh, it will have. He'll be rattled all right. But we need more. He needs to be tipped right over the edge.'

'But what else do you want to do? That was pretty bad what I did to his car, and you did the badger thing. Let's leave it for now and–'

'We will *not* leave it for now. We need to keep up the pressure. Now just be quiet for a few minutes and I'll tell you what you're going to do, okay?'

Lavender sighs. When Gran's in this mood there's no arguing with her. 'Okay, I'm listening.'

Chapter eight

Thank God the weekend is on the horizon. Matt's had a shit few days. He's had to walk to school through the driving rain and wind blowing a hooley, because it's taking forever to get the tyres done on his car. Something about ordering the right ones – Matt's no clue about cars; he sees them as a necessity to get from A to B. Then the heating system at the cottage's playing up, and to top it all, he thinks he's getting a cold. Matt shuts an exercise book, sets his marking pen down and looks at his watch. It's four o'clock. Can he sneak out of school early? It is Friday, after all, and he's worked late every night since he started the job.

He's just about to step out from his classroom into the corridor, when he hears Jessica's voice booming at some unfortunate cleaner. She's the last person he wants to run into, so he ducks back inside and waits for her to pass. Her tapping heels stop outside his door and he pictures her looking in through the glass partition. Matt's hiding in the recess behind the door and heaves a sigh of relief when the heels tap-tap on down the corridor. Outside he finds it's stopped raining and hurries through the playground, a bundle of exercise books under his arm, planning a relaxing bath and an evening doing nothing – unless the heating is up the spout, then he'll go to the pub.

Matt's beginning to feel like a regular in the Driftwood Spars. He's got to know the barman well enough for a pint of Doom Bar to be set in front of him without having to ask, and he's on nodding terms with one or two of the other customers. The best thing about this evening though, is the cosy atmosphere as he sits on a comfy chair warming his toes by the fire. His stomach is full of a wonderful dinner and he's loath to venture back out to his cold little cottage. If they don't fix the heating over the weekend, he's going to threaten to leave without paying the rent and find more comfortable accommodation.

Yawning, Matt stretches his arms above his head and closes his eyes. When he opens them again, Lavender Nancarrow's breezed through the door, pulling the cool salt air behind her like a train. She looks stunning as usual. Matt closes his mouth and watches as she orders a drink. A deep blue velvet dress under a tasselled multi-coloured shawl would look stupid on anyone else. But on her it's perfect. There's a jewelled comb in the back of her hair, which she's piled up in soft curls on top of her head, and though she's wearing make-up, it's subtle, understated. A few men are watching her too and Matt feels strangely protective. If she's wary of men, she might feel under threat. Should he go up and talk to her? He's not sure. They didn't have such a great meeting the other day, and it might freak her out.

As he's deliberating, she pays for her drink and turns towards the comfy seating and the fire. She sees him and smiles, comes over and stands opposite. 'Matt, isn't it? Is it okay if I sit here, or are you with someone?'

Matt's so surprised she's come over, he takes a few seconds to respond. 'Er, no, please take a seat. Great to see you again, Lavender.' He gives her what he hopes is a winning smile, not a rictus grin.

Then a guy saunters over. He's tall, with dark spiky hair, good-looking – and knows it. He leans in to Lavender. 'Hey, beautiful. How's tricks? Not seen you for a few weeks.'

Lavender shrugs. 'Okay, Jamie. How's your gran?' She looks about as interested in him as she would be in having dental work without anaesthetic.

'Annie's well. She met up with Morvoren the other day, had a nice little chat. Just tell your gran I totally understand.' He looks Matt up and down as if he's scum and then back to Lavender. 'Speak soon. And I'm just over there if you need me.' Jamie indicates the bar with his head and walks away.

Lavender rolls her eyes at Matt, takes a sip of her wine and sets the glass between them on the table. 'No idea what planet Jamie's on sometimes.' She smiles and takes another sip of wine. 'I must apologise for my rudeness the other day. You must have thought I was nuts just rushing off like that.'

'I have that effect on women.' Matt smiles again and hopes the line's not too cheesy.

She laughs. 'I'm sure that's not true.' She slips off her shawl, showing that the dress is sleeveless and that she has a delicate tattoo – sprigs of lavender winding round and down her left arm. Then she tips her head to one side, gives him a sheepish grin. 'My gran's to blame for my sharp exit.'

'Right?' Matt wonders whether to act totally dumb or come clean. Lavender's honest wide eyes prompt him. 'Yes. Morvoren Penhallow doesn't like me, I must admit. She wants me out of the village, me being a Trevelyar. God only knows what we've supposed to have done though.' He spreads his hands, sits back and watches Lavender's face.

Lavender mirrors his pose. 'Yes, I'm afraid she and your gran had a run-in back in the day.' A mischievous smile lights up her face. 'I think they fought over your granddad.'

'My granddad?' The thought of anyone fighting over old Terry is preposterous to him. It's hard to picture him a young man.

'Yeah. Apparently, your gran pinched him from mine.'

Matt laughs. 'I had no idea.' Then he remembers the damage to his car, the badger, and stops laughing. 'So you're telling me that your gran wants me out because of an old squabble over a man? She was pretty vile to me in this pub not so long back.'

Lavender sighs. 'The first cut is the deepest, don't they say?'

'Even so. To harbour a grudge for what? Fifty-odd years?'

A shrug. 'Yes, but there we are. And more importantly, there's also some old feud between the Penhallows and the Trevelyars going back centuries.'

'What old feud?'

'I'm not sure of all the details. Anyway, Gran told me to avoid you if I ever met you because of your relatives and the fact that you were taking up a job in our school, which could have been given to a Cornishman.'

Matt's temper is rising, and he takes a swallow of beer. Why is Lavender sitting with him if that's the case? 'You think this too?'

'Not so much as her... but my gran does have a big influence on our wider family.' There's an uncomfortable silence while Matt wonders where to go next. Then she says, 'But having thought about it, I think she's mistaken where you're concerned. You have a kind face.'

That's something, he supposes. 'Thanks. But I can't get past the fact that your gran would damage my car and warn me off with a badger head, all because of some old feud and the fact that my gran nicked her bloke.'

Lavender's mouth fell open. 'Damage to your car and a badger? What do you mean?'

Matt tells her.

'That's ridiculous. My gran's nearly eighty. I think she'd have a bit of trouble smashing headlights and slashing tyres.' She laughs, but Matt detects no humour in it.

Matt notices a plaster on Lavender's finger and hates where his thoughts go next. 'She could have had help.'

Lavender narrows her eyes. 'My gran might be a lot of things, but she wouldn't stoop to those levels. Nor would she get anyone else to.' Her voice is cold, harsh. Then she grabs her shawl, wraps it round her and stands.

Shit. He doesn't want her to leave. Why did he say that? 'Hey, sorry. I'm just shaken by what's been going on lately. Please sit down and have your drink.'

There's hesitation in her eyes, but then she sighs and sits back down. 'Okay. But only until my friend gets here.' She looks at her watch and to the door.

'What time is she supposed to be here?'

'Ten minutes ago. Kelly's not a great timekeeper. Mind you, she's married now, got a little one. I expect she's fallen asleep.'

Matt knows the answer but asks, 'You're not married, or with anyone?'

'No, not yet. My gran thinks I'm in danger of being on the shelf. I'm only bloody twenty-five.' Lavender rolls her eyes.

'I've got five years on you.'

A smile. 'You really are on the shelf then, unless there's a Mrs Trevelyar?'

Matt's heart twinges. 'Not any more. She died.'

'Oh no! So sorry. Hope I didn't upset you.'

Matt shakes his head and musters a smile. 'No, it's fine. People don't expect me to be a widower at my age. It still hurts but…' He feels a lump in his throat, so drowns it with beer and changes the subject. 'After you'd gone the other day I looked in the window of your shop. You're a stunning artist!'

A pink hue floods Lavender's cheeks. Obviously self-conscious, she briefly covers her blush with her hands. 'Oh, thanks, that's nice of you. The business is doing quite well. We had quite a few tourists this year and they bought loads of my paintings.'

'Excellent. What are you working on now?'

'Another seascape. They sell best, and I adore the sea. I live in a cottage right next to it. No matter what the weather, I have a beautiful ever-changing seascape right outside my window.' She spreads her hands to illustrate.

Matt tries not to stare at the webbing between her index fingers and thumbs. How unusual. Mostly he tries not to stare at her eyes, her mouth. She's even more beautiful now she's enthusing about her work. Captivating. 'It's obvious you're inspired by where you live. I adore the ocean too. We came to Cornwall lots when I was a kid. My grandparents missed it so much – my gran especially. Living here now… it feels like I've come home to my roots. I belong here, know what I mean?'

'Hmm.' Lavender looks away, stony-faced, pulls her mobile out of her bag. Matt wonders what he's said to upset her. 'Oh,

Kelly's not coming. I got a missed call and a text. The baby's unwell.' She shoves the phone away and drains her glass.

'That's a shame. Can I get you another drink?'

'No thanks. Must be off.'

'You okay?'

She avoids his gaze and stands. 'Yeah, fine.'

Damn it. She'll be out and away before he can do anything. He blurts, 'Will you consider coming out for a bite to eat and a drink one evening, Lavender?' Bite to eat – he sounds like bloody Jessica! She looks at him and away. No chance of that then.

'Not sure, Matt. My gran would be livid for a start.'

'Ask your gran. The more the merrier – she might realise I'm not the devil's spawn if she gets to know me.' *God, don't let her say yes to that bit.*

Lavender laughs. 'I can't see that happening. But why don't I think about it and give you a ring?'

As he puts his number into her phone, Matt tries to stop an ear-to-ear smile breaking out. Wow. He never thought he'd get so far with her after what she'd said. 'Great. Give me a ring in a few days, yeah?'

A quick nod and half-smile. 'Okay. See you, Matt.'

Matt watches her leave, heads turning in her wake. They have no chance, and he has very little. But at least there's a glimmer of hope. Lavender Nancarrow is certainly a woman he'd love to know better. He just prays that Morvoren Penhallow doesn't stick her evil nose in and kill the glimmer of hope dead in the water.

Chapter nine

August 1956

Morvoren can't decide whether she likes Elowen more than she's jealous of her. Elowen makes her laugh; she's funny and so nice too. A great friend. Jealousy is a very ugly thing, her mother says. And it is. Morvoren tries so hard to push it away, but every time she sees her blue-eyed friend toss her glossy blonde curls and flash that movie-star smile, she wants to slap her, push her over in the mud and hack her hair off with her dad's sheep shears. Elowen is only fifteen, for God's sake, a kid really in age – but her curves would give Marilyn Monroe a run for her money. Morvoren, two years older, has a figure like a boy and nondescript gravy-coloured hair. No matter what she does with make-up she looks like a pantomime clown, so she doesn't bother mostly. Her mother doesn't approve of 'war paint' anyway.

Insects hum in the meadow grass and a cow moos in the pastureland down the valley. Beyond that, the ocean's cradled in the arms of the hills like a precious sapphire and Morvoren's heart swells with love for Cornwall. Setting down her basket in the grass, she sits down to wait for Elowen. How lucky she was to be born here, because there's no finer place. She can't understand those who want to venture elsewhere. Towns scare her. All that bustle and car fumes – why anyone would want to make a home there is beyond her.

The old ways are best. Natural. Nature has so much to offer those in the know, and she's learned that from Mother and Grandmother. They worry that the old ways will die out, because the youngsters of today aren't interested. Their heads are too full of Elvis and rock and roll. But they shouldn't worry, because Morvoren's interested, and so is Elowen.

That's how they were drawn together. One day Morvoren was walking the meadows and woods, just like today, with her basket. She was picking herbs, flowers and berries for potions and medicines when in the distance she'd seen Elowen doing the same. Even though they'd not had much to do with each other in school as they were different ages, they'd got talking and had been fast friends ever since. There was even a bit of unspoken rivalry between them over who knew most about herbs and flowers.

Morvoren thinks about who will receive the potion she'll make with today's offerings and feels her face flame. She's made love potions for others, but never for herself. And if her mother knew which man she meant to give it to, she'd be banished from the house.

Elowen appears at the bottom of the field and runs up to meet Morvoren. She moves so gracefully, like a young doe. The sun's glistening on her curls, her cheeks are rosy, lips pink and full, like her figure. Jealousy uncoils in Morvoren's belly, opens its jaws, but she sends a bolt of good thoughts down to quiet it and stands to greet her friend. 'Hello, thought you weren't coming!'

Elowen takes a moment to catch her breath. 'I know. I stopped to pick a few leaves on the way, but my mum made me late by getting me to churn the butter and then clean the chickens out! I need to get another job before I turn into a farmer.'

Morvoren frowns. 'Nothing wrong with farming. It's what I do. What my family have done for generations.'

'Yeah, mine too.' Elowen shoves an errant blonde curl from her eyes. 'And it's great that you love it. But I want something more from life. A bit more interesting, you know?'

'Well, working in the interesting chip shop didn't suit, did it?' Morvoren sighs.

Elowen wrinkles her nose. 'No. I stank of fish and chips – couldn't stand it!'

'Then what's next?'

'I want to try hairdressing. There's a job going in Perranporth, but I've heard that Gilly's going for it and she's had experience.'

'That's no way to get ahead, is it? You have to think you're just as good as the next maid. Better, even!' Morvoren laughs and walks on.

Elowen catches up. 'Yeah, you're right. I'll get that job if it bloody kills me.' Then she looks in Morvoren's basket. 'Oooh, who's the love potion for?'

Bloody hell, this girl's good. Morvoren looks in Elowen's basket. 'Who's got the cold?'

'I asked first.' Elowen runs ahead on the narrow path through the woods, stops Morvoren passing. 'Is it for Helen? She's in love with Barry, but he's not interested.'

'Not telling. And anyway, it might not be a love potion.'

'It is. There's rosemary, lavender, a few rose petals, primrose, wild fennel, g–'

'Some of which can also be used for sleeping potions.'

'Where's the valerian or camomile? Can't make sleeping potions without those.' Elowen raises a delicate eyebrow.

Morvoren snorts and pushes past. Heat races up her neck and she doesn't want Elowen to see, or she'll put two and two together. 'Come on, it will be teatime soon and we've not got much.'

'It's for you, isn't it? I can tell!' Elowen yells behind her.

Morvoren stops so quick her friend bumps into her back. She turns to face her and hisses, 'What if it is? Not a crime, is it?'

'No. But I want to know who the boy is.' Elowen's eyes are alight with excitement, thirsty for secrets.

'Well, you can want,' Morvoren snaps.

'You *have* to tell me.'

'Why?'

'I'm your best friend.' Elowen does a winning smile.

'Who says?' Morvoren tries to stop her lips copying Elowen's. 'Me.'

Elowen looks so mischievous that Morvoren's smile breaks through and she turns back to the path, crushing the wild garlic underfoot, the oil pungent in the air. Over her shoulder, she says, 'Okay, yes, it's for me.' Her friend shrieks with excitement so she hurries on, 'But I'm *not* telling you the name of the boy, because if I do, the potion won't work.'

'Is it Graham? I bet it is.'

Morvoren says nothing, just shakes her head.

'Or Peter? He's lovely. Looks a bit like Dean Martin.'

Morvoren laughs. 'Dean Martin? If he does, then I'm the queen.'

A giggle from behind. 'Hmm. I wonder who it could be… Mind you, I know who it certainly isn't. Terry Trevelyar. I think he's the most handsome lad in the village. Clever too. My mum says he'll go places, that one. But he's out of bounds for you, cos of your feud.'

Morvoren's heart jumps. *Elowen likes Terry?*

'Why aren't you saying anything?'

'Eh? I told you I wasn't telling you who it is.'

'Yes, but the other two I mentioned before Terry – you shook your head and then said Peter wasn't like Dean Martin. You went quiet when I said about Ter–'

'Course it's not him! Now can you bloody shut up!' Morvoren deliberately stamps on a clump of garlic flowers and quickens her pace.

'Hey, no need to go crackers. I'll shut up now… Oi, Mor, wait for me!'

Morvoren doesn't answer, just keeps on stomping down the path, her heartbeat quicker than her steps. There's a storm in her head and anger fuels the lightning bolt she imagines striking down that little bitch hurrying along behind. If Elowen goes near Terry, then God help her.

Chapter ten

Lavender's rearranging the display in the window of her shop. Nobody has been in this morning so far and it's almost eleven. She tells herself it's normal for mid-September after the main tourist season has tailed off, yet it makes the day drag when there's nobody at all. She wonders if the shop is a waste of time in the autumn and winter. Once she's paid rent and heating and electric she doesn't make much. It's a good job her main income is over the spring and summer. Oh well, she'll just get on with painting in the back and hope someone comes in soon.

Half an hour later, inspiration is out the door and beckoning her to go for a walk on the cliff path. *Might as well take the canvas and do it in the fresh air, lock the shop for a few hours and pop back around three.* As she's packing up, the doorbell tinkles and her heart lifts. It crashes again when she hears, 'Lavender, it's only me!'

Gran. *Not today, please.* 'Hi, just going out to paint. I need a bit of inspiration.'

Gran's face falls. 'Have you got time for that? You have to prepare for tomorrow, don't you?'

'Prepare? How long does a phone call take?'

'But what if he says no? You have to make it a sure thing.'

'Trust me, he'll jump at the chance of a drink. He was very keen the other night. Took me all my time to be civil. I could have slapped his face when he said he belonged here. The cheek of him.'

'I bet.' Gran's gaze slips away from Lavender's and she looks at a painting of the old schoolhouse. 'I was just thinking – it might be better to invite him to your cottage for dinner. Then you could do the deed without the danger of anyone seeing. The Driftwood's a bit public.'

'What? Him and me on our own in my cottage? Have you gone nuts? Isn't he supposed to be violent with women?'

'Just his wife, I think,' Gran says absently and continues to study the painting.

Lavender's temper grows hotter. 'You *think*? Oh. That's okay then. I'm perfectly safe!'

Gran turns to face her. 'He won't do anything silly if he's as smitten as you say. He'll want to do everything by the book. Talking of which...' She gets the ancient book from the shelf. 'How long will it take you to concoct a potion?'

Lavender throws her hands up in exasperation. 'I have no idea. Not long.'

Admiration fills the other woman's eyes. 'No, it never does. You are the best, my girl, and that's the truth. I was good in my day, that bitch Elowen too – but it comes more naturally to you than anyone I have ever seen practice. And I've seen a few.'

Lavender knows this isn't just Gran flattering. She's always had a gift for potions, since Gran taught her to recognise the first healing leaves when she was five. Lavender's always known how much of this, that or the next thing to add without looking at the book. It came by instinct. Besides, the book is going on for a hundred and fifty years old, and she prefers not to use it if she can help it in case it falls apart.

Gran's looking at her as a robin views a worm. Those sharp hazel eyes might sit on a concertina of wrinkles, but they miss nothing. Lavender packs her wet brushes and catches her webbed thumb on the bristles. She splays the extra skin and rubs the paint off with a tissue. Cruel children whisper 'freak' in her head and she shoves the memory away. Matt Trevelyar didn't seem to think she was a freak the other night. She'd seen him looking at her hands but there was no trace of disgust in his eyes. All of a sudden, this whole venture seems ridiculous to her.

'You know, Gran, I'm not sure I want to go ahead with this potion. I mean, what if he reacts badly? Much as I don't care what happens to him, given the monster he is – I don't want to be a murderer.'

Gran coughs out a wheezy laugh. 'There's not a chance you'd do that, my beauty. You're too skilled, clever.'

'There's always a chance. Everyone reacts differently.' Lavender folds her arms, stands her ground. Gran's obsessed, but she won't take the fall if anything goes wrong. And to suggest that he comes to her house? The two of them alone. Does she care more about driving this man out than her own granddaughter's safety?

Gran slaps her hand down on the shop counter and Lavender blinks. The old woman can still scare the shit out of her, even now. 'Look here, my girl. This man beat his wife until she couldn't take life no more. Then he molested little girls – *you* know full well what that's like! Do you want him to do it to our little ones? Where's your backbone!'

Lavender's stomach turns and tears well up behind her eyes. Memories surface of that day at school again. The day when… She closes her eyes, shoves the scene into a dark cupboard, bolts the door. 'Okay! Okay, I'll ring him and invite him to dinner tomorrow if it makes you happy.' Her voice sounds thin, wobbly, and Lavender hates it.

Her gran sticks her chin out, bangs the counter again. 'Aye, it do make me happy. Ought to make you too! The sooner that sick devil Matthew Trevelyar is gone from here the better we'll all be.' She sweeps out of the shop, slamming the door behind her. Lavender covers her ears against the jangling of the doorbell and leans against the counter until silence returns. The canvas waits on the table, but all desire to paint has gone.

***

Matt's just arrived home from school when his phone rings. His heart leaps when he sees Lavender's name. 'Hi there, Lavender. How are you?' He walks to the window and looks out over the fields, excitement building in his chest as if he's a teenager again.

'Good thanks, Matt. I was wondering if you'd like to come for dinner tomorrow evening?'

Bloody hell! Does she mean at her house? 'What, you're going to cook for me?'

'That was the plan.' Lavender's laugh sounds nervous.

'How nice!'

'I'd wait until after you've tasted it before you make a judgement.'

'I'm sure it will be wonderful.' Matt plonks himself down on the sofa, kicks his shoes off. 'Can I bring anything?'

'No, just yourself. About seven?'

'Yes, great. Looking forward to it.' Matt's smile is so wide he can hardly speak.

'Okay. Bye, then–'

'Er, I need your address.'

She laughs. 'Of course you do. I'm a few miles from you, so you'll need to drive. It's Headland Cottage on Atlantic Spur Lane. Go right to the end and the cottage is on the left. There's only two houses on there, can't miss it.' She gives him the postcode and hangs up.

Matt notices his daft grin in the dining room mirror and laughs out loud. Who'd have thought it? Lavender Nancarrow asking him to dinner. He must be pretty special given what Jessica had told him about how she was with men. *That Jamie bloke in the pub the other night didn't stand a chance, but she obviously likes me.* Then he tells himself off. Tomorrow might be a test to see if he's a gentleman… so he has to be on his very best behaviour. Matt can just imagine the old witch Penhallow going berserk when she finds out. Unless Lavender hasn't told her of course. Matt's glad he has to drive to Lavender's, because he can only have a glass of wine. The last thing he wants to do is get merry, because he tends to say things he shouldn't when he is. Last night, after he'd spoken to her, he was a bit worried that things were moving too fast. Dinner was a huge thing so early in a… what? A relationship? They didn't really have one – so it was a bit odd. Besides, did he actually want a relationship? Then he'd told himself to just see where things went.

Lavender wasn't just anyone, she was one of the most beautiful and interesting people he'd ever met. He'd be stupid to say no.

***

Outside her house, he looks at the flowers he'd purchased from the garage and wishes he'd got chocolates too. Do they look too droopy? They hadn't a lot of choice and he wanted to bring something as well as wine. He looks at the bottle of red in his other hand. What if she only drinks white? She was drinking white the other night at the pub, so... The door opens as he's contemplating.

'Hi, Matt. I thought I heard a car pull up.' Lavender's standing in the hallway wearing a flowery dress. Sunflowers on a red background would look garish on anyone else, but Lavender rocks it. Her hair's loose, cascading over her shoulders, and she gives him a warm smile that lights up her face. She eyes his gifts.

'Hi Lavender. I brought you some flowers and wine.' *Well, duh. She's not blind.*

'Thanks, that's so kind.' She takes the flowers. 'Come inside.'

Matt's only just set foot inside Lavender's home, but he wishes he had a place like it. From the patio doors, there's a panoramic view of the ocean, a field or two and a rugged cliff over which the sun's setting. The inside walls are made from huge stone slabs, upon which some colourful fabrics hang. There's similar fabrics woven into the rugs on the stripped floors, and in the wide chimney breast, an open fire. The furniture has seen better days, but the old leather overstuffed sofa works so well in this setting. The cottage is perfect.

'Wow, what a wonderful view, and a wonderful home too,' Matt says, slipping his jacket off and hanging it on the back of a kitchen chair.

Lavender turns from arranging his flowers in a yellow ceramic vase, a smile on her lips. 'Thanks. I love it. My granddad used to rent it out when I was a girl and I always said I'd like to live in it one day. When he died he left it to me in his will.'

'That must have been a lovely surprise.'

'It was. Not sure Gran was that pleased, though. I think she was going to sell…' Lavender's words are cut short by the stream of water gushing into the vase. Matt thinks she realised she was telling him too much about her gran. That wouldn't do, given she and Matt are enemies. 'Please take a seat at the table. It won't be long now.'

Lavender sets the flowers down on the big farmhouse table and hurries back to the kitchen. Matt scrapes out a chair and sits. Then he stands up again and takes the top off the wine, pours a little into a glass by a set place. 'Hope you like red?'

'Love it. It'll go well with the beef stroganoff.'

'Lovely. It smells divine!' Divine? How pretentious. *Just act normal, Matt.* He pours himself a glass and takes a sip. His pulse quickens. Why is he so nervous? 'Can I help at all?' he calls through to where he can see Lavender crouched in front of a cupboard.

'You can come and drain the rice if you like.' She smiles and hands him a colander.

A few minutes later, he's feeling calmer. He always feels better when he's doing something and together they have carried in plates, dishes of salad, rice and home-made bread. Now they're sitting opposite each other, and he's taken by her beauty again, her face aglow in the candlelight.

'Cheers, Lavender,' he says, raising his glass.

'Cheers, Matt. Now dig in before it gets cold.'

He does as he's told and finds the food is delicious. The conversation flows easy between them and they share their backgrounds and interests on a perfunctory level. Once or twice Matt notices the extra skin between her thumb and index finger and wants to ask about it. Instinctively he knows that would be a bad move at this stage. She surprises him therefore by saying, 'I know you're dying to ask about my webbing. You keep looking.'

Matt glances at her face, but there's no trace of discomfort in her eyes. Just openness. 'Um. Only if you want to tell me. It's none of my business.'

'It isn't, but I don't mind. I was born with it. My gran has it between her index and middle fingers. Mum wanted me to have the op to remove it when I was a kid, but Gran wouldn't hear of it. She says those who've got it have a special relationship with nature and the sea. Dad went along with his mother.' Lavender pauses, shrugs. 'I don't care now, but it was pretty grim when I was at school.'

'Did the other kids bully you?'

A cloud passes over her eyes and she takes a sip of wine. 'They did. Sometimes I didn't want to go to school because of it, but Gran said I had to go in and show them all I wasn't bothered. She said it would make me strong… and I think she was right.'

'Kids can be cruel.'

'And adults.'

The pointed look she gives him is fleeting, but Matt's convinced she meant her words for him. He swallows a mouthful of food and asks, 'In what way?'

'Just in general. I don't have many friends… I have the webbing and dress differently. I'm committed to using herbs, plants, nature's gifts, to heal ailments, create well-being. Some say I'm a witch like my gran.' She smiles but he can't see warmth in it.

'Is she a white witch?'

'If being an authority on herbs, healing and plants makes you a white witch, then yes.'

Matt shifts in his seat. Was that an admission of Morvoren being a witch? Is he having dinner with one? Does it matter if he is? Struggling for something positive to say, he offers, 'There's a lot to be said for holistic methods of healing nowadays. So many conventional drugs can harm the body, I've read.'

'That's true.' Lavender tears a hunk of bread and dips it in her stroganoff sauce. How refreshing to see no inhibitions. 'Too many chemicals can do more harm than good.' She pops the bread in her mouth and chews, stares into the middle distance and says, 'How did your wife die?'

Taken aback by her abrupt change of topic and matter-of-fact tone, Matt takes a moment, pushes some rice around his plate. 'She had a serious illness.' Even now the word 'cancer' sticks in his throat.

'Mental illness?' Lavender takes a sip of wine, fixes him with a cold stare.

'Eh? No. What make you say that?'

She shrugs. 'People talk. I heard she was depressed.'

'Which people?' Her attitude and manner are beginning to piss him off.

'I can't remember now. Don't tell me if it upsets you.' Lavender avoids his gaze, picks up her wine glass, circles her finger around the rim.

Matt's struggling to cope with her abrupt manner. Why has she suddenly switched her personality? But if she wants the miserable truth, she can have it. 'My beautiful wife and soulmate Beth, died of leukaemia after a three-year battle. When she was first diagnosed, she was pregnant – we agreed she should terminate so she could have chemo, to give her the best chance of survival... but it was for nothing in the end. That still hurts. I often wonder whether our child would have been a girl or boy... what they'd be like now as a five-year-old.' There's a tremor in his voice so he takes a drink of wine and notices he's nearly finished the glass.

'Oh dear. That must have been tough, sorry,' Lavender says, and starts to clear the table. She sounds about as sorry as a fox with a free pass to a henhouse. She shouts from the kitchen, 'Apple pie or cheesecake?'

Is she for real? He's just opened up to her, and she's behaving as if they'd been talking about the weather. If she doesn't alter soon, he's out of here. He shouts back, 'Surprise me. Just going to the loo!'

Upon his return, on the table there's hot apple pie and cream and another glass of wine. Matt sits down and pushes the wine to the side. 'Thanks, but no thanks. I'm driving.'

Lavender gives him a sweet smile and seems back to normal. 'It's a dessert wine, non-alcoholic. Made it myself.' She takes a spoonful of pie.

Matt smiles and does the same. Then he takes a sip of the wine and finds it a bit too sweet but very pleasant. 'Hmm. The blackcurrant tones compliment the apple pie perfectly,' he says in a plummy accent.

She laughs and soon they're talking about anything and everything, just as naturally as they were before she went weird on him. She pours him another glass of the wine and they go to sit by the open fire, Lavender on the sofa, him in the armchair. It's so cosy here. His place is warm now they've fixed the heating at last, but it lacks the cosy feel... Matt could listen to Lavender talk all night. Her voice is so soft and that subtle Cornish burr... He closes his eyes, lets it wash over him and thinks what a wonderful evening it's been... mostly anyway, apart from the little blip. He opens his mouth to ask her something... but he can't for the life of him remember what he wants to say...

Chapter eleven

September 1956

Morvoren can't quite recall when she fell out of hate and in love with Terry Trevelyar. It was probably last year at the farmer's dance when he'd walked in looking like he'd just stepped out of a Hollywood movie. With his slicked-back hair and quiff, wearing a leather jacket, he could have been Elvis, without a word of exaggeration. Those blue, and dare she think it, come-to-bed eyes had sent a fire through her cheeks and other places it had no business being. It was shameful the way he made her feel.

Tonight would be the night that he'd fall in love with her too. There'd been precious little opportunity to be anywhere near him for months, even though she'd tried her best to bump into him around the village. These attempts were awkward and painful on her part. On these occasions she asked if he was well in a stiff little voice, and he just grunted – looked at her as if she'd been something on his shoe. Unsurprising, given the bloody feud that had gone on for far too long now.

Nearly two hundred years of hatred and loathing between their two families. Their parents didn't speak to each other, and when she and Terry found themselves in the same class at school, the two sets of parents had forbidden the teacher to allow them to play together. Yes, what the Trevelyars had done was despicable, but wasn't it time to put the quarrel to bed? Morvoren's cheeks flare again and she hurries into the harvest festival dance.

The village hall is swollen with what looks like almost the entire population of the village. Good. That will make her less noticeable when she sidles up to Terry. The young ones are jiving in the middle of the room while the older ones knock back the home-made cider and look on disapprovingly. There are some little kids playing with a pumpkin and racing about with a scarecrow, but as yet she hasn't spotted the object of her desire. Oh. There he is by the apple bobbing barrel, pint in hand, leaning nonchalantly against a timber post. He's chatting to a group of his mates and her pulse quickens at the sight of him.

How to get near him though? The place is packed, but she can't just wander up to him and chuck her potion in his drink, can she? He'd notice something like that. As she's wondering, Elowen breezes through the door with her parents and bumps into Annie, spilling her sherry in the process. That's it. That's the answer. Thank you, Elowen! Morvoren takes a deep breath, smooths her purple taffeta skirt and sets a course for Terry. As she gets near him she trips and pushes him in the chest, sending his drink flying through the air.

'What the bloody hell you doing, maid!' he yells.

'Sorry! Must've tripped over something. I'll get you another.' Morvoren dabs at a few spatters of ale on his jeans with a tissue and his mates guffaw.

'Oooh, watch where you're touching him, love. He'll come over all unnecessary!' one of them says, which sets them all off again. Terry's not laughing.

'Leave it.' He brushes her hand away, anger furrowing his brows.

'I'll get you another. What you drinking?'

'I'll not take a drink from a Penhallow.'

'Oh come on. Don't be like that.'

'No, Tewwy, sweetie pie, don't be wike dat!' the same joker says, and the rest fall about laughing.

'Pale ale. A pint,' Terry growls and turns his back.

There's a crush at the bar, which is just what she needs. Nobody sees her slip a vial of liquid from her pocket and tip it into the pale ale, give it a stir with her finger. Turning, she makes her way back to Terry just as Elowen spies her across the hall, yells her name and waves like a windmill. *Shit. Go away.* The last thing Morvoren wants is a vison in scarlet turning up just as she's about to look into Terry's eyes as he takes the first sip.

'Mor! Mor! Hang on, I can't get through!' Elowen's yelling as she threads her way through the dancers.

Morvoren pretends not to hear and hurries the last few feet to Terry, holding the pint out to him like a trophy. 'Here, Terry. And sorry again.'

There's only a couple of his mates here now – the joker's dancing and Terry looks less furious. 'Right. Cheers,' he says, looking vaguely interested in her, but he doesn't drink.

She looks right into his eyes and gives him her best smile. He smiles back and raises the glass to his lips.

'Bloody hell, that was a right squash getting through that lot!' Elowen chimes in her ear. 'Didn't you see me, Mor?'

Morvoren swallows a torrent of abuse, looks at her friend and through gritted teeth says, 'No. I was getting a drink for Terry.' She looks back at Terry. The glass is still poised but he hasn't drunk, and her stomach rolls. He's not looking interested in her any more. He's not looking at her at all. He's looking at Elowen. Or should that be drooling?

'Elowen, isn't it? Mark's little sister?'

Elowen turns pink and nods.

'You've grown up, ain't you?' Terry gives her a heart-stopping smile and raises his glass to his lips again.

No. Noo. Don't drink it while looking at her. LOOK AT ME. Morvoren feels sick, weak-legged. 'You still play football on Saturday afternoons, Terry?' she says, putting her hand on the arm holding the drink, hoping to distract him.

Terry shakes her off as if she's an annoying fly. 'Oi. You'll spill my drink again.' He barely glances in her direction. His eyes seem welded to Elowen's.

Elowen says, 'Mark can't play on Saturdays now as he works out at Perranporth, at the butchers.' To Morvoren's horror, she gives a little pout with her full pink lips and pats her blonde curls.

Terry's gaze shifts to Elowen's ample bosom spilling over the dress and back up to her face. 'Well, next time I see him I'll tell him what a doll he has for a sister.' Then he does the beautiful smile again and takes a long pull of his pint… and the bottom falls out of Morvoren's world.

She watches the two of them for a few minutes, chatting away as if they're the only two people in the place. They might as well be for all the notice they take of anyone else, so wrapped up as they are in each other. Morvoren can't stand it. She mutters something about getting a drink, but they don't respond. They're oblivious to her. To anyone. She turns and runs to the door, but before she goes through it, she takes a glance back over her shoulder just in time to see Terry kiss Elowen's cheek. That's it then. It's worked. The strongest love potion she's ever made is a huge success. *Well done, Morvoren, you stupid cow!* Running outside, she's glad to find it's raining. She never lets anyone see her cry.

Chapter twelve

Tap, *tap, tap*. Matt's at the bottom of a deep pit. It's pitch-black; something's holding him there. *Tap, tap, tap*. What's that noise? It sounds like knuckles on glass. There's no glass here. There's nothing. He needs to get away, go up… There's a light – just a pinprick so high… How will he get there? *Tap, tap, tap*. Then there's a muffled voice. What's it saying? He strains his ears.

'Matt! Matt! Wake up!'

Wake up? He is awake, isn't he? Are his eyes open? He can't tell, but he can see the light, so they must be. Matt looks at the light and pushes his feet to the floor, except he can't feel a floor, but then he's rising, drifting up to the light. The voice is getting clearer and the light's getting brighter until it's blinding. 'Ow, fuck!'

What the hell? Matt rubs his eyes and focuses… on a steering wheel. He's been asleep in a car. His car? He rubs his eyes again and turns his head to look outside and sees Betty from the newsagents tapping on his window.

'Matt. Thank God, you're awake! Get out of the car!'

He must still be dreaming. Must be, because he's naked. Naked in his car with an empty whisky bottle on his chest. He shifts in his seat and the bottle thumps to the floor. Matt covers his modesty with both hands and stares at his lower body. Bloody hell… There are red lipstick marks all across his stomach and thighs.

'Bugger off! I won't tell you again!' Betty yells.

Matt's head jerks to the windscreen. There's a teenage boy crawling on the bonnet, pointing a phone at him, eyes alight with mischief. Betty cuffs him round the head and the lad jumps down, runs off laughing. Inside his stomach, a tide of nausea begins to rise. Shit. He needs to be sick. Matt's hand shoots to the door handle but it's locked. He flicks the central locking button and tumbles out into the cold air; his legs won't support him. It's too late. On his knees he's helpless to move as he retches and vomits into the gutter.

'Oh, God. What a state you're in, lad,' Betty says, and he feels material cover his back. 'You'll have to slip my coat on until we get you off the street. It's too late to keep this a secret I'm afraid, cos there's been three kids taking photos of you. I heard the commotion as I was walking to work just now.'

Matt tries to say something, but his lips won't move. He allows himself to be helped into the coat and led along the side street where he appears to have parked, and onto the high street and into Betty's shop. In the back kitchen, bewildered, he slumps onto a chair while she puts the kettle on. Resting his head in his hands, he says, 'I... I don't know what the hell happened, Betty.'

'Hmm. Looks like you had quite a night.' She sets a mug of tea down on the little table and sits opposite. 'What were you thinking, lad? Getting in that state and driving? You're a teacher, a respected member of the community. It won't do. Look at the state of you.' She shoves a small mirror along the table.

With a shaking hand, he picks up the mirror and can hardly believe what he's seeing. His hair's wild, there's more lipstick marks on his neck and his mouth and his eyes are bloodshot – haunted. Matt looks into Betty's concerned brown eyes and feels tears push behind his own. What a fucking mess.

'You *have* to believe me, Betty. I have no clue about what happened or how I ended up like this in my car. I feel like I've been drugged. When you tapped on the window I was having a weird dream and found it hard to open my eyes. And I *never* drink and drive. Ever. The last thing I remember is that I was at Lavender's house for dinner. We had a nice meal and sat by her fire for a chat. The next thing I remember is you tapping on the window.'

'Lavender Nancarrow asked you to dinner?' Betty frowns, looks sceptical.

'Yes. I know that sounds unbelievable given what she's like, but she asked me. She'll remember what happened.' He stands up. 'I have to go and…' A pain blooms over his right eye and the room tips. He sits down again with a thump.

'You'll be going nowhere 'til you've come round and had a proper sleep. I'll ring for my Laura to come in to take over the shop and then I'll run you home.'

Matt's moved by this woman's compassion. Not everyone would be so kind, considering how he was found. 'Thank you, Betty. You're a real friend…' Then a thought occurs to him. 'Did you see my clothes, or my phone, wallet?'

'Didn't have time to look. Might be in the car. You drink that tea and I'll go and see.'

While she's gone, Matt examines his body. The lipstick marks are smudged mostly, but one or two are perfect imprints. Too perfect. It's as if they've been stamped on his skin. He wets a paper towel, and he's scrubbing at them when Betty comes back in.

'Lucky for you your clothes were in the back seat, and your wallet and phone too.'

'Thank God.' Matt takes them from her and flicks through his wallet. 'Nothing taken. Whoever did this to me wanted humiliation, not money.'

'Did it to you? Haven't you considered the possibility that you just got drunk, Matt, and you and Lavender had a bit of fun together?' Betty crosses her arms and sighs.

Matt considers this for all of two seconds. 'There's no way. She's not that kind of girl, and even if it was true, how they hell did I come to be naked in a side street alone?'

'Perhaps she woke up in a similar state, was ashamed of what she'd done and legged it.'

'But why would we be in the village? Why didn't we just stay at her house?'

'No idea.' Betty shakes her head. 'Now if you'll excuse me, I'll open the shop. I'll take you back when Laura gets here. It's nearly eight o'clock on a Friday morning and we've been shut half an hour.'

Eight? On a Friday morning... Realisation slams into Matt's consciousness. 'Shit, it... I should be at school.'

Betty turns at the door. 'Yeah, but you can't go in today. Not in your state. I'd call in sick and do it now. They'll not be too pleased you left it so late.'

Matt gets dressed in the small toilet in the offshoot. Maureen, the school secretary, was not happy when he told her he'd felt unwell all night and had just thrown up – that was why he was so late calling in.

But Betty is right. He can't go in today. The churny stomach is calming down a bit, but his head's throbbing and there's a vile taste in the back of his throat. It's a mixture of vomit and blackcurrants. He can't remember eating blackcurrants.

Ten minutes later, Laura, Betty's daughter, arrives with Betty's two-year-old grandson, Oliver. Betty picks him up and showers him with kisses. 'He's 'ansome, ain't he?' she says to Matt, her homely face beaming with pride.

'He sure is, Betty.'

Laura's not beaming. The young mum hangs her coat up, eyes him with disdain and takes her phone out of her pocket. 'I think you should know that the state you were in earlier is all over social media.' She scrolls down the screen and holds it out to him.

The churny stomach resurfaces and he takes the phone in trembling fingers. It's Twitter... There are various tweets of photos of himself from different angles, asleep behind the wheel naked, the whisky bottle on his chest.

@bigman21 OMG this is the new teacher!!
@Mumofthreesprogs I'm gonna RT! Dirty bastard's
not going anywhere near my kids!
@KLMorsley89 WTF?? If he's not sacked I'm keeping
my kids home. Fucking disgusting!

The floor's coming up to meet him and he hangs onto the back of a chair. Breathes in through his nose, out through his mouth. Laura takes the phone from his limp hand. 'There's more on Facebook. Wanna see?' she snaps.

Matt shakes his head. He has no words.

'Matt says he can't remember what happened, Laura,' Betty says, obviously trying to smooth the situation.

'Not surprised with a bottle of whisky down him!'

Matt looks at Laura, sees a mixture of disgust and venom in her eyes. 'It's true, Laura. Someone must have done this to me... drugged me. I never get like this. I don't even like whisky!'

Laura holds her hands up. 'Good luck with getting people to believe that.' She turns to her mum. 'Right, you'd better take him home. I have to be at playgroup with Oliver soon.'

***

Lavender's not answering her phone. After the tenth attempt at calling, he chucks his mobile down on the bed. He's not leaving a voicemail. No. He wants to gauge her reaction straight away. Matt decides to have a shower, but halfway through, he hears his phone ringing. Great. Wrapped in a towel, he hurries into the bedroom to answer it, hoping it's Lavender. Just as he gets to it, it stops ringing. Matt thumbs to the missed calls. Shit. It wasn't Lavender. It was Deborah. News travels fast. Matt sinks down on the end of his bed. There's a voicemail. He can guess what the headteacher has to say will not be what he wants to hear.

'Matt, it's Deborah. I hear you're sick. I'm not surprised, having seen your photos all over social media. Please call me immediately.'

His finger hovers over her number but he can't bring himself to call. Why would she believe him? Why would anyone? Throwing it down, he goes to finish showering, just as it rings again. Matt leans his head against the steamed-up mirror in the bathroom and lets it go to answerphone. When he checks, it's Deborah again.

'I'm assuming you're home. I'm coming over... This won't wait. I'll be there within the hour.'

Matt swears and throws the towel across the room. This is going to be bad. Very bad.

Chapter thirteen

The doorbell rings. Matt sets his coffee cup down and goes to answer it – the condemned man walking to the gallows. The hall mirror tells him he looks more human, but his brain and insides feel like alien territory. When he opens the door, Deborah looks at him as though she can actually see his insides and steps past him quickly. In the kitchen she whirls round, folds her arms and raises an eyebrow. She doesn't need to say anything.

'If I were you, I'd feel exactly the same,' Matt says in a voice that sounds like he's trying to talk down a suicide jumper.

'Really? And how do you think I'm feeling?' Deborah snaps.

Matt pulls out a chair at the table, waves a hand at it, but she ignores him.

He sits instead; he can't trust his legs. 'Angry, bewildered, disappointed, betrayed…' He raises his hands and lets them fall with a slap to his thighs.

Deborah leans her back against the sink. 'Pretty much, yep. Any excuses at all?'

'Yes.' Matt swallows and wonders how the hell to start. She's glaring at him and he feels about five years old. 'Look, I went to dinner with a friend last night. I had one glass of wine. The rest was non-alcoholic. The next thing I remember is waking in my car on a side street in the village… in the state you must have seen in those photos. That's all I remember… I swear on my family's lives and—'

'A friend?'

'Lavender Nancarrow.'

Deborah rolls her eyes. 'Might explain the lipstick, Matt?'

'No! We did nothing like that. We aren't even boyfriend and girlfriend.' Now he sounds five years old too.

'Right.' She shifts her weight from one foot to the other, drops her hip. 'And your explanation for it all is…?'

He shrugs, looks away from her searching dark eyes and at his feet. 'I was set up. Drugged, stripped and left on display for all of St Agnes to see on a Friday morning.'

Deborah's snort of derision's followed by, 'Why on earth would someone want to do that?'

Matt looks back at her, keeps his gaze on hers. 'Because they want me out of town. I didn't tell you, but on my first day here I had a severed badger head left by my front door as a warning, and a sign telling me to fuck off back to London. Then not long after that, I had my car tires slashed, the paintwork scraped and the headlights smashed in. Now this.'

Deborah's mouth drops open and she pulls out a chair opposite. 'Why the hell didn't you tell me? What did the police say?' She sits down with a thump, her expression much more sympathetic.

Embarrassment floods up his chest and sets his face on fire. How dumb was he not to have reported the car? He still hasn't sorted out the CCTV for the cottage either, has he? Matt sighs, looks at the floor again and says in a small voice, 'I didn't want to worry you with it. I reported the badger, but not the car. Couldn't see the point as they had no clues the first time. Just thought it would be a lot of hassle for nothing.'

'Oh, Matt. That was *really* stupid. If you'd reported it, this latest incident would have been more believable. You'll have to report it straight away. Ring the police right now.'

Matt looks up. 'Why should they believe me any more than you did? I don't blame you, by the way. I'd have thought the same. You saw the photos and jumped to one conclusion… You're a work colleague… a friend, so what chance do I have with the police?'

'I don't know, but they'll have to investigate if you register a complaint with them. There might be drugs in your system and fingerprints in your car. Someone must have driven you into town – so CCTV might have picked them up. They'll probably interview Lavender too. See if she can shed any light.'

For the first time since he'd woken up that morning, Matt begins to have some hope. Then he thinks about his car and groans. 'Betty's husband drove it over here for me just before you got here. If there was any evidence, it would have been mucked up, wouldn't it?'

Deborah stands up, smooths her dress. 'I don't know, Matt. But what I do know is you must call the police and tell them what's happened, or there'll be no chance in you coming back to school any time soon.'

Matt stands and faces her, his pulse quickening. 'I was wondering about that situation...'

She looks him in the eye. 'I had to suspend you, Matt. I had a quick chat with the governors this morning and we could see no alternative. It does look a bit more hopeful now I know the background to it – but we'll just have to see what the investigation throws up.' Deborah pats his shoulder and heads for the door.

Matt follows her. 'I guessed as much. Again, I don't blame you. I just wish whoever it was didn't hate me so much. At first I thought it was Morvoren Penhallow. I had a run-in with her. But she couldn't have done this to me... unless she had help.' Lavender's change of mood and scowling face from last night presents itself, but he pushes it away. It pushes back. Who else could have drugged him? She had the perfect opportunity.

Deborah asks about the run-in, so he tells her – adding what Lavender told him too.

'I can't see that old Morvoren would go so far, even if there is a feud and your grandma stole her man. I mean, it's evil. Something like this could ruin your career, finish it for good even...' Deborah's words run out as she sees the look of dismay on Matt's face. 'Let's hope for the best, eh? Try not to worry too much.'

As Deborah drives away, Matt raises his hand in farewell and then leans his head wearily against the door post. Any hope he has drains into the wet gravel and evaporates in the strengthening autumn sunshine. The headteacher is right, he must register with the police and then try to speak to Lavender again. She must know more than he does. The uncomfortable suspicion of her involvement whispers in his ear again. Shelving it for the moment, he finds his mobile in the bedroom and calls the police.

The police sound less than enthusiastic but say they'll send someone out in the next few hours. They tell him not to have a shower or wash his clothes. The first ship has sailed, but he takes his clothes back out of the laundry basket and shoves them in a carrier. Next, he calls Lavender yet again. Still no answer. The voice of suspicion grows louder. Despite not wanting to, he leaves a polite voicemail. Then he changes his mind. He'll ring again and this time he'll leave one she can't ignore. 'Lavender, please call me as soon as possible. The police will probably be calling to see you today about what happened to me last night.'

Five minutes later she calls. 'What's wrong, Matt? Why are the police calling?' She sounds rattled big time. Good. Serves her right for ignoring him. He tells her what's happened. 'Oh my God, Matt. How terrible for you!'

'Yeah. Therefore, the police will need to ask you some questions about how I was last night. What time I left – those kinds of things I'd imagine. I was sober when I left, right?'

'Yes, as far as I know. You'd had the one glass of wine… but seemed okay.'

'Seemed okay?'

'Yes. But then I don't know you well, do I?'

What the fuck? 'You can surely see if a person is drunk or sober whether you know them or not?' If she's like this when the police ask her stuff, he's sunk.

'No need to get mad, Matt. Okay, yes, if I had to say, I'd say you were sober…'

'Sorry. Didn't mean to snap. I've had a trying morning so far, as you can imagine.' The last thing he wants is to get on her wrong side. God knows what she might tell the police.

'Must have been dreadful. How do you think you got in that state? Did you go and buy a bottle of whisky and... meet a woman?'

Her voice sounds innocent enough, but he thinks she's trying not to laugh. He swallows anger and says in an even tone, 'I certainly didn't. I can't remember anything since sitting chatting to you by the fire.'

'Then how do you know what you did, or didn't, do?'

A reasonable question. One which the police will ask. 'Look, I've never felt so out of it before. It felt different to any hangover ever. It's like I was out of my body for a while as I woke up... like I'd been under anaesthetic... drugged.'

'Drugged? But how?'

This time Matt's sure he hears a muffled snigger and his blood ignites. 'I don't know, Lavender! Why don't you tell me?'

'What?'

'You heard me.'

'You're suggesting I drugged you?'

'It's possible.'

'So is you leaving mine, getting out of your head and meeting a tart somewhere!'

'Why can't I remember anything since leaving yours, then?'

'How the hell should I know? Why would I want to drug you?'

'Maybe your gran knows. Maybe you were in it together. You drugged me and then hoped I'd be found – lose my job... be driven out?'

'Oh please. Do you really think me and my gran could be capable of doing something like that? You're bloody delusional! Goodbye, Matt.'

'No, wait...!'

Too late... *Well played, Matt*. She's liable to stick the boot in now when the police call. She might say she thought he was under the influence, make all sorts of shit up about him. He throws the phone at the bed and sits on the edge of it, head in hands, goes over everything that happened last night for the umpteenth time.

What if that non-alcoholic wine was actually alcoholic? Or what if Lavender put something in it? Coupled with her attitude just now on the phone, the more he thinks about it, the more convinced he is that she is the only one who could have got him in such a state. No doubt the old crone Penhallow helped too.

A flame of embarrassment shoots up his cheeks when he thinks of them stripping him and putting lipstick marks all over his body. The perfect pouty ones – Lavender will have done those, won't she? She's an artist after all. Matt can't see her stooping so low as to put lipstick on and kiss him herself, especially as she's so jumpy around men... yeah right. A real shrinking violet, that one. For some reason the juxtaposition of shrinking violets and bold Lavender in his head makes him laugh. Hysteria, he expects.

Matt goes into the kitchen and pulls a can of beer out of the fridge. Then he shoves it back. That would be really stupid with the police about to arrive. But then he is really stupid, isn't he? Monumentally so. He's not been the sharpest pencil in the box lately. Arrogance and ego had made him think someone like Lavender would select him above all other men, ask him to dinner, want to be a friend... more than a friend, he'd hoped. Any notion on that score is dead in the water. Good job too, if she's a flaming nutcase, joining forces with the old witch and stooping to these levels just to see the back of him. After the car was vandalised Matt had decided that if Morvoren Penhallow wanted a fight she could have one. She's hands down won this battle... and the way he's feeling right now, she might just win the war too.

Chapter fourteen

October 1956

Morvoren's picking blackberries in the hedgerows. There's precious few left now at the end of October, but probably enough to make a pie later with the glut of apples in the orchard. Her mum says she's the best pie maker for miles around, and Morvoren has to agree. She does make excellent pastry. Since the dance, she's not had much enthusiasm for baking, or eating. She's not had much enthusiasm for anything... apart from sobbing her heart out, late at night, into her pillow. Mum caught her snivelling while she was milking the cows the other day, and she had to pretend she was getting a cold. Morvoren doesn't think she fooled her though, because ever since, she's felt her mum's eyes on her – watching her like a hawk.

An extra plump blackberry tumbles down the little pile in her basket and Morvoren picks it out, holds it up. It's juicy, perfectly shaped and smells delicious. It reminds her of that little bitch Elowen, and she squishes it hard between forefinger and thumb, relishing the feel of it crushed, destroyed against her skin. If only it were so easy to get rid of Elowen.

In the five weeks that have passed since the dance, she's been to Morvoren's house every Monday and Wednesday. At those times, Morvoren told her mum to say she was out. There's no way she could speak to the little witch without trying to strangle her. Each time Morvoren spotted Elowen wandering the highways and byways foraging, she hid until she'd passed. Once great friends and potion makers, they were now great enemies. Elowen has no clue about the change in their relationship, but she soon would have. They can't avoid each other forever.

Morvoren told her mum that she was fed up with Elowen and didn't want her hanging round any more. She hoped Elowen would get fed up of pestering soon and get the message. Mum hadn't liked lying, but she'd done it for her daughter. It wouldn't last forever though – Mum would get annoyed if Elowen kept it up. Just because Elowen hadn't seen Morvoren didn't mean *she* hadn't been seen. Morvoren's loyal friend, Annie, had become a great spy. She'd dutifully reported back to Morvoren any sightings of Elowen and Terry together, even though it had broken her heart to hear Annie's reports of the two of them in the pub, laughing. Worse still, out walking the lanes while stopping to kiss under the harvest moon.

The blackberries have stained Morvoren's fingers and she licks them, rubs them on her old shawl. When she looks up, she's shocked to see Elowen has seen her. She's running down the hill a little way off, waving and grinning like a fool. 'Morvoren! Where the hell have you been?'

Morvoren turns back to her picking. There's a prickling sensation along her spine; she knows this meeting will be the showdown that's become unavoidable. Elowen's by her side now, panting like a little dog. Morvoren looks at her. Turns the corners of her mouth down and spits on the ground, a few inches from Elowen's shoe.

Elowen looks at the spit and furrows her brow. 'Hey. What's up with you? I've been searching everywhere for you – went to your house loads of times, but your mum said you weren't in. She seemed a bit cagey the last few times.'

'You saying my mum's a liar?'

'No… just thought it was odd that each time I came to yours, you weren't in.' Elowen steps back a bit and puts her basket between them as if shielding herself from Morvoren's glowering stare. 'I looked all round our usual places too – you were never there, and it's been ages since the dance. That was the last time I saw you.'

'Yes. I remember it well.' Morvoren scowls into Elowen's bewildered face then adds, 'And how is the gorgeous Terry Trevelyar? Seen anything of him?'

Elowen's face beams so bright, it looks like it's lit from within by a thousand Sunday church candles. Morvoren wants to snuff them out, grind them into dust. 'That's why I was searching for you. I was so excited I couldn't wait to tell my best friend about it all!'

'Who's your best friend?' Morvoren's voice is icy.

'Eh?' Elowen's big blue eyes grow moist. Her bottom lip quivers. 'You, of course, you daft thing.'

'Might have been, but no more. You're just a little bitch who's out for all you can get, no matter who you hurt.'

Elowen's mouth drops open and tears spill from her eyes, rolling down her cheeks. 'I've got no idea what you're on about, Mor. Tell me what's wrong.' She goes to put her hand on Morvoren's arm, but Morvoren bats it away. Hard.

Morvoren thrusts her neck out, puts her face inches from Elowen's. 'As if you didn't know!'

Recoiling as if she's been slapped, Elowen says, 'I don't know. I honestly don't!' There's fire in her eyes now and hot angry tears course down her face.

'Then I'll spell it out for you.' Morvoren's voice is barely a whisper but the fury in every syllable is deafening. 'You stole the man I love. Stole him right in front of me while I stood there like a fucking idiot.'

'What? You love Terry? But the feud...' Elowen stops, shakes her head in bewilderment.

'Sod the feud! You can't help what your heart does, can you?'

'But why didn't you tell me?'

Morvoren coughs out a bitter laugh. 'Because I thought you knew! That day in August we were out in the meadow and you noticed my love potion. You guessed it was for Terry.'

Elowen shakes her head. 'No I didn't. I did wonder at first, but you said it wasn't him! Told me to shut up.'

'That's because of the feud. My parents would have gone nuts if they found out I liked him. I wanted to make him fall in love with me before I shared how I felt.'

'Okay, so how could I possibly have stolen him, if I didn't know!'

'I think you knew deep down…' Morvoren's conviction of her friend's guilt is wavering now, but she can't stop. Jealousy is in the driving seat and it's flooring the accelerator. 'You stood there at the dance, coming onto him like a tart as he drank his pint. The pint with my potion in it. He was looking straight at you… at YOU not me.' Morvoren jabs her finger into Elowen's chest.

'Oi! Stop it! If I had known about the potion I wouldn't have gone anywhere near him!'

'No, because you are so innocent and virginal, aren't you?'

Elowen's eyes narrow and she takes a step forward. 'Course I'm a virgin. Nothing to be ashamed of.'

'Yeah. So why do you dress like a prostitute with your tits hanging out – tight skirts, high heels?'

'Why are you being so cruel? We were best friends…' Elowen says, almost to herself.

'Well we aren't now. And cruel? You're the cruel one, taking my Terry, you cow.'

'Your Terry? Don't make me laugh. And that love potion wouldn't have even worked – you're crap at making potions compared to me.'

'Fuck off. I saw the way he looked at you after he drank it, you stupid tart!'

Elowen's eyes are dark with anger. There are two spots of colour on her cheeks, on an otherwise white face. She throws down her basket, thrusts her neck out. 'That's because he was looking at *me*. He'd have to drink a barrel of love potion for it to have worked with you! Look at the state of you – bloody scarecrow!' She jabs a finger into Morvoren's chest.

Jealousy stops driving at a hundred miles an hour in Morvoren's head, and crashes into rage, into unadulterated fury. 'Scarecrow!' she bellows. 'I'll give you scarecrow!' She launches her basket hard at Elowen's head, then pelts her with the blackberries. They split into her hair, her face. 'Now who's the scarecrow?!'

Elowen falls to the ground but soon jumps up, her face and hair streaked purple, her eyes filled with rage. From her mouth comes a string of expletives and a guttural roar which turns Morvoren's bowels to water. She sounds like some primeval animal. When her return launch comes, it's brutal and unexpected. Elowen's stronger than she looks, and each blow she lands on Morvoren's face and body is a punch, not a slap.

Morvoren pictures Terry kissing Elowen, finds her resolve and gives back as good as she gets. She has the benefit of six inches in height, and soon Elowen's under her, pinned to the damp grass, her face a mess of blood and blackberry juice. 'Stop it, Morvoren! That's enough now!' Elowen yells, after taking another vicious jab to her chin.

Morvoren's relieved because she doesn't know how much longer she can keep this up. Her face feels like an elephant's walked over it. She flicks away a long thread of snot and blood dangling from her nose and says, 'Do you surrender?'

A sigh. 'If it makes you happy. Just get off me, for God's sake.' Elowen turns her head to the side and spits blood into the damp, trampled grass.

Both women stand and dust themselves off. Elowen picks up her basket and gingerly touches her swollen cheekbone and split lip. 'It will be interesting telling everyone how I got these,' she says, contempt in her eyes.

Shit. Morvoren hasn't thought of that. Terry will know… everyone in the village will know, and soon! 'That's not fair. You started it!'

'Me? I might have poked you, but you started the whole bloody fight with all your bullshit about Terry, and me stealing him. People will laugh their socks of at that one.' Elowen turns and stomps away down the hill.

'No! No, don't tell everyone, Elowen. I'll be the laughing stock of the village…' Morvoren hurries after her. 'My parents will go mad!'

'Oh, poor little Mor. My heart bleeds for you!' Elowen tosses over her shoulder as she walks.

'Please, Elowen!' Morvoren hates the whine in her voice, but she'll say anything, do anything, to stop her secret getting out.

'Sod off!'

Morvoren catches up to Elowen, grabs her elbow, makes her stop. 'Look, all I can say is I'm sorry for what I said about you. It was wrong. But if you tell anyone, you'll be the one who's sorry!'

Elowen smiles and her cut lip oozes fresh blood onto her chin. 'I'm already sorry. Sorry I was ever friends with a complete maniac.' She shakes her arm free and continues on her way.

Morvoren watches Elowen hurry down the hill, until she climbs over the five-bar gate and becomes just a suggestion on the distant country road. Then despair snakes its arms tight around her chest, grows too heavy to bear. She sinks to the grass and lies flat, looking at the turbulent clouds gathering overhead. Swirls of grey, white and charcoal buffet together, tormented by a merciless wind. Merciless. Merciless gossip will be the wind to her dark clouds before the day is out. How will she hold her head up in church, the market, anywhere? What will her parents say? She'll bring shame on them. Humiliation.

A river of tears escapes from the corners of her eyes and roll down her cheeks onto her battered face, the salt in them making her wince as it seeps into the many cuts and grazes. *Damn Elowen to fucking hell!* How *dare* she take her life, her love, and rip it up into tiny pieces – scatter it around the village for all to see. She won't get away with it. Will not. One way or another, Morvoren will make her pay.

Chapter fifteen

It's three o'clock before the police show up. Matt looks through the kitchen window just as the car door opens… Oh joy, it's PC David Cross. Unaccompanied this time – no female officer. Certainly no detective with him. Great. His case is obviously a high priority then. Matt opens the door before Cross can ring the bell, ushers him inside and offers tea, which is accepted.

The officer parks his behind on a kitchen chair, puts his hat on the table and takes out his notebook. 'Not having much luck since you moved here, eh, Mr Trevelyar?'

'You could say that.' Matt tells him about the vandalising of his car too.

'Hmm. That was a bad move, not calling us about that. You needed a crime number, so you could have–'

'Yes, I know. I have been really stupid. I just didn't want the hassle of it all… There was no way the culprit would have been caught anyway. I need to get CCTV set up.'

'Might be an idea, yes. Especially in the light of this unfortunate incident.'

Matt nearly laughs in his face. Unfortunate incident? How about total fucking tragedy? 'Do you think they'll try something else?'

'Hard to say. Now let's go through what you said on the phone.' Cross checks the story about everything that happened – it doesn't take long.

'Have you spoken to Lavender Nancarrow yet?' Matt asks.

'I have. She says you went round for dinner, left about ten… and as far as she knew, you seemed pretty sober.'

'As far as she knew? Surely it was obvious – I only had one glass of wine. Well, and that stuff she gave me.'

'She said you had non-alcoholic wine.'

'Yes. But I reckon she put something in it.'

'Yes, Ms Nancarrow mentioned that you'd spoke on the phone, said you said she'd drugged you.' Cross narrows his eyes. 'That's quite an accusation, Mr Trevelyar.'

'But that's the most logical explanation. Her grandmother will have roped her in because she's carrying on some ancient bloody feud, and she's still fuming about my gran stealing her bloke. I mean, can you see me driving from Lavender's house, stopping off in the village, necking a bottle of whisky, meeting a woman and then getting it on with her in my car? Where would I have got the whisky from and met a woman at that time of night?'

Cross purses his lips and shrugs. 'You could have already bought the whisky and met the woman before last night... arranged to meet her after you'd left Lavender's. It's possible...'

'Possible, but not true.' Matt can feel the heat of his temper rising along his neck. 'I never drink whisky, and when I woke this morning in the car I felt completely weird. Like when you wake from an operation, you know?'

'Can't say as I do, never having had one... but I take your meaning.'

'And I'd never risk my job like that. It's not just a job, it's a vocation. Or was...' Matt rests his head in his hands.

'You've been suspended, I expect?'

'Yes.'

'Hmm.' Cross scribbles in a notepad for a few minutes then raises his head, looks closely at Matt. 'Have you washed since the incident happened?'

'Yes, I had a shower. I felt filthy. I'd been sick... just didn't think...'

'Ah. That's washed away any crucial evidence that might have been present then.'

No shit Sherlock. 'I know. I do have my clothes bagged up though – they're not washed.'

'Okay. That's a start. How about the car? Is it still down by the newsagents?'

Matt sighs. 'No. Betty's husband brought it up here.'

'Right…'

'Can't you do me a blood test? See if there's some weird shit in my system?'

The officer frowns. 'It is quite a few hours now since the incident… It would be doubtful we'd find anything.'

'Well if you'd come this bloody morning I might have stood a chance!'

Cross pulls his neck back, his expression matching his name. 'No need to get angry, Mr Trevelyar. We have to prioritise the most serious incidents, what with the cuts and all.'

'This isn't seen as serious?' Matt's incredulous.

'It is to you, of course. But there hasn't been a crime committed, has there?'

'No crime? I was drugged, stripped and left in my car with lipstick all over me. That's not a crime?'

'But we only have your say so on that. You weren't sexually violated at all, were you? Or beaten. If you were, it would be a different matter.'

'So you're telling me because I wasn't raped or beaten up, you're going to just do nothing?'

'No, Mr Trevelyar. I'm telling you that it isn't as high a priority as it could be. I'll ask you to make a statement, and then I'll see what my superior officer is prepared to do, given what we have to go on.'

'Which will be my statement, Lavender's statement and my clothes.'

'Um… yes. Unless I can get them to authorise a blood test.'

'Doubtful though, hmm?' Matt says in a sarcastic manner.

Cross just taps his pencil and looks thoughtful. 'There might be the possibility of trying to catch your car being driven from Ms Nancarrow's on CCTV.'

Matt's hopes rise. 'Yes, I wondered about that. There's also my phone and wallet, which were on the back seat on top of my clothes. Betty brought them in from the car, but if we rule her fingerprints out, and mine of course, there might be some that belong to whoever did this. Lavender most probably.'

'It's worth a try. I'll put them in an evidence bag and take them into the station.' Cross finishes his tea while Matt writes his statement and then he puts his notebook away. 'I'll be in touch, Mr Trevelyar. And for what it's worth, I am very sorry you've ended up in this awful predicament.'

'Thanks. So am I. If we can't prove any of this, I can't see my teaching career resuming any time soon.'

'Let's hope it all blows over in time.' Cross looks about as convinced of that as Matt is. At the door he turns and says, 'I'll ring you soon to tell you to come into the station if we're going to do the bloods. Bye for now.'

Matt watches him drive away and in his heart of hearts knows there will be no phone call. He knows the force is stretched – he reads the news, knows what they're up against. Funds are directed at murder, rape, theft… serious crime. There's certainly no money for stupid men who get themselves into ridiculous situations.

The next three days are some of the worst Matt can remember, barring his wife's last few weeks of life. He stays inside, orders takeaways, watches endless TV to try and block out what's happened. Deborah phones once to ask if there's been an update, but there hasn't been. PC Cross hadn't phoned back, as Matt knew he wouldn't. He did say he'd be in touch by the end of the week though. The end of the week is tomorrow.

Matt flops down on the sofa and searches for the remote. Netflix might have a film that's worth a look. The TV goes on but he can't see the screen properly because the sun's angling in through the window. About to close the curtains, he stops, lets his hand fall. It's eleven o'clock in the morning on a lovely September day. Why is he hiding away as if he's the one who's done something wrong? The more he hides, the more people will assume he's guilty.

Matt ought to be walking the cliff paths, taking in the salt air and planning his next move, not skulking inside like a prisoner in his own home.

Ten minutes later, he steps out onto the gravel drive, rucksack containing biscuits and a flask of coffee on his back, and stout walking shoes on his feet. A jackdaw swoops onto a nearby wall and has a heated argument with a ginger cat. The cat wins and the jackdaw flies off over the fields. Perhaps he ought to go into the village and have a heated conversation with Ms Nancarrow? She's the key to the truth, he's sure of it. But who would be the jackdaw in that scenario? Him probably, especially if a customer came in. Everyone would have seen him on social media by now, and Matt would be the evil schoolteacher terrorising poor little Lavender.

As he nears the village, Matt keeps his head down and quickens his pace. His best bet is to hurry through and get onto the cliff path as soon as he can. The last thing he wants are any snide remarks from people, or worse. He shudders when he remembers some of the comments on Twitter about what needs doing to him. Probably idle threats, but who knows? As he passes the baker's shop he feels a thump on the back of his head and something hot slips down his neck and inside his hood. Grabbing at it, he turns just in time to receive a sausage roll square in the face. He wipes the greasy pastry from his nose and cheeks and looks at what's in his hand – half a pasty.

'Shame it's not a brick, you prick!' a young man dressed in a safety vest and overalls yells. A gang of similarly dressed men howl with laughter and one hurls a half-eaten bread roll which lands at Matt's feet. A plump woman comes out of the shop, trying to calm the situation. And though his fight is trying to take over the flight instinct, Matt grabs the opportunity to hurry on. There's no way he wants to be photographed fighting in the street. That would be the living end.

At last on the cliff path, he realises he's shaking. It's not with fear, but fury and a sense of terrible injustice. Fucking Lavender and Morvoren – they have to answer for this. But how? Matt sets off at a brisk pace, focussing on his feet stomping along the rocky path, blood pumping in his ears and murderous thoughts in his head. The stiff offshore breeze is blowing in from the choppy ocean to his right, but the sun's unseasonably warm and takes the chill from it. Soon his gut and fists start to unclench, and he stops to take in his surroundings.

A seagull or two hover as if on invisible strings over an azure and turquoise ocean, tipping their wings occasionally to adjust their bodies to the breeze. Far below, a spit of a yellow beach is beset by huge rollers rushing in and smashing against the majestic ancient rocks. The force of the waves is so hard Matt can feel the vibration in his legs. He steps closer to the edge, and just for one moment imagines what it would feel like to push Lavender off into the water. She wouldn't last long, especially if she smashed her head on the black jagged rocks on the way down. Then he shakes the image away. What is he becoming?

Matt takes the back roads home as much as he can through the village, his hood up, head down. Luckily no one spots him, or if they do, they don't say anything.

Once inside he sticks the kettle on and then his phone rings. He doesn't know the number.

'Mr Trevelyar? It's PC Cross here.'

Matt's heart lifts. 'Yes?'

'I'm just calling to say I'm afraid the CCTV cameras haven't caught your car at all. Whoever drove back from Ms Nancarrow's must have used only the back roads.'

Matt's heart sinks. 'Hmm. Someone who knows the place like the back of their hands.' *Their webbed hands.*

'Probably…'

'Definitely.' Matt sighs. 'So that's it then? What about my wallet and phone? My clothes?'

'Nothing. The only prints on those were yours and Betty's. Nothing on the clothes apart from lipstick. No hairs, nothing.'

'Okay… well, I'm sunk then.'

'I hope not, Mr Trevelyar. People have short memories, and it will blow over eventually...'

'I know you're trying to be nice, PC Cross, but you know as well as I do I won't work in my school again. Maybe not in any school.'

'Again, I hope that's not the case. Sorry we couldn't have done more.'

Matt ends the call and puts the kettle on again. He doesn't know why, because he doesn't want tea. He doesn't want anything apart from his job back... his life back. He'll have to phone Deborah and tell her the latest, such as it is. And then what? That would depend on what she says. He expects she'll have to consult with the governors. Therefore, his fate depends on a few parents, local dignitaries and a pompous ex-headmaster. His chances? Slim to none.

Absently sipping his tea, he decides that once he's spoken to Deborah, he'll head back to London for a bit – see his parents, his grandparents. They know nothing of his news. They'll be so upset... but maybe Elowen might have an idea about Morvoren. What her weak spots are. From the depths of despair and darkness he needs to find his fighting spirit, pull it up into the light. He needs to prove he isn't some drunk womaniser, needs to show he's fit to teach. Okay, given the strength of local feeling against him, maybe not in this village, but somewhere. Matt knows the only way he'll achieve his aim is to expose the real culprits. He also knows that will be easier said than done.

Chapter sixteen

Lavender's being spoiled with a lavish afternoon tea – her reward for such a successful mission. Gran's fussing over her like an old hen, can't do enough for her. 'Now, my love. Are you sure you don't want more cake? Annie's baked it specially for you. She's so proud of you for driving that evil man out of the village. Shame we can't tell everyone here what you did, but at least we know, eh?'

'You helped too, Gran… and Jamie.' Lavender picks up her second piece of chocolate cake and takes a bite. The fact that Jamie appeared that night as if by magic has really bothered her. Gran organised it without telling Lavender, which was a bit sneaky. She doesn't trust him. The more people who know about all this, the more chance it has of leaking out.

'I didn't do much, and Jamie only stripped him, helped get him to the car. You did the rest – bloody genius with herbs you are.'

'I'm not bad.'

'Not bad? You're the best!'

Lavender smiles at her gran's obvious pride in her granddaughter. 'Maybe. The thing is, how can we be sure he's gone for good?'

Gran's bushy brows knit together, and she pours more tea. 'We can't be absolutely sure. But my source says he's gone back to London. He's not going to be teaching at the school for the foreseeable, that's for sure. Don't know if it's permanent, but it bloody well ought to be. The villagers won't have it. Not after what he did.'

'Except he didn't do anything, did he?' Lavender says. 'We did.' She raises an eyebrow at her gran.

'No.' Gran points a fork at her. 'But don't forget what he did to those young girls in London, and his poor wife.'

'I'm just saying. And I haven't forgotten, that's why I agreed to it all in the first place.'

They eat their cake in companionable silence for a while, then Gran says, 'What do you think about young Jamie?' Gran's tone is evasive, false. It makes Lavender feel uncomfortable.

'In what way?'

'He's handsome, isn't he?' Gran's eyes shift about the room like anxious butterflies, finally settling on Lavender's face for a few seconds, and then down to her plate again.

'I guess so. Why?'

'He's set to inherit the business too.'

'And?' Lavender's getting more worried now.

'And he'd be a good match for you. Annie says he's besotted.' Gran's butterflies become bolder, stay focussed.

'A match? What century are we in? And I don't want a man, thanks. I'm happy as I am.'

'You're going on for twenty-six! You need to start thinking about settling down, having children. We need to carry on the Penhallow line.' Gran sits back, folds her arms.

Lavender can hardly believe what she's hearing. 'Settling down? I don't want to bloody settle down... and Penhallow? Not sure if you've noticed, Gran, but my surname is Nancarrow.'

'Yes, but you're a Penhallow right enough. It's in your blood.' Gran slurps her tea and sighs, looks into Lavender's eyes and says, 'I can see why you'd be a bit worried about settling down. I know you've only been out with a few men and because of what happened when you were a kid, it didn't last. But Jamie will take that into consideration... Annie's had a talk to him about it and—'

Lavender almost chokes on the cake. 'She did what!'

'Now don't get upset.' Gran holds her hands up. 'The lad has to know what he's getting into.'

'Getting into?' Lavender thumps her fist on the table. 'There is no way I'm going to be romantically involved with Jamie. NO WAY! Do you hear me?'

'But he's in love with you.' Gran's voice, on the surface, is soft, pleading, but Lavender detects steel running underneath.

'I don't care if he were to show up here with a million pounds in a gold carriage and propose. I'm not interested.' Lavender takes a calming breath, looks Gran directly in the eyes. 'And that's the end of it, okay?'

'Not sure he will see it that way.' Gran sniffs, folds her arms.

'Really? That's tough.' Lavender sips her tea and then remembers something about Jamie from the night she was in the pub with Matt. 'Hang on… a week or so ago in the pub, Jamie said to tell you he understood. What did he mean?'

Gran shifts in her seat, shrugs and says, 'Not sure. Unless it was that if he sees you with Matt, not to worry. I told Annie you had to be with him to achieve an end. Jamie agreed to help us out when I phoned him the night you administered the potion. Good job, because just you and me could never have got him in the car.'

Bloody hell, all this planning behind her back was practically Machiavellian. 'Seems like you, Annie and Jamie had it all plotted out, long before I agreed to it.'

Gran shrugs again and pours more tea. 'Had to be done.'

The way she says that sends a shiver down Lavender's spine and she doesn't know why. She thinks for a moment and realises Gran will stop at nothing to get her way. To win the battle. Lavender feels like a pawn in her game. Of course, she too wants Trevelyar permanently out of the village, because he is a wife beater and child molester, but she's beginning to feel manipulated – controlled. All this Jamie stuff has rattled her. Is she the prize in some bizarre matchmaking exercise? Because Jamie helped with Matt, is she expected to reward him by agreeing to become his girlfriend, his wife?

'Had to be done? Makes me wonder if you're just caught up in all the intrigue and excitement. I mean, life must be pretty boring for you sometimes, Gran.'

Gran turns her mouth down at the corners. 'How dare you! This isn't a game, you know.'

'Really? Because I was wondering if that's exactly what it is to you.'

'Eh? Have you forgotten about the way he treated his wife and those girls – the feud?' Gran's voice is trembling with fury.

'No danger of that.' Lavender holds her head high. 'You tell me every day. But I think the main thing you're still angry about is the way his gran nicked your man.'

'Don't be ridiculous!'

Lavender watches red blotches appear on Gran's neck, a sure sign that she's lying. 'I'm not being ridiculous. You are punishing him, mainly because of what his gran did.'

'I'm warning you, girl. Hold your tongue and show some bloody respect.'

'Respect has to be earned.'

'I'm your grandmother!' Gran stands up, places her palms on the table, leans across it and glowers in Lavender's face.

'Really? Thought you were my pimp the way you're trying to give me away to the highest bloody bidder!'

The slap comes so hard and fast that Lavender's head rocks to the left, her hair tumbling over her face. She raises a tentative hand to her smarting cheek and glares at her grandmother. 'It's a good job you're an old woman or you'd get the same back!'

Gran raises her hand again, but obviously thinks better of it. 'Remember who you're talking to, young lady!'

'I know full well!'

'I'm warning you. If you keep this up, you'll be sorry,' Gran growls.

'What you gonna do – make me a potion?'

Gran's face relaxes. She tries a smile and says softly, 'Don't be stupid. We're in this together – you're my brilliant and talented granddaughter and I love you. You sent Trevelyar packing and if the bastard ever shows his face back here, I know you'll step up to the plate again. Next time we have to be sure he won't be able to come back.'

The chill is back with reinforcements. 'What exactly do you mean by that?'

'The only good Trevelyar is a dead one.'

The horror of those words delivered as calmly as if she were talking about the weather pulls Lavender to her feet. She picks up her bag and coat. 'I'll be going now. I suggest you have a think about what you've just said.'

'And I suggest you have a look and see where your loyalties lie!' Gran calls after her as she hurries out of the door.

***

An hour's stomp along the cliff path has done nothing to calm Lavender's temper or allay the feeling of unease regarding Gran's obsession with Matt Trevelyar. Her face, contorted with hatred, surfaces in Lavender's mind, as do the words 'the only good Trevelyar is a dead one...' Would she actually go that far? Perhaps the hatred really is just to do with Gran's personal history – not what Matt has recently been up to at all. Lavender sits on a bench and looks out over the ocean. The breeze whips strands of hair across her face, so she tucks them behind her ears and twists the rest into a ponytail. She's out of sorts, but the expanse of choppy sapphire water, framed by a sandwich of yellow sand and grey sky, starts to work its magic. There's a few dark clouds gathering in the west, and Lavender sucks in a deep breath – salt and seaweed. At last, calm spreads through the pent-up twisty ball that's formed in her chest, and as she releases the breath, a plan begins to form.

Gran's mysterious 'source' needs to be tracked down and questioned. It has to be someone who works at the school, or someone who knows someone who does. This is the only way she'd be privy to what Matt had done in London. At the back of Lavender's mind there *is* a friend or relation of someone at the school. A friend or relation that Gran knows... but who is it? The post office is hovering at the back of her mind too. Kevin Parry runs it, and as far as she knows, he and Gran aren't big friends – nor does he have anything to do with the school. He's not old enough either, only around fifty-odd, because didn't Gran say that the source had suffered at the hands of a Trevelyar in the past?

The post office won't go away though, so Lavender decides to go there, see if anything will jog her memory. She'll have to hurry, because it will be shut in half an hour.

***

Kevin's sorting through some birthday cards as Lavender walks in. He smiles and carries on, leaving Lavender unsure how to open the conversation. She goes over to the envelope shelf and pretends to look at them, then she says, 'You okay, then, Kevin?' *Lame but hey ho.*

'I am thanks, my lovely. Can I help you with anything, Lavender?' He kneels down and pulls out a drawer full of cards in cellophane, frowns at a picture of a cat in a hat and looks up at her expectantly.

'No, just looking for a few envelopes.' She smiles and waves at the envelopes to emphasise her comment. Dear God, he must think she's away with the fairies. He goes back to his task and she stares at his shiny bald pate. 'Have you always run this place then?'

Kevin looks up again, rubs his short grey beard and says, 'For the last twenty years. My dad ran it before that. Why?'

'Just wondering.' Lavender's sure she's on the right track now. 'Oh... I think my gran might know him. What's his name?'

'She ought to know him. They were at school together. John Parry's his name.'

John Parry? Yes, she remembers Gran talking about him now. He's normally in the pub propping up the bar, or walking an old whippet almost as old as himself through the village. But there's a bit missing... Lavender looks up to the left, puts her head on one side, pretends to think. 'Hmm. I think she might have mentioned him. Did he have anything to do with Penhallow School?'

Kevin shakes his head. 'Not apart from being a pupil there once, like Morvoren. But my sister has been the school secretary for the past few years.' He smiles and gets to his feet. 'Decided on an envelope?'

Lavender can tell he's obviously tired of this Q&A game. Probably wants to close the shop. She buys three envelopes, unnecessarily, because she's got exactly what she wants, and it isn't envelopes.

***

John has his eyes shut and so does his dog. The pair are at a corner table – well, the dog is half under it – and John's got his hand around an empty half-pint glass. Lavender slides into the bench opposite him and the dog opens one eye. She reaches down and strokes it, saying in a loud voice, 'Hello there, boy!'

John jerks awake, looks at her as if she's an apparition. 'Where did you come from?'

Lavender chuckles. 'I'm just saying hello to your lovely dog here. What's his name?'

John's weather-beaten face concertinas into a gummy smile and he pats the dog absently. 'Name's Bullet. He was as fast as one back in the old days, weren't you, lad?'

Bullet opens the other eye and yawns.

Lavender says, 'He looks tired, bless him.'

'Aye, he will be. We walked round the village and that's about all either of us can manage nowadays.' John rubs his eyes and sits back in his seat. 'How's Morvoren doing?'

'Her usual self, thanks. Fighting fit.' Lavender strokes her tender cheek.

'Always was a firecracker, your grandma.'

'You were at school together, weren't you?'

'Yes. Since we were… 'bout four. That means we've known each other best part of seventy-five years.' John laughs. 'Old bloody crocs.'

'Wow, that *is* a long time! Your daughter works at the school now, doesn't she?' Lavender says, hoping that she doesn't sound too nosy.

'Yes. Our Maureen loves it there.' John looks at his empty glass, longingly, so Lavender asks if he wants another. He protests, but she insists, and soon he's gulping down a pint and telling her his life history. It takes a while for her to get a word in edgewise, but as he's yawning, she jumps in.

'Gran told me you were wronged by the Trevelyars years back. Bet you weren't very pleased to hear there's another teaching at the school. Well, he's not exactly teaching now, is he?'

John frowns and scratches his head. 'Not wronged so much, really. It was this young Trevelyar teacher's grandma – Elowen. I was in love with her, but she wasn't never more than a friend to me. I should have come clean about how I felt, but I was too shy.' John sighs. 'Always regretted it. Anyway, she chose Terry Trevelyar, and that was that. Your grandma was livid, because she was in love with him. It was a right old scandal at the time!'

'Yes, Gran did tell me some of it.' Lavender hurries on before he goes on about all the ins and outs. 'Serves this Matt Trevelyar right, if you ask me.' She lowers her voice conspiratorially and leans across the table. 'Him being a wife beater and pervert. I mean, who wants a man like that in the village?'

John pulls his neck back and wipes froth from his mouth with the back of his hand, looks at Lavender in bewilderment. 'Wife beater and pervert? That's the first I've heard. Our Maureen tells me he's a lovely man, bloody good teacher. She believes him that he was set up – stripped naked in his car.' John shakes his head and looks into his pint. 'A terrible business.'

Lavender wishes she had a pint. She needs a drink. More than one. She swallows hard, takes a deep breath, tries to slow her quickening pulse. 'Really? I heard his wife killed herself because he beat her, and he molested girls at his school in London.'

John's jaw drops, and he shakes his head. 'No, no. That's not right at all. Maureen said his wife died of leukaemia. And they wouldn't let a bloody paedophile teach at our school. Even I know that, and I'm not up on school rules!'

Lavender feels like a prize idiot. She should have known too, shouldn't she? It stood to reason. But she'd let Gran's stories in without question. Just as she always had. What Gran says, goes.

Well not any more. How many more lies has she swallowed over the years?

'Who did you hear this rubbish from?'

Lavender shakes her head, drops her gaze to Bullet, who's gone back to sleep. What does she say now? Gran will be furious if she drops her in it. But isn't it about time she was dropped in it? The hideous things Lavender has done to an innocent man, because she believed the lies. Her stomach rolls at the thought. Poor Matt's been humiliated, might have lost his job permanently, all because of herself and the witch of a grandma she's been unfortunate enough to be saddled with. Besides, the way she'd behaved towards Lavender earlier is still fresh in her mind. If Morvoren Penhallow isn't stopped now, there's no telling what she'll do. *The only good Trevelyar is a dead one...*

'Lavender, did you hear me? I said who–'

'I heard.' She lifts her head and wipes away angry tears. 'I heard it from my gran. She told me that you'd told her. Must have bent the truth a bit though, eh?'

'What?' John's raised voice snaps a few heads in their direction. He lowers his voice again, says, 'All I told her was that there's a new Trevelyar teaching at the school. I knew she hated them because of the old feud and what happened with her and Terry. I told her my Maureen says he seems nice though and that the poor lad lost his wife from leukaemia. That was it, I swear.'

She nods and pats his hand. 'Don't worry. I believe you, John. I just wish I hadn't believed her.' Lavender stands up to leave.

John beckons her closer and she leans in. 'Why are you so upset, love? Has Morvoren got something to do with all this mess the lad's in?'

She so wants to tell him. Wants to blurt out all of it. But how can she? She'd be in it right up to her neck and that would be the end for her. There'd be no coming back from that. Imagine the wagging tongues. Half the village already think she's a weirdo. And she might end up in prison for all she knows. She ought to be, given what she's done. No. Gran had made sure that if she went down, she'd pull her granddaughter under too. *Very clever, Morvoren.*

Lavender pats John's shoulder. 'No, don't worry. I'm upset about something else... me and Gran aren't getting along lately. I can't go into it all though. Please don't mention any of this to anyone, especially Gran. She'd be very embarrassed if she knew that I know she's made stuff up. I worry for her mental health... Anyway, I'll see you, John.' Then she strokes Bullet's head and hurries out into the cold evening air.

Chapter seventeen

Matt steps off the tube into the London rush hour and hails a taxi. He can't be bothered getting a bus, as he's been travelling six hours already. Six hours to get from Cornwall to the capital – nuts. He could almost get to the USA in the same time. The car would have been a little quicker, but he'd wanted to relax. Too much stress makes Matt a dull boy. He's had enough of that over the past few weeks.

Shit. The taxi flies past him down the street. Matt sighs, pulls his coat collar up against the bitter fume-filled wind. Crowds swarm in and out of the tube station, shops, cafés, all in a rush to be somewhere, see someone, do something. He used to be one of the crowd; now he's used to a slower pace. But for how much longer?

In a taxi ten minutes later, he thinks again about the meeting he'd had with Deborah a few days ago. She'd been very sympathetic and told him she did actually believe him that he'd been set up, but having said that, it might be better if he sought a post elsewhere. The governors discussed it all at length and the parent governors had said the feeling amongst the majority of parents was that if Matt came back, they'd remove their children.

Deborah it seemed was in a terrible position. She didn't want to lose such an able and hitherto well-liked teacher. But in the end, she would have to put her school first. Imagine the scandal if the kids walked out en masse. It would be on the local news; it might even make the nationals. At least this way Matt could apply for other jobs relatively shame-free. Deborah, of course, would write a good reference. He totally understood her decision– he would have done the same – and so Matt had done the honourable thing and resigned.

The taxi draws up outside his old terraced Victorian family home in Hackney. There are no lights on and Matt hopes his parents are in, as they have had new double-glazed doors fitted since he left and he hasn't a key. Maybe it wasn't such a good idea to make a surprise visit after all. Paying the driver, he jumps out and hurries up the path. After a few moments ringing the bell, his hopes are dashed. Serves him right for not calling ahead. Matt looks down the street to the café on the corner. He could wait in there, or do the ten-minute walk to Gran and Granddad's. An image of Gran's comfy kitchen and home-made cake presents itself and the choice is made. His grandparents might not be in either, but once again he decides not to call as he likes to surprise them.

A similar Victorian terrace waits at the end of the avenue, but this time there's a welcoming light escaping around the margins of the blind at the bay window. Matt lifts the door knocker and lets it fall three times. The blind shifts an inch and he sees a partial view of Gran's face looking out at him. Then the door flies open and she's standing there, tears in her eyes, a huge smile on her face and her arms outstretched. 'Matt! My darling boy!'

Matt walks into her embrace, and for the first time in a long time, he feels safe, wanted. 'Hello Gran. Thought I'd come and surprise you.'

She holds him at arm's length. 'You certainly did that all right. Did your mum and dad know you were coming?'

'No. Nobody does. Just been there but they aren't in.'

'Yes, they've gone for an early tea.' She ushers him inside and follows him along the hallway to the kitchen, which is just how Matt pictured it in his head. On the table is a fresh batch of scones and a chocolate cake. 'They've taken your granddad with them, then they're going to the cinema to see that new *Star Wars* film. As you know, I'm not a fan.'

Matt shrugs his coat off, sets his rucksack down and sits at the table. 'Yes, I remember.' He nods at the baking. 'I expect you'll be wanting someone to share these with you?'

Gran laughs and hugs him again. 'It's as though I knew you were coming. I wasn't going to bother baking until tomorrow, but I did it anyway. Tea?'

Matt nods and feels the knots in his neck start to loosen, the burden of worry lighten. He watches Gran bustle about the kitchen and marvels at her energy. What is she now – seventy-six, seventy-seven? She looks and acts a good ten years younger. Mind you, Matt knows she must dye her once naturally blonde hair nowadays. That would make the difference to her overall appearance of youth. Her bright blue eyes sit on a multitude of crow's feet, but they are still alive and full of an intelligent curiosity.

They talk of this, that and nothing in particular until Matt has finished a huge slab of chocolate cake and a scone. Then Gran says, 'You're on October half-term already then? Thought it was later in the month.'

Matt sighs and takes a few sips of tea to wash his scone down. 'Not exactly.'

'Not exactly?' Gran cocks her head to one side, furrows her brow.

'Not at all, to be honest.' He swallows hard and looks at her. 'I've resigned.'

Gran's cup clatters against the saucer. 'What? But that's all you've ever wanted to do.'

Matt leans his elbows on the table, rests his head in his hands. 'It is. I've had a spot of bother in St Agnes.' For the next half an hour or so he tells Gran exactly what's been happening with much interruption, expletives and exclamations of surprise from her.

'Why the hell didn't you tell me that Morvoren was out to get you, lad?' she asks, banging her hand on the table.

'I didn't want to upset you. Besides, I wasn't totally sure she was behind it… I have no proof. Nor about Lavender.'

'That badger head has Morvoren written all over it… besides, who else could it be?'

'That's the conclusion I came to.'

'She's never forgiven me for taking your grandad. Not that she even bloody had him in the first place! Stupid vindictive cow!'

Matt takes her hand, squeezes it. 'Don't get beside yourself, Gran. I–'

'Damn woman! Hides behind the two-hundred-year feud, always has, but that's just an afterthought.'

'What exactly happened in this feud?'

Gran sighs, takes a sip of tea. 'The story goes that Jory Trevelyar, your great-great… I don't know, maybe five great grandads ago? Well, anyway, he's supposed to have lost some land in a card game to Kenver Penhallow – Lavender's five times great granddad. There was a big row at the time, as Jory said Kenver cheated. There was no proof, but Kenver Penhallow was well known for it and Jory never forgot it. Whenever he crossed paths with Penhallow, he made snide comments and sometimes they came to blows. The next part of the story goes that it continued to fester in his head for years, until one day he got blind drunk and set fire to Penhallow's barn to teach him a lesson. The tragedy was, Penhallow's youngest child was in there with a sheepdog that was ailing. They both died.'

A cold finger ran the length of Matt's neck and arms. 'Oh my God! Did he do it?'

'He said not, but his wife is supposed to have admitted to the priest that he did. She couldn't live with the burden and left Jory. This of course added weight to his guilt and Kenver Penhallow was already convinced because of what had gone before. Two weeks after the barn burnt, taking the child and dog, Jory Trevelyar was found at the foot of a cliff with his neck broke.'

'Bloody hell!'

'Yeah. Grim, eh?'

'And the Trevelyars and Penhallows have been at each other's throats ever since…' Matt says, the shock evident in his voice.

'Yes. Though I doubt these days it will mean much to anyone, save the old bag Morvoren… perhaps Lavender. Who knows? When we were kids, by order of their parents and grandparents, the Penhallows weren't allowed to play with the Trevelyars, or sit at the same table in school. But by the time Morvoren was seventeen she was ready to bury the feud, cos she'd fallen for your grandad.'

'You reckon that's the main reason she wants to drive me out?'

'Undoubtedly. You look so much like he did back then for a start. Must be like rubbing salt into her wounds, seeing you and knowing I'm your grandma. We were great friends, you see, but she thought I'd deliberately betrayed her. Stole her man with a love potion she'd brewed. Stupid bitch.'

Matt snorts in derision. 'Yeah, you're not kidding. Lavender said they both know about herbs and stuff. All this white witchcraft is a load of claptrap.'

Gran gives him a half-smile. 'I didn't mean it like that. I meant that she was crap at potions… compared to me that is.'

His jaw drops. 'You used to do all that stuff too?'

'Still do. Not as much, mind you – can't go wandering, picking ingredients in the fields here in bloody London. But I do get them from time to time. Mostly from herbalists. Mix and match my own remedies. Great for my aches and pains.'

'The things you do learn…' Matt shakes his head in bewilderment.

'I was the best in Cornwall, I reckon. Morvoren knew it too. Hated it… hated me in the end as it turned out. We fought over your granddad in a field. I mean a physical fight – blood and snot everywhere.' Gran tries a smile, but her eyes hold no humour.

'Blimey! What happened?'

'She accused me of knowing she loved Terry, but going after him anyway. She'd put the potion in his pint and he drank it while I was talking to him. I'd interrupted them at a dance. If the recipient of the potion looks at the opposite sex while drinking it, they fall in love with them.' Gran shook her head. 'Not even sure that's the case, but that's what we believed back then. But as I say, she was rubbish at potions and Terry just fell for me anyway… and I him.'

'But if she was in love with him, wasn't she worried about the reaction from her parents, because of the feud?'

'That's why I never suspected she could like him! I told her this, but she wouldn't have it. Anyway, we fought and then she begged me not to tell anyone why. We were both covered in bruises and scratches, so we'd have to say something. I was so furious with the way she'd talked to me and the cruel names she'd called me… I told her I'd spread it around the village… and I did.' Gran's voice has taken on a dream-like quality, and she's staring over Matt's shoulder as if watching the long-ago scene replay on the wall behind him.

'Wow! Did everything kick off?'

'You could say that. Her parents more or less disowned her for a while. She was a laughing stock amongst our peers and she withdrew into herself even more than she had before. Not long after, me and Terry both had a fox head left on the doorstep, your granddad and my parent's vehicles were vandalised and pig shit and a maggoty dead rat were posted through the door.'

'Nice. That's why you said my badger head incident had Morvoren written all over it?'

'Yes. It really got to me after a while, so the next year when I fell pregnant with your dad and your granddad got the chance of the London job, I was more than happy to leave.' She held a finger up. 'Don't get me wrong, it ripped the heart out of me to leave Cornwall, but I was desperate to leave Morvoren far behind me… I've never forgiven her for forcing me out.'

'But wouldn't Granddad have wanted to go anyway? You said in the past that he was ambitious and wanted more than the traditional farming, fishing and quarry work round Cornwall.'

'He might have. But I would've talked him out of it, if it hadn't been for Morvoren.' Gran winks and laughs. 'I could always wrap Terry round my little finger.'

Despite the situation, Matt had to laugh too. 'You always could make me laugh when I was sad, Gran.'

'I'm your gran, that's my job.' She reaches across the table and pats his hand. 'Can't bear to see my beautiful boy hurting.'

'I'll be okay… just need to figure out how to prove Morvoren and Lavender got me in that state – set me up. I was hoping a visit back here might have shed some light on her antics and what she's capable of. You've certainly just done that. She won't beat me though.'

'Good! Glad to see you've not lost your fighting spirit.' Gran offers him more cake but he declines. 'Any ideas so far?'

Matt leans back in his chair, stretches. 'Not beyond going back to the village and making sure they know I'm going nowhere. That should bring Morvoren out of the woodwork, given what you've told me about her driving you out back then. I've some savings, so can get by for a bit. There's no point in applying for jobs in the area until I have some evidence of what she's capable of. Some kind of proof linking her to me being naked and "drunk" in a car. I reckon she'll not rest until I'm gone… so she's bound to try something else. I'm going to get CCTV fitted and try to catch her in the act.'

'I could come back with you. Her quarrel's with me after all.'

Matt's horrified by that suggestion. God knows what Morvoren would be driven to do. 'No way! I'm not getting you involved.'

'Ha! I'm already involved. Have been for sixty-odd years.'

'You know what I mean. I won't have it, Gran, okay?'

'Okay.' Gran nods and squeezes his hand. 'But if you need advice or help, I'm always here at the end of the phone, day or night. Remember that.'

'I'll remember. And I might hold you to it. The more I know about Morvoren Penhallow, the better it will be.'

Gran's mouth becomes a thin line and a determined light deepens the blue of her eyes. 'Wise words. Know thine enemies, lad. Because Morvoren and her ilk are surely yours.'

Chapter eighteen

There's a cat dancing on the roof. She can hear its claws scraping on the slates... But cats don't dance, do they? Lavender opens one eye and realises she's coming out of a dream. The clock says it's almost 9am but it's so dark. Her senses focus, and she realises that rain is pelting down, hence the cat dance. She pulls back the curtains on a scene from *The Tempest*. Trees bent double, seagulls battling against the fierce wind, a boiling ocean and charcoal clouds tearing across the sky chased by a storm. No wonder it's so dark. At least it fits her mood over the last few days. Lavender's tried to process John's news and plan the next step with Gran, but so far, she's not had the guts.

Over breakfast she rehashes the whole thing again. How could Gran do that to her? Her own granddaughter, who she's supposed to love so much? Lavender feels used, sullied... violated even. It's not too strong a word. She's been used against her will. Used as a tool to destroy a man. An innocent man. A man who'd never beaten his wife but instead lost her to a terrible disease. A man who'd never abused children. And now his career is gone, his respect and reputation destroyed. He's been humiliated, ridiculed and everyone for miles around despises him. And why? Because Morvoren Penhallow lost out in love, sixty-odd years ago.

In her heart she knows she should just cut all ties with Gran, but that would be so hard to do to a woman who's been in her life forever. Lavender's considered telling her parents about it all, but what then? It wouldn't change what's happened, would it? Besides, she's worried about the truth getting out. Mum and Dad won't intentionally tell anyone, but one little word to the wrong person... She can't chance that. Lavender finishes her toast and stacks her plate in the dishwasher. She'll go and see Gran, have it out with her and then tell her she's washing her hands of her. Difficult or not, the relationship has to end because Morvoren Penhallow is poisonous.

**

Gran's cheery smile freezes on her face as she opens the door and sees Lavender's grave expression. 'Hello, love. Come in out of this awful weather... Not working today?' She steps aside and ushers Lavender inside.

'No. I haven't opened the shop for a few days. Had too much on my mind.'

Gran nods. Her eyes fill and she puts a trembling hand to her face. 'Oh, right. Me too, love... because of the last time you came round... our terrible argument. I have been wondering why I'd not heard from you, because I rang you a couple of times, to apologise for slapping you... I know I shouldn't have. I left a message on your answerphone–'

'I know you lied about Matt Trevelyar.' Lavender takes her wet coat off and puts her umbrella in the sink. She folds her arms and glares at Gran. She can't be doing with all this fake sympathy Gran's trying to pull off. She's seen it before.

'Lied?' Gran frowns, picks up the kettle.

'Lied. And I don't want tea, thanks. I won't be staying long.'

She fills the kettle anyway, flicks it on. 'What on earth's got into you? I said I'm sorry for slapping you. Everything just got a bit heated over Jamie and–'

'You lied about the things Matt's supposed to have done.'

Gran's neutral expression falters and she repositions the mugs on the work surface. 'What on earth are you talking about?'

'You know exactly what I'm talking about. The fact that Matt's wife died of leukaemia and he's never abused children!' Her voice cracks on the last word. 'How could you lie about something like that?' She throws her arms wide, sticks her neck out. 'Oh wait. It's because you wanted me to do your dirty work for you, and there was no better lie to tell me than that one, was there?'

Gran stops making tea, shouts back, 'He did! My source told me.'

'John Parry, you mean?' Lavender pauses and watches Gran's face closely. Oh, she's good. A moment's shock passes behind her gran's eyes, then the bewildered expression is back. 'We had a lovely little chat in the pub about it all. He said what a lovely man and great teacher his daughter Maureen thinks he is. Maureen also thinks he must have been set up because what happened was so out of character.'

Now Gran's shock is more than fleeting. It seeps down from her eyes, slackens her jaw. Gran slumps into a kitchen chair. 'Um... how... how did you find out my source was John... know where to find him?'

'That's it?' Lavender says, incredulous. 'That's the first thing you have to say? Not, "Oh God, I'm so sorry I have been such a fucking witch and roping you into it all. It was inexcusable. How can you ever forgive me?!"'

Morvoren sits there just staring into the fire for a few moments. Then she passes her hand over her face and gives Lavender a level stare. 'Because I'm not sorry. Not sorry at all. He is a Trevelyar and evil at heart. It wouldn't be long before he'd do something despicable – so I lied to make sure nobody came to harm. He's gone from the village – that's all that matters in the end.'

'He's an innocent man.' Lavender bangs her fist on the table. 'Innocent!'

'How can he be innocent – he's a Trevelyar!'

'Have you heard yourself? You sound deranged. It's time this ridiculous feud ended, and you need to let go of the fact that Matt's granddad chose someone else instead of you. Because that's what it's all really about, isn't it?'

'Of course not. It has something to do with it, but it's not the main reason!' Gran's face is a mask of fury now and she's grasping the edge of the table, heaving herself upright. 'If you ask me, you're sweet on him.' She jabs a bony finger at Lavender. 'If you are, you can think again. There's no way I'll allow it. You have a perfectly lovely man just waiting for the word, but you don't want him, oh no. Instead you're prepared to throw yourself at a disgusting Trevelyar! Remember the old saying – 'don't trust a man of neither field nor farm, for he will only do you harm."

'What on earth are you going on about?' Lavender can't believe what she's hearing. When has she ever given Gran cause to think that she might like Matt? When he was at hers for dinner that fateful night, she did find him good company and certainly attractive, but only in an objective way because she thought he was guilty of hideous things. Now he's innocent, she can see him in a different light, but nothing will ever come of it because of what she'd done to him.

'Don't give me all the shocked round-eyed rubbish!' Gran jabs her finger through the air again and grabs Lavender's wrist. 'I knew from the off you fancied him. When you spoke his name, your eyes sparkled and your voice purred. Matt this, Matt that… disgusting.'

Lavender pulls her wrist free and is tempted to slap the old crone. She's sure she never behaved in that way around Matt. 'You need your bloody head looking at. You've gone nuts.' Lavender shakes raindrops from her coat and picks up her umbrella. 'I can't stand to look at you. I'm leaving now, and I don't want to have any more to do with you. Ever.'

Gran follows her down the hall. 'Eh? You can't do that! I need you to help me get rid of him again if he dares to show his face back here! And I mean to end him once and for all.'

Lavender whirls round, her wet coat slapping Gran's arm. 'If you ever do anything more to that man, I swear you'll be sorry.'

Gran affects a high-pitched mocking tone and raises her hands, wiggles her fingers in the air. 'Oooh… I'll be sorry?' Then her voice drops, becomes threatening. 'You trying to threaten me, girlie?'

'Yes.' Lavender speaks quietly but there's menace in her words. 'If you *ever* do anything to hurt him again, I will make sure you pay. I will not stand aside and see an innocent man hounded and harmed. You used me as a tool in the most despicable manner – but never again.' She shrugs her coat on and opens the door to the storm. Immediately, a tumble of leaves blow into the hall and rain drenches the mat. 'I'm leaving now. Don't contact me or try to see me.' Then she turns and hurries down the path and through the gate. Over the wind she can hear the old woman shrieking and wailing for her to come back, but she ignores it and strides on.

Chapter nineteen

Matt's been back a day and has spent his time skulking indoors. Though it's a daunting thought, he has to go out and be seen about the village. He needs Morvoren to know he's back and here to stay. A playful wind chucks a handful of leaves in his face as soon as he steps outside, so he pulls his hood up as protection against it and the prying eyes of nosy villagers. Ten minutes later he's on the high street and so far, so good. Nobody has spat at him or thrown rotten eggs, but there's time yet. Matt hunches his shoulders and keeps his head down, then hurries into the newsagent to see Betty. He could do with seeing a friendly face.

'Matt! I was only thinking about you yesterday,' Betty says from the top of a stepladder. She's sorting out some magazines and flaps one at him. 'Have you been away?'

Matt looks round the shop and sees they are alone apart from an elderly lady bundled into a padded green jacket and wearing a faded red headscarf. She's thumbing through a book, her glasses perched on the end of her nose as if engrossed. Something about the angle of her head makes Matt think she's not at all interested in the book, but flapping her ears for gossip. Well, good. She might know Morvoren and pass on a few tasty morsels to her. He goes nearer to the woman, pulls his hood back, pretends to look at some pens. 'I went to London for a couple of days to see my parents and grandparents. It was ages since I'd seen them, and I wanted to tell them all about this awful situation some evildoer has made for me here in the village.'

'I bet they were really upset, bless them,' Betty says, coming down the ladder and putting a pile of magazines on the counter.

Matt notices the woman give him the swift once-over then go back to her book. 'Yes. Gran especially. She used to live here as a girl, you know. Think I told you?'

'You did, yes. My mum remembers her. Elowen, wasn't it?'

The old woman nearly drops the book but side-steps a bit closer to himself and Betty.

'Yes, that's right. My granddad's from here too – Terry Trevelyar. They were both shocked and disappointed that one of their own is being hounded in this way.'

Betty tips her head at the old woman and widens her eyes at Matt. Then she lowers her voice slightly, but not too much. 'I'm not surprised. It's an awful business. I've been spreading the word to anyone who comes in the shop that you're innocent. Been telling them you're from Cornish stock too. A few are on your side now. Let's hope we can get a few more,' Betty says, and smiles at the old woman who has sidled up again. 'You okay there, Annie?'

Annie pretends not to have heard and affects a deep sigh while squinting at a page.

Betty moves closer. 'Do you need help choosing a book, Annie, my love?'

'Hmm?' Annie says, looking up at Betty while tucking a stray grey curl under the headscarf. 'Talking to me, Betty? I'm miles away.'

Matt thinks she's never been to drama school.

'You okay with that book?'

Annie looks at the book and across at Matt. 'No. I won't bother with it. It's a load of old tosh. Never could be doing with romance – not up my street.'

Matt smiles. 'I'm sure you've had your share of it in the past. A handsome woman such as yourself.'

Annie's cheeks turn crimson and she laughs and fans herself with the book before putting it back on the shelf. 'Flattery will get you everywhere, young man.'

Matt laughs too and says, 'My grandma came from here. Her name's Elowen. Did you know her?'

Annie puts a hand to her mouth, wide-eyed. 'You're Elowen and Terry's grandson? Well I never!'

Betty, standing behind Annie, rolls her eyes at Matt in a meaningful way and goes behind the counter. Both of them know she'd overheard their conversation just now. 'Yes, we were just saying, Annie, how upset they both are. Poor Matt has been wrongly treated – he's had to leave the school. I'm sure you've heard all about it.'

Annie bobs her head and offers a sympathetic expression. 'If you're that schoolteacher who was found in the altogether and drunk in his car, then I must admit, I have. But it's terrible if you weren't to blame and that. Who might have done such a thing?'

Matt twists his mouth to the side. 'I don't know for sure, but I have a strong suspicion Morvoren has something to do with it and perhaps her granddaughter too.'

Annie's small brown eyes light up with excitement. 'Well I never!'

'But I'm not going to be driven out of the village. I like the house I'm in and feel close to my roots here. I want to try and persuade the villagers I had nothing to do with what happened to me.'

Betty nods. 'I know you're a friend of Morvoren, Annie. Do you know anything?'

Matt hides a smile. Great – he's hit the jackpot. He gives Annie a questioning look and sighs.

'I... I... me?' Annie jabs a finger at her chest, and raises her eyebrows so much they disappear into her headscarf. 'No. No, I don't know anything.' The crimson cheeks are back and glowing like embers. 'But she's an old woman like me. She wouldn't harm nobody.' Annie coughs, looks at the floor and makes her way to the exit. 'Be seeing you both.' She waves over her shoulder and leaves.

Once the door closes behind her, Matt and Betty burst out laughing. 'The old mare will be in Morvoren's house spilling it all before you can say gossip,' Betty says.

'And that's exactly what I wanted. If Morvoren thinks she's driven me out, she's got another thing coming.' Matt picks up a newspaper and digs into his pocket for change.

***

On his way back home, his feet take him across the road and towards Lavender's shop. On the way into the village, he'd deliberately taken the long route to avoid her, but once again, despite everything, he feels drawn to her. His head justifies it by saying if she sees him, she'll pass it back to Morvoren and then he can be doubly sure the old crone knows he's back in town. He takes a glance through the window. Lavender's there behind the counter, elbows resting on the desk, propping her chin up on interlinked knuckles. She's a faraway look in her eyes and a face so full of melancholy it stops Matt in his tracks. He pretends to look at a painting, but he's quickly aware he's been spotted. To his surprise, she looks relieved and runs to open the door.

'Matt! You're back.'

He eyes her smile and obvious delight at seeing him with a good degree of confusion. 'Yes, I'm back,' he says in a flat tone, shrugs and stays on the threshold.

'Please come in and have a cuppa. I've been worried about you…' She steps to one side and ushers him through. Her smile falters as he steps inside, and her colour comes up. 'There's also some apologising to do.'

Matt raises an eyebrow at her and stands in the shop, uncertain of what to do next. This is not what he was expecting at all.

Lavender turns the shop sign to closed and leads the way into an offshoot kitchen. She offers tea and he accepts. Then he keeps a very close eye on her as she makes it – he doesn't want to end up naked and drugged in his car again. 'I don't know where to start, to be honest,' she says in a quiet voice as she hands him a mug and sits down.

Matt sits on an old stool at an even older table. Giving her a direct look, he says, 'Being honest might be the way forward.'

Lavender takes a sip of tea then sets it on the table. She squares her shoulders as if preparing for something unpleasant and takes a big breath. 'Yes. I will be. Firstly, will you please accept my deepest and sincerest apology for believing the hideous lies I was told about you? I believed almost without question.' She shakes her head. 'Never again.'

'Let me guess,' Matt says, shifting in his seat and trying to keep his cool. 'The lovely Morvoren told you these lies?'

She just nods, bites her bottom lip, looks at the table.

'What lies, exactly?'

Lavender lifts her head, her eyes flitting to his and away. 'She said you'd beat your wife and she'd killed herself because she couldn't take any more... and that you abused children at your last school.'

Anger grows in the pit of his stomach and explodes in his chest. 'She said what?!' Matt bangs his cup down and rakes his fingers through his hair. He could hardly believe his ears. No wonder she couldn't care less when he'd told her about his wife the evening he'd been with her for dinner. And was this girl stupid? How the fuck did she think he got a teaching job if he'd abused kids? 'You think that schools normally employ paedophiles, then?'

'No... but I wasn't thinking. She said you'd talked you way out of it. Dismissed it as rumour. Gran's always had this hold on me and she knew which buttons to press.' Lavender looks at him briefly and he can see her eyes are brimming with tears. She wipes them away and clears her throat. 'You see, I was abused when I was ten by a teacher at Penhallow School. He asked me to stay behind for a moment at the end of the day and he put his hands on me, made me do things to him...' Her voice falters and her eyes fill again.

Matt's anger abates as what Jessica told him about Lavender is put into perspective. No wonder she won't let men near her. He puts his hands up. 'Hey, that's terrible. You don't have to tell me what–'

'I do!' Lavender jumps up, dashes angry tears away with the back of her sleeve and then folds her arms tight across her chest.

'I do, because only then can you forgive me. I'm so furious with myself...'

Here is where she tells me she's involved. Matt sighs. 'Why are you so furious with yourself? What did you do?'

At this, Lavender puts her fists into her eyes and rubs them, shakes her head. 'I wish I could do something to clear your name,' she sobs.

'Perhaps you can?' He feels desperately sorry for what she went through as a child and being under the influence of Morvoren to this extent, but at the same time he wants his life back. What kind of a grandmother would do that to a grandchild? 'Was Morvoren the one who forced you into it? Did you drug me that night, strip me naked? Or did she do it with help from elsewhere?' He takes her silence as indecision. He watches her struggling to answer, her face a mask of anguish. 'Lavender, did you drug me? I asked you on the phone the day it happened, and you said something along the lines of "Why would I?" And that I was delusional. You never actually said no. So that wasn't a straight answer, was it?'

She lowers her hands from her face and walks to the door. 'I'm sorry, Matt. I can't say more... I need to open the shop again. People will wonder why I've closed at this time.'

Shit. She was so close to spilling something then. Matt follows her through the shop, wondering if she might come clean another time. He would make it his business to try and get a confession soon. Halfway through the door, he turns to her and says, 'I'm so sorry for what that sick bastard teacher put you through as a child. I'm also sorry for the way you've been manipulated by such a cruel relative... but I'm glad that you know the truth about me too. Perhaps you'll do the right thing soon and help me clear my name?'

Lavender won't meet his eyes. She looks out of the window and says to the other side of the street, 'I'll do all I can to make sure everyone knows what a lovely man you are and that you've been set up... Goodbye, Matt. And I'm so sorry once again.'

As he walks away down the cobbled pavement, his mind is in turmoil. Lavender's obviously in this up to her eyes, but she won't admit it because she'd be in serious trouble – maybe even get a jail sentence. And she'd have to involve Morvoren too. He kicks a stone at a hedge lining the narrow lane leading to his cottage, and a few startled sparrows take flight. The best thing to do is keep on trying to tease a confession out of her. He thinks it's possible, because she'd been so close just now. If he fails, he'll go to the police with what she's just told him about Morvoren. At least that's something. Lavender might deny it in front of the authorities, but hopefully, if she's as sorry as she says she is, he might be lucky.

Chapter twenty

Matt's wandering through town again the next day, just to have some fresh air and to get out of the cottage. Without gainful employment he's going a bit stir-crazy already. He's been online to look at possible surveillance equipment, and can't decide what to get. There's so much to choose from. Inside, he could have spy cameras hidden in air fresheners, radios, light switches, smoke alarms, all sorts. They can be linked to Wi-Fi and can be accessed by smartphone too. Outside, the cameras are very discreet nowadays – unlike the big obvious ones his parents had back in the day. They can include motion detectors and work on infrared at night. Matt's not bad at technological stuff, but it might be best to let the experts fit them.

Outside the baker's he comes to a halt, the smell of fresh Cornish pasties wafting into his nostrils acting as an invisible lasso. About to go inside, he recalls that the last time he walked by here, he was attacked by those nasty yobs... but after a quick glance around and a peep inside, he decides the coast is clear. Behind the counter there's a middle-aged, thick-set man with a sour expression. He's wiping down the counter and eyes Matt from under salt-and-pepper bushy brows. 'Afternoon,' the man says, chucking the cloth down and folding his hairy arms over his considerable paunch. 'What can I do for you?'

Matt thinks he sounds as if he wants to do nothing at all, judging by his offhand tone and stance. 'I'd like a pasty please.' He tries a polite smile.

The man shakes his head and sighs. 'What kind? We got so many types, can't just say you want a pasty.' He sweeps his meaty hand at the rows of pasties inside the heated glass container.

Matt dips his head and reads the labels. 'A steak one please.'

The man rolls his eyes. 'Large, medium, what?'

'Large.' Matt decides not to add 'please'. Why's the man being so rude? He must believe the gossip about him.

The man gets some metal tongs and tosses a pasty into a white paper bag. 'Four pounds fifty.' He sets the bag on the countertop and holds out his hand.

Matt gives him five pounds and waits for change. The man tosses fifty pence on the countertop and turns his back. This is to be expected, and though it's going to be hard, Matt needs to be prepared for it and meet this kind of behaviour head-on. It's why he's come back after all. 'You know, the rumours you might have heard about me aren't true,' he says, picking up the bag and change.

The man turns round. 'Yeah, so my mother-in-law says. You were tellin' her all about it in the newsagents yesterday.' There's mockery in the man's eyes, and a touch of menace too.

Matt opts for the polite response. 'Oh, Annie's your mum-in-law? Lovely lady, and I can assure you—'

'I don't want you to assure me of nothin' cos you're a liar. Annie's been friends with Morvoren since they were kids. She'd never do nothin' like that.' The man leans on the counter and sneers at Matt. 'And Lavender's my lad Jamie's intended – so you'd better watch your mouth accusing her of stuff, Mr Trevelyar.'

Intended? What the hell? He's about to ask the lout what exactly he means by that, but he can see there's no point. The man's face is set into a grimace, his eyes shadowed under the eyebrows. He's fierce and ready to do battle.

'I can see there's no point continuing the conversation, Mr…?'

'Bob Penhale's the name. Not sure you've a need to know it, cos I don't want you back in my shop in future.' Bob picks up the cloth and continues with his cleaning, so Matt turns and walks out.

From a bench he stares down the road towards Lavender's shop and chews things over, both metaphorically and physically. The pasty is one of the best he's tasted, which is annoying, given the baker. Is Lavender actually going to marry Jamie Penhale? Because 'intended' usually meant intended to marry – or at least it used to in the olden days. Lavender was decidedly disinterested in Jamie in the pub that evening though… Perhaps that was just for show to trick Matt into thinking he had a chance with her. If he'd thought there was anything between the two of them, he wouldn't have gone round to hers for dinner, would he? And why does he care? His main priority is getting her to admit what she'd done – if indeed she had. But would she help? There's only one way to find out. Matt finishes the pasty and sets off to Lavender's shop.

It's a dull afternoon and as he gets nearer, he sees there's no light on. Once outside, he sees a sign on the door.

Sorry, gone painting. Back tomorrow! If you need me desperately, email me at lavenderbluedilly@yahoo.com.

Matt needs her desperately to help clear his name, but he can hardly say that in an email, can he? Perhaps she's gone to the coastal path with her easel. She'd mentioned to him she often does that, so should he go looking for her? Matt looks down the street towards the sea and a cold wind whips through his hair. No. She could be anywhere. Seems futile. He looks back at the sign on the door and sighs. What now? An image of a good book, a glass of wine and a roaring fire's presented by the comfort side of his mind, and he decides to pop in the bookshop, buy a book and head for home.

As he's stepping out of the bookshop, he hears his name on the wind. A woman's calling him, but she's some way off. The voice is familiar, but he can't place it. He quickly takes a look over his shoulder, just as the voice registers. Shit, it's Jessica! There she is hurrying up the street towards him, a parcel under her arm, black coat flapping like the wings of a huge carrion crow. No! He cannot stand to be in her company right now. Can. Not. Matt pulls his hood up, ducks down a side alley and then he runs for his life.

***

Matt wakes in his armchair, in darkness apart from the glowing red embers of the fire – his book is on his lap, his wine glass empty. Leaning across to the side table, he flicks on the lamp and looks at the clock. It's nearly seven. He's been asleep over an hour… 'bout time he made some food. The fridge presents an uninspiring bunch of onions, cheese, a handful of tomatoes, one large potato and half a dozen eggs. An omelette frittata type thing? Again. A 'big shop' needs to be organised for tomorrow, much as he hates it. He's just about to chop a tomato when he hears the doorbell ring. Immediately his hackles are up. There's nobody round here who would want to just drop by for a friendly chat… What if Bob and Jamie have brought a few mates over for a game of football? If they have, he'll be the ball.

Tiptoeing down the hall, he wishes he'd fitted the fucking spy cams – then he'd know who is outside just by looking at his phone. He's been thinking of doing it for too long. Wondering and prevarication never solved anything, did they? Action is needed now. Ordering them and getting someone to fit them was his number one priority tomorrow.

He presses his ear to the door just as the bell rings again. Then he hears a muffled, 'Matt? Matt, it's Jess!'

Oh no. Why can't she take a bloody hint? He almost wishes it was Bob and the team instead… almost. Matt opens the door. 'Hi, Jessica.'

Not waiting to be invited in, she waves a bottle of wine and a big brown paper carrier bag at him and pushes past. 'I saw you in town earlier, shouted you, but you didn't hear. I didn't know you were back from visiting your folks.' She makes a beeline for the kitchen as if she's a homing device. 'Anyway, I took a chance that you'd not eaten yet and got us a Chinese.' She sees the unchopped onion on the board with the knife by its side. 'Oh, good. Just in time!'

Matt can't cope with a full-on missile attack this evening – well, at any time really. But how the hell can he say no now? She's already taken off her coat and stuck some plates in the oven to warm. 'Er… I'm not that hungry, actually, Jess–'

'Nonsense!' She turns to him, her black bob swinging, red lips stretched into a huge smile revealing those pearly whites. 'Everyone knows that Chinese isn't too filling.' She holds up the bottle of wine. 'Now. Where do you keep your glasses?'

An hour later, despite his reservations, Matt is kind of enjoying the evening. Jessica has taken his mind off things a little, even if they did talk about it briefly until he changed the subject. She's caught him up on what's been happening at school and he's been asking about his favourite pupils. Apparently, some of the kids believed the stories, but most said because he was such a cool teacher, they thought he must have been set up somehow by a bad person, as Deborah and Jessica had mentioned in assembly. Matt's heart swelled with gratitude at that.

Jessica divides the last of the wine between their glasses. 'I know you changed the subject earlier, and you haven't been returning my calls… but I do want to help, you know? I know you didn't get yourself into that state, and totally believe you that someone set you up.' She raises her glass to her lips and regards him over the rim. 'Deborah says she thinks it must have something to do with Lavender "oddball" Nancarrow.'

Even though he agrees, he doesn't like Jessica poking fun at Lavender. 'Yeah, but she's a vulnerable woman, manipulated by her evil witch of a grandmother. And thanks for your support, by the way. I didn't call you back because I've been in a dark place. Still am to an extent really.'

Jessica reaches across the table and covers his hand with hers. 'Poor Matt. Of course you are… I hope I've managed to cheer you up a bit this evening.'

He gives her a brief smile and withdraws his hand to pick up his glass. 'You have, thanks.'

'I was worried you wouldn't be back, given what happened and that your relationship with Lavender is over.'

'Relationship?'

Jessica raises her perfectly groomed eyebrows and fixes him with her green catlike stare. 'Well… yes. Deborah tells me you were over at her house for dinner that evening.'

'It was dinner – once. We hadn't got as far as a "relationship".'

'Hmm. But you wanted one, yes?' Jessica takes another sip of wine.

'No… yes, I don't know.' Matt rakes his hair. 'It's irrelevant now anyway because she's obviously up to her eyes in it. Her and Morvoren.'

'Is that why you came back? To try and prove it, get reinstated?' Jessica sits back, crosses her legs, and he's treated to an expanse of thigh as her skirt rides up.

He looks away and into his glass. 'That's the plan… I'm not sure about the getting my job back bit, but a job in teaching, yes.' He drains his glass and gets another bottle from the fridge. He pours more for both of them as she's getting a taxi, apparently. It's Saturday after all tomorrow. 'It does seem a bit more hopeful now too, because Lavender confessed her grandmother tricked her into believing I was a paedophile and a wife beater.'

At this, Jessica gasps and is all ears. He fills her in about what Lavender told him the day before. Not the bit about her being molested by a teacher, but all the rest of it. It's a relief to share what he knows and the wine's helping to loosen his tongue.

'So she's definitely behind it then. It's obvious!' Jessica says triumphantly when he's finished.

'No. Morvoren's behind it – but yes, I think Lavender was instrumental in drugging me. The stripping me bit too – but I'm not sure how two slight women, one being almost eighty, could manhandle a dead weight into a car. I'm six foot two and nearly fifteen stone.'

Jessica licks her lips and gives him a look which can only mean one thing. He feels like a prize bull. Her gaze intensifies, it's like she's pulling him closer with her eyes… She does have stunning eyes. 'I think you need my help, Matt,' she purrs. 'I'll go round and see the old crone. The young one too. See what I can find out.'

Matt shakes his head. That's the last thing he needs, Jessica striding in and stirring up a hornet's nest just when he's getting close to tipping Lavender into a confession. Why did he have to open his big mouth and tell her everything just now? Because he's lonely and wants comfort, that's why. 'No. I know you're being nice and want to help. But I want to do this my way... and on my own. But thank you.'

He stands and picks up the empty plates and cartons, but she stops him by taking his arm and leading him into the living room. 'I'll sort the dishes – you just stoke the fire and relax on the sofa. You've had a rough few weeks – let me take care of you, hmm?' She pats his shoulder and goes back to the kitchen.

Matt jiggles the poker in the fire and does as she suggests. He closes his eyes and stretches his legs out to toast his toes in front of the leaping flames. It's not been a bad evening, actually. At least he's not had to spend it alone for a change. A few minutes later he feels the weight of Jessica sit beside him on the sofa. She's very close, as he can smell her perfume and hear her breathing. Matt keeps his eyes closed. Perhaps she'll take the hint and get that taxi... It must be gone ten by now. Then her lips brush his and his eyes fly open.

'What are you doing?' He moves away slightly, looks into her deep green eyes inches from his own.

A slow, seductive smile. 'Isn't that obvious?'

He starts to protest, but her mouth stops his words and a quick hot tongue flicks against his own. Matt feels the heat of her hand stroke down his belly and come to rest on his thigh. No... This isn't a good idea. With huge effort, he pulls back. 'Jessica, I don't think–'

'No. Don't think, Matt. Just let your instinct guide you... Give in to me.' Jessica's eyes are full of lust and her mouth's so close, so inviting. He closes his eyes and does as she asks.

Chapter twenty-one

Matt wakes to the smell of toast and coffee. There's someone moving about in the bedroom. He rubs his eyes and wonders if he's still asleep, then last night smacks into his head like a wrecking ball. Jessica. He slept with Jessica. Shit. What had he been thinking? She's wrapped in a towel and pulls the curtains back. Matt yanks the covers over his head and his stomach rolls. He hadn't been thinking, had he? At least not with his head.

'Wakey wakey! Toast and coffee for you, sir.' Jessica pulls the covers from his head and sets a tray at the end of the bed. 'Come on. Sit up and eat… We need you to build your energy back up, don't we?'

Matt heaves himself up and gives her a weak smile. 'Thanks.'

She sticks her bottom lip out. 'You seem a bit lacklustre this morning. A big change from last night. God, it was amazing!' A lascivious smile, and then she sinks her even white teeth into a slice of toast.

Matt avoids her eyes, takes a sip of coffee. Amazing? Was it? Flashes of her naked body come back to him in various positions… She'd done all the work – he'd been lazy, until he'd sent his mind elsewhere. Elsewhere to Lavender. Lavender's eyes looking down at him, her mouth on his body, her hair stroking his chest as she'd moved lower. Then he'd taken charge… tightly closing his eyes to keep Lavender in his head. That was both unexpected and unfair on Jessica. But then, he should never have slept with her, should he? It only happened because she'd caught him at a low ebb, and it had been a *very* long time since he'd had a woman in his bed.

'Cat got your tongue?'

He smiles again, unsure of what to say.

She nods at his uneaten toast. 'I was going to make bacon and eggs but you've no bacon. Not enough eggs for scrambled really, so...' She looks at him sidelong... 'I'm rambling, aren't I? I'm a morning person. Seems like you're not.'

Matt bites into his toast. 'It takes a while for me to wake up.'

She lets the towel slip to reveal full, pert breasts. 'I can wake you up when you've finished that, if you like.'

He has to stop this right now... She drops the towel completely now and slips into bed beside him. Matt puts the tray to one side, gets out of bed and puts his robe on. 'I'm so sorry Jessica... but I think last night was a mistake. I'm not ready for a relationship, especially not with all this going on.' He shoves his hair back and folds his arms, gives her what he hopes is a kind smile.

Jessica pulls the quilt up to cover her breasts. Her face is on fire, her eyes flashing with fury. 'Well thank you *very* much! Pity you didn't say all that last night.'

Matt turns his back, sits on the edge of the bed. 'Yes, it is a pity. I'm really sorry.'

'So am I. Seems like you took what you wanted and then just dumped me in the morning... typical bloke.'

Eh? That was hardly fair. She was the one who did all the running. Matt sighs. 'I did say I didn't think it was a good idea. Actually, I didn't get that far, because you jumped on me... told me not to think about it.'

'Whatever.'

Matt walks round the bed to face her. 'Hey. Let's not fall out. We had a great night together, but can we just leave it for now?'

She looks up at him, her bottom lip trembling. 'For now? Does that mean there might be a chance for us in the future?'

Why does she have to make it so difficult? He shrugs and gives her a quick smile. 'Who knows? Let's just see.' Then he goes to the bathroom and turns the shower on. With any luck she'll be gone when he's done. What a mess. As if his life's not in enough turmoil without this. But he only has himself to blame, doesn't he?

Twenty minutes later he comes out of the bathroom and tiptoes to the foot of the stairs to see if the coast is clear. The cottage is in silence and there's a note next to the kettle.

Matt,
  I made a quick exit. I'm walking into town and getting a taxi home from there, as things are very awkward between us. I hope there will be a chance for us when you've sorted your life out. You know where I am. Jess xxx

Relief fights with shame in his head and shame just gets the edge. He hates hurting people and letting her down gently has resulted in her thinking there might be a future for them. Why can't he just sort himself out? He needs to be firmer with people and more decisive in what he's doing. Thinking of which, he's going to organise those spy cams right now. Then he's going to see Lavender and demand that she tell him everything. Otherwise he'll bring the police back to her door, then she'll be sorry.

***

Lavender opens the door a crack, shading her eyes from the late afternoon sunshine. 'Hi Matt. I'm a bit busy right now.'

'Really? This won't take long.' He pushes the door open and, ignoring her protestations, marches into the living room. If Morvoren's here she'll get it with both barrels. She's not. Shame. He's in the mood for a showdown.

'You can't just barge in here!' Lavender grabs her phone from the sofa. 'Leave now, or I'm calling the police.' There's a tremor in her voice and Matt can tell she's bluffing.

'Go for it. The more the merrier.' He flops down on the sofa, puts his feet up on the coffee table. 'I'm sure they'd be delighted to hear all about Morvoren's lies.'

Lavender holds the phone to her chest and then sets it down. She walks round to face him. 'Okay, I won't call them. But as I said, you can't just barge in here like this, Matt. I'm shocked that you would... I didn't think you were so aggressive.'

Matt gives a humourless bark and springs to his feet. He's absolutely incredulous. 'Are you for real? After what your grandmother did to me, with your help.' He stabs a finger through the air at her. 'Because you *must* have helped her, Lavender. You have the cheek to stand there and accuse *me* of being fucking aggressive!'

Lavender's lip trembles and her eyes fill. She slumps into the armchair and begins to sob. Matt wants to say sorry – it's not in his nature to be such a bully – but he can't. He needs answers, and so it's just tough if she's upset right now. After a while she grabs a tissue and dabs her eyes. 'You should leave, Matt. You're scaring me, and I have nothing to say to you.'

'Oh, I think you do, young lady. I won't hurt you, but I need answers and I'm not leaving until I get them.'

Lavender just shakes her head and looks hopeless. Broken.

Matt decides to try a softer approach… He's a trained teacher, after all, and has learned that being too shouty doesn't always work when dealing with difficult situations. Scared children often retreat, and Lavender looks exactly like one at the moment.

'Look, Lavender. Try to put yourself in my position. You tell me Morvoren told you hideous lies about me and lo and behold, I wake up naked in my car the very morning after I spent an evening here with you. The other day at the shop you were beside yourself with remorse, but stopped just short of confessing. My heart goes out to you for what happened to you in the past, and the way that bitch of a woman manipulated your emotions. You're a victim as much as I am. But if you tell me the truth, I promise we'll think of a way to keep you out of trouble with the police. Morvoren can take the fall. She deserves nothing less.'

'I have washed my hands of her. She's poisonous.' Lavender wipes her eyes and blows her nose.

This gives Matt heart, but he must handle it carefully. She's avoiding the confession – slowly, slowly catchy monkey. 'Rightly so. How did you find out that everything she'd told you about me was a lie?'

'I had my suspicions last week. She seems to be totally obsessed with you, even though you left the village. Also, there's a man here that she's trying to get me matched up with as if I'm a prize at a fair! Lots of plotting with this guy and his family behind my back.' Lavender tosses her hair, her eyes flashing, deep purple flecks in their depths. 'Can you believe that? I was starting to feel totally controlled by her.'

Matt nods. 'I can believe it actually.' He tells her about his encounter with Jamie's dad at the bakery. Relief swells in his chest at the knowledge there's nothing between Jamie and Lavender. He needs to keep a check on it. The woman sitting opposite might be his heart's desire, but she helped to ruin him too.

'Intended? I'm his fucking intended?' Lavender slaps the arm of the chair. 'How dare he. How dare they all! It's flaming medieval…'

'Yeah. That's my thinking. Bloody outrageous… So how did you find out about the lies?' Matt adds the last bit as he sits back on the sofa and crosses his legs, hoping to draw her into a false sense of security.

Lavender sighs and mirrors his pose. 'I found her "source", or the guy related to her. It's John, Maureen the school secretary's dad. Seems like Gran found out about you from him but twisted all the information she had about you.' She rolls her eyes. 'Not just twisted it – altered it beyond all recognition. John was so shocked when I gave him my version. He said Maureen thought you were a great teacher and hates what's happened to you.'

Matt nods, leans forward, his elbows on his knees, and gives her a direct stare. It's now or never. 'And what exactly did happen to me?'

Lavender shakes her head and covers her mouth with her hand as if she needs extra help to keep the words in.

'Come on, Lavender, do the right thing. As I said, we'll think of a way to keep you out of trouble. We might have to bend the truth, but I'm willing if you are.'

She sits staring into his eyes for the longest time, then she sticks out her chin, says, 'Yes, you deserve the truth. I can't see as how I'll be kept out of trouble, but it's the right thing to do. I put a sleeping potion in the wine I made. Once you were out, Gran came round, and Jamie – though I didn't know he was coming. Another bargaining chip, I expect, when they spring the fucking marriage arrangement on me.' She sighs. 'Anyway, he stripped you and Gran did the lipstick smudges. She stamped some on with a little rubber lip thing that she found in an art shop. I didn't see you when you were naked, if that helps.'

Matt flops back and covers his face. At last! But how the hell can he keep her out of trouble and still clear his name? It will take some thinking about. And that shithead Jamie was involved. It stood to reason. He clears his throat. 'Thank you for being honest… I knew someone else must be involved, because you and Morvoren couldn't have lifted me into my car when I was out cold by yourselves. Who drove me into town?'

'Jamie. I was going to in the original plan, but he said he'd do it.' Lavender's eyes have filled again, and tears spill over onto her cheeks.

'Right…' Matt stands and walks towards the kitchen. 'I'm going to make us a cuppa and we'll put out heads together, work out what our story should be.'

An hour and a half later, they have fleshed out a story. The only one that might work, but it still doesn't put Lavender totally in the clear and Matt hates it. He runs the story again in his mind as he watches her open a packet of biscuits for their second cup of tea. They will say Morvoren encouraged Lavender to be friendly to Matt, as she decided it was high time the old feud was put to bed, because Lavender confessed to her that she liked Matt, but was worried about what her gran would say. She was really pleased Morvoren gave her blessing. Morvoren said Lavender should invite him to dinner, and even supplied her with home-made non-alcoholic wine… In the wine was the love potion that Morvoren had used years ago on his grandfather, when unfortunately, the wrong woman benefitted. Now there was a chance to put right the past…

Only, there was sleeping potion in the wine, not a love potion, Lavender was told later. Morvoren put it there. When Matt passed out, Lavender had become worried and had just been about to phone an ambulance when Morvoren and Jamie burst in, did what they did, and threatened Lavender, said she must keep quiet, or they'd both deny it and put all the blame on her. They had airtight 'alibis' from Annie and Bob. They had both been round at Annie's playing cards all night. Lavender had been horrified at what they'd done, but then they'd told her hideous lies about Matt to justify it. Lavender believed them for a time until she started getting suspicious of Morvoren's obsession. She'd been mortified about what had happened, and eventually told Matt the truth, even if it might mean she'd get in serious trouble for hiding it.

Lavender came up with a problem during their discussions of the 'story'. Why hadn't she drunk the wine that night? Matt would have noticed, surely? Matt solved that one – because she had poured it in the kitchen and brought the glasses in. Hers was normal red wine. That would work. Matt crunches into a biscuit and watches Lavender dip hers in the tea. Their story might work... but would she get off scot-free?

She sips her tea and looks at him. 'What are you thinking?'

He tells her.

'I think I have a better chance of getting off now than I did before you arrived today. I think our story works, and believe it or not, I was considering going to the police and telling the truth next week. I feel better about doing that now. But if I go to prison, then so be it. Living with the guilt is eating me up... And I know it means dropping Gran and Jamie in it up to their eyes, but they deserve it. They have this "alibi", but if it goes to court, I bet they'll trip themselves up under cross-examination. Gran is no good at lying to people's faces. She gets flustered and loses her temper.'

Matt's heart goes out to her. She's willing to risk her liberty to do the right thing. 'The thing is, Lavender, even if Morvoren and Jamie don't get punished because of the so-called alibi, I'd be happy with clearing my name and maybe getting my job back here. I would put in a good word for you, say that I believed you, that you were completely innocent, and you were manipulated. The lies they told you helped you to keep the truth a secret because of what happened to you as a child…' Then he stops. 'Hmm. You might not want people to know.'

She shrugs. 'It's about time people did know. At the time I never told a soul… I was too ashamed. The teacher left a few months later and I tried to get on with my life. I told my parents a good eight years after, when they asked why I never had a boyfriend and ran a mile when boys showed interest. I told them never to breathe a word of it to anyone – Dad told Gran, and predictably she went nuts. In my case, there was nothing much anyone could do about it by then, of course. Dad did tell the education authority and they said the teacher was currently in prison. He'd abused another few girls in another school and somebody had spoken out. So now I don't care who knows. It wasn't my bloody fault, I've nothing to be ashamed of, and at least people will know I'm not "weird". Sodding Jamie already knows – thanks to dear old Gran.'

Instinct leads Matt over to Lavender and he sits on the arm of her chair. He places his hand on her shoulder and says, 'This must be really tough, but you are doing the right thing. You're so brave and we'll get through this together. I'll do all I can to help if you let me.'

Lavender looks at him and places her hand over his. 'Thank you, Matt. It makes me feel better that I have you in my corner… I'm so lucky to have your support given what I've done.'

Matt kneels in front of her. 'Hey. Look at me. As I said, you've been manipulated for years and used by your grandmother… You're as much of a victim as I am.'

'Not sure that's true… but thanks for saying so.' Lavender leans in and brushes her lips across his cheek.

Matt looks into her eyes and she doesn't look away. He swallows hard and looks at her mouth. Is he misreading the signals? The air between them is charged with electricity and suddenly she cups his face in her hands and presses her lips to his. Kissing her back, he can feel his desire growing and pulls back a little as he's scared of frightening her.

He says, 'I'm sorry… This might not be such a good idea at the moment. Our emotions are all over the place and I don't want to take advantage of you.'

Lavender shakes her head and places a forefinger on his lips. 'I kissed you first, remember?' She moves her finger from his lips and traces the contours of his jawline. 'I've wanted to kiss you since the first day we met.'

Matt can't believe his ears. 'You have?'

'I have.' Then she kisses him again, and this time he doesn't hold back.'

***

Morvoren stamps her feet and rubs her arms. She's been waiting behind the hedge lining the lane to Lavender's cottage for the last hour and twenty minutes. It will be dark soon and her old bones won't tolerate the damp, cold autumn air. When she saw that bastard Trevelyar's car outside Lavender's, she couldn't believe her eyes. She'd sneaked up to the back window and seen the two of them sitting there all comfy cosy, having a chat like two old friends. It had taken all her resolve not to burst in there, but she wants to have the element of surprise. Lavender can't know that she's been seen. If she knows, she'll be on her guard. If Trevelyar doesn't leave soon, she'll ring Jamie. He'll have something to say.

Five minutes later, she's about to head home when the door opens and Trevelyar comes out, stops on the path and pulls his coat on. Lavender's leaning against the doorpost bathed in the soft yellow oblong of light like some ethereal fairy. She's smiling and then laughs at something he says. When he leans in and places a kiss on her mouth, it takes all Morvoren's strength not to fly over there and strike him. *So much for her being shy of men because of what happened in the classroom. She's obviously got over it now – the slut!*

He walks to the car and they wave to each other before he gets behind the wheel. Then he backs up and toots the horn before driving away. Morvoren ducks her head and waits for him to pass her hiding spot. When she looks back, the door's shut and the porch light goes off. Her legs feel wobbly and her pulse is rapid. She needs to go home, take some deep breaths on the way.

Morvoren's worst fears have materialised... a granddaughter of hers and a Trevelyar. How could she! Even though she and Lavender had a falling out, surely she must have known it wouldn't last, that they'd be friends again soon? Because they are blood. Blood binds, bonds – connects one generation to the next. But after everything Lavender knows about the past, about the feud, she's prepared to lie down with the enemy. Morvoren stomps from the field into the lane, a multitude of emotions writhing like a rampant vine in her chest. Sorrow, disbelief and fury. Fury feels best. It's cleansing, gives her strength and the resolve for what she must do. She hawks and spits on the road in disgust. If Lavender prefers a stinking Trevelyar over her own family, her traditions, her roots... then so be it. When he meets his end, she can go to hell with him!

Chapter twenty-two

Matt's ridiculously pleased with the CCTV setup. He can access views of both inside and outside remotely from his phone, and only the trained eye can detect the ones on the front and side of his cottage. It all cost an arm and a leg, so the ones at the back of the house will have to wait a bit. The trouble is, at the back is an old shed on a scrap of lawn accessed by a rickety gate from the lane – so it's very easy to get into the garden undetected. Intruders wouldn't be able to get in, however, unless they came around the side, and then they'd be picked up easily by a camera under the roof, about halfway down. It had two lenses also. One angled to the back, the other to the side. If the old witch tried to damage his car again, or leave any more beheaded animals, she'd be caught on camera, no trouble.

He's also ridiculously pleased about himself and Lavender. The way she just leaned over and kissed him the other day still won't go into his head properly. Matt's afraid he'll wake up and find it's all a dream. The kiss had progressed to more, but then she'd pulled back, saying she wasn't ready, but she thinks she will be soon because she likes him so much. Apparently, he's the first man she's ever considered 'making her boyfriend'. Matt found that so endearing and old-fashioned… refreshing. Both agreed to take everything slowly, but his head is full of her during all his waking hours and she walks through his dreams too.

They're meeting tonight for a meal at the Driftwood and he can't wait. Lavender wanted to go to the police the day after they'd got together, but he said to wait until they were sure the story was as good as they could get it. Next week will be soon enough. Part of him is delaying because he's worried she'll get into trouble, despite everything they plan to say. So, for this reason, he's reluctant to go ahead – and because he wants to get to know her better without all this drama hanging over them. They will have to go through with it, however, if he's to hold his head up in the village once again and get his career back on track.

Three hours later, the mirror tells him he's trying too hard. It's a meal at the local pub, not dinner at The Ritz. He's still too early, but wants to spend time getting the look just right. Matt takes his suit and tie off and loosens his hair from the band. It's almost past his shoulders now – too long even for him. A trim at the village barber goes on his mental to-do list. The black jeans and dark red shirt he's discarded on the bed get dragged back on and he looks at himself again. His gran once said his granddad looked like Elvis when he was a young man. When he saw her last week, she said Matt reminded her of him sometimes, so he scrapes his hair back and does an Elvis pose. Yeah… he has the hair colour, the eyes, possibly the nose. The mouth is a bit fuller though. Satisfied he'll do, he wiggles his hips and belts out a few verses of 'Jailhouse Rock' before leaving the bedroom.

***

Peering round the side of the shed, Morvoren watches Trevelyar through the uncurtained upstairs window. He's dancing. What a prick he is! Must love himself, gyrating in front of the mirror like that. Just like his grandfather: a pompous, posing fucking peacock! Her pulse races and she can feel palpitations drumming in her throat. Closing her eyes, she takes a few deep breaths. The shed smells of wet wood and rusty hinges. *Calm down, Mor, you can't get overwrought. You need your wits about you.* She's not felt fighting fit lately; these palpitations are getting more frequent. She has a nasty cough too, off and on. Still, she's nearly eighty – if she's not long for this world, it makes her all the braver to do what needs to be done. There's a slight pang in the old heart about what has to be done regarding her granddaughter, but then she's made her bed.

A few minutes later, the kitchen light comes on and she can see Trevelyar washing up. He'll be making his tea in a minute and that's when she'll strike. This thought gives her energy. A surge of power strips back the years, smooths her aches and pains, and she's seventeen again, ready for anything. Ready for revenge. And how fitting for the young Trevelyar to go in this way. His bastard of an ancestor started it – but she'll finish it.

She eyes the large plastic container of liquid near her feet. It nearly defeated her on the way here. She'd concealed it within her innocent-looking shopping trolley, and she'd dragged, pulled and pushed the weight of it from her car, parked a mile away, all the way down the lane. Morvoren sniggers into her hand. It won't be heavy soon, though, will it? And what an unholy surprise it will be for Matthew Trevelyar.

Chapter twenty-three

The mirror tells Lavender she's trying too hard. She's going for a bite to eat at the local, not to a nightclub. She strips off the tight black dress with the plunging neckline and slips on her usual floaty apparel. Red's a change for her. She rarely wears it, and she thinks it's a good contrast to her blond hair and lavender eyes. The black dress is back on its hanger, but should it be? She strokes the velvet and reconsiders… It is very smart and has a swirly hem, and most of all, it's very sexy. Her reflection shows her rosy cheeks and guilty eyes. Sod that. What has she got to feel guilty about? She's a grown woman about to meet a man she cares about. The past is the past and she's ready for the future.

The black dress is off the hanger again and held in front of her; she strokes the velvet and unzips it. Matt's kisses from the other night play over in her head again and a silly smile curls her lips. For the first time in her life, she hadn't wanted to run away from a man's embrace. It had felt natural and normal, so she can't be a freak, can she? As she pulls the dress over her head, the smile disappears. If only they didn't have the confession to the police to contend with. How long will their happiness last if she gets arrested, possibly jailed? *All the more reason to make the most of the time I have now.*

Then there's a knock at the door. *Great. If that's Gran, she can piss off.* She hurries downstairs, grumbling to herself.

'Hi, Lavender. Not sure if you know me?'

Lavender looks at the smartly dressed woman on her doorstep. A dark asymmetric bob, green catlike eyes and red lipstick… She's seen her before, but can't quite place her…'I'm not quite sure…?'

'I'm Jessica Blake, the deputy head at Penhallow. I think we met once at a fundraiser for the school?'

Ah yes, that was it. Lavender remembers not warming to her at all. 'Of course, yes. I donated a painting for it, didn't I? What can I do for you this evening, Jessica?'

'Um, can I pop inside for a mo?' Jessica rubs her hands together as if she's cold.

'Yeah, but I'm going out shortly.' Lavender stands aside and waves her along the corridor and through to the kitchen. What the hell can she possibly want?

Jessica's gaze sweeps up and down the black velvet dress and she shrugs. 'You off somewhere nice?'

'Meeting a friend.'

Jessica raises an eyebrow and looks at the dress again. 'No probs. This won't take long.'

It might seem rude not to offer Jessica a drink, but if she does, the woman will stay longer. 'Take a seat,' Lavender says, gesturing to a kitchen chair.

'I'll stand, thanks.' The pleasant tone has gone, the smile with it. 'I'll come straight to the point. Do the right thing by my boyfriend, or I'll make your life very unpleasant.'

'What are you on about… and boyfriend? I don't know your boyfriend.'

'He's Matt Trevelyar.' Jessica folds her arms and glowers.

Lavender's legs go weak and she sits in a kitchen chair. She can't speak… can't think. There's treacle where her brain used to be. All she can hear is *He's Matt Trevelyar* on a loop. Must be another Matt, because Matt is with her… isn't he?

Jessica leans against the wall. 'Anyway, there's no doubt you've been instrumental in bringing about his downfall – meaning his suspension and consequent resignation. How could anyone sink so low as to target an innocent man because of some stupid feud? The kids have lost a great teacher because of you, and half the village think he's a pervert. You should be ashamed.'

Lavender sighs and wonders what Matt's told her. Has he mentioned Lavender's confession? The best policy is to keep quiet, even though all she wants to do is rage, scream and yell. How could Matt do this to her? All the time he was kissing her the other night he knew he was someone else's boyfriend… It didn't seem possible. It felt so real. How could she be so wrong? She also wonders if she has enough strength to stand up. She grabs the edge of the table and rights herself. 'Can you leave now, please? I have nothing to do with any of that.'

'I'm not done yet. Matt told me your grandmother tricked you into believing he was a wife beater and child molester. I reckon that gives you plenty of motive – plus your stupid old feud too.'

Lavender's relieved Jessica doesn't know about her confession, which makes her think she needs to get to the bottom of Jessica and Matt's relationship. If they were so close, wouldn't he have told her the whole thing? She owes it to him not to just believe this pompous, pushy woman. After all, they were colleagues. Couldn't he have talked to her just as a friend? Maybe Jessica is making their relationship out to be more than it is.

Feeling stronger now, she looks Jessica in the eye and says, 'As I said, I'd like you to leave.'

'I'll leave.' Jessica stops leaning against the door post and saunters down the corridor towards the front door. Over her shoulder, she says, 'But if you haven't been to the police by this time tomorrow, your name will be dragged through this town, and your creature of a grandmother's too. Everyone will know what kind of people you are… if they don't already. Then Matt will go to the police.'

At the door, she turns and glares at Lavender. Lavender shakes her head. 'Dear oh dear. I don't know Matt that well, but he doesn't strike me as the kind of man to let his' – she sweeps Jessica top to toe with a contemptuous gaze – 'girlfriend do his dirty work for him. I think he might have told me all this himself – not sent you.' Lavender folds her arms and looks Jessica up and down again. 'In fact, Miss Blake, I do believe you're not his girlfriend at all.'

'You can believe whatever the hell you like!' Jessica snaps, but Lavender has clocked the shifty slide of her eyes, the bristle of her shoulders. She was right. Jessica is hiding something.

Lavender narrows her eyes and suddenly leans in, her face inches away from Jessica's. She recoils, fear in her eyes. 'What's wrong? I'm only opening the door for you… Did you think I was going to bite… or put a spell on you?' Lavender raises her webbed fingers and wiggles them in Jessica's face.

Jessica flashes her eyes and makes her escape, nearly tripping over her high heels in her hurry to get away. Lavender smiles. Sometimes being seen as a witch has its benefits. Her smile fades as she considers what to do next. Should she just carry on and meet Matt as arranged in an hour or so? Or should she call him now and clear things up over the phone? If she had to hear he actually *was* Jessica's boyfriend, standing there in a sexy black velvet dress in the middle of a crowded pub would be so humiliating. Lavender picks up her phone and takes a deep breath.

Chapter twenty-four

Jessica sits in her car at the end of the lane leading to Matt's cottage. It's almost dark and a few dead leaves scatter themselves along her windscreen. There's a stiff breeze out there and the stars look cold and hard in the navy sky. Twice now she's got out of her car and then got back inside again. It's the prospect of humiliation that's anchoring her to the seat. What she should do is march up to his door and tell him exactly how she feels about him. Tell him about the little bitch Lavender too… embellish what's just happened. Say she threatened her, slapped her face. But then he might be angry that Jessica went to Lavender's house in the first place after he expressly told her not to the other night. He might calm down when she tells him she did it because she loves him, is looking out for him.

Tears well in her eyes and she pulls the sun visor down with the little mirror on it to dab at her mascara. Turning up at Matt's door looking like a panda isn't the look she's going for. She curses him under her breath. Why does she always fall for the wrong men? Her ex-husband was a philandering bastard – broke her heart time after time. Matt is the complete opposite, but he doesn't care for her at all. Not really. He slept with her because she was there and practically gave herself to him on a plate. But he *was* interested in Lavender, wasn't he? Oh yes. Jessica saw the look in his eyes when she asked him about their relationship on Saturday night. The way he says her name too – soft as silk. Bitch. Lavender was meeting a friend? Yeah, right.

Out of the car now, she pulls the collar of her grey winter coat up around her ears, wraps her red scarf around her neck and clicks the key fob to lock the door. At first her footsteps are quick and light, her conviction spurring her up the lane to her heart's desire. She will tell him the extent of her feelings and, once inside the house, allow her instinct to guide the rest. The main thing is that she stops him going to meet Lavender fucking Nancarrow. Jessica's gut reaction on seeing Nancarrow dressed in the black velvet dress was immediate. She was going out to meet a man. No woman dresses like that to meet a friend. It had to be Matt. How Jessica knew this she didn't know – but she did, and that was that. Soon they'd be cosied up together talking about Jessica – poor deluded old Jessica. But if she got to him first, spun a tall tale, he'd have his doubts about Goldilocks. And doubt can be built upon… raised up until it becomes a strong tower of mistrust.

Matt's cottage comes into view in the distance, a cosy yellow light in the downstairs windows, and her pace slows. Her feet want to turn back and go the way they've come. But his car's there – at least she knows he's in for sure. When she'd turned in to his lane earlier, she saw a man hurrying away round the corner, towards the village. It looked a bit like Matt, but it was dark, and she'd been driving, so she only caught a glimpse. But even if Matt was in, it could all go horribly wrong, couldn't it? He might turn her away at the door. And on the other hand, he might not. Jessica stops and squares her shoulders. Faint heart never won fair gentleman, did it? She sets off again, picks up the pace, until an acrid taste settles in her throat. Smoke. Wood fire? No, it smells more like petrol…

Covering her mouth with her scarf, she hurries towards the cottage, her heels wobbling on the uneven ground. Shock encircles her guts and squeezes. Hard. The cosy yellow light she thought she could see downstairs isn't light at all. It's fire. The whole ground floor seems to be alight and there's no access through the blazing front door. Fishing in her bag for her phone, she punches in 999 and alerts the fire brigade. Then, from round the back of the house, black acrid smoke billows towards her on the wind. It grabs her by the throat, forcing her to take small shallow breaths through the scarf. The sensible thing to do would be to wait for the fire brigade and sit in the car, but instinct drives her. If Matt's in there she needs to help him.

One side of the house is totally inaccessible due to the wall of thick black smoke; the other side isn't too bad. There's smoke, but not enough to stop her. Hurrying past the high hedge and fence, she places the flat of her right hand against the damp stone wall of the house to guide her way through a sudden cloud of smoke. Eventually she stumbles down the side and out the back. She can just make out what looks like the remains of a garden shed. It's gutted, but there's one or two remaining struts glowing red, the wind sporadically sending a shower of sparks skyward. Jessica needs to get past it to the back door. Was there a back door? There must be… mustn't there? She can't remember. Maybe there's a side door around the other flank of the house, because there's only a window on this side.

Unsure of her next move, through a gap in the smoke, Jessica sees a black shape by the collapsing shed. She thinks it's a man because of the height and build, and he's bending over something on the ground. She removes her scarf, yelling, 'Matt! Matt, are you okay?' Coughing, the man straightens up and turns in her direction, but she can't make him out. 'Matt!' The smoke obscures her view again, so she runs to where she thinks he is, spirits rising, her heart pounding in her chest. *Thank God he's alive and out of the house!*

The smoke shifts again… The figure's moving away… He's carrying something. Or is he? It's so hard to make anything out. Then there's an excruciating pain in her calf as her shoe twists and takes her ankle with it. Jessica bites her lip to stop a cry of pain and finds herself prone on the lawn, just feet from the last two flaming struts of the shed. Fuck! She needs to get away before the damned things fall on her. Upon testing her weight, a white-hot shard of pain bolts from ankle to thigh, and this time there's no stopping the scream she sends up into the smoke-filled sky. 'Matt! Matt, I need help!'

There's no reply. All she can hear is the crackle of flames and the pop of wood in the struts as the knots in it burn through. She'll have to drag herself back the way she came, and fast. Inch by agonising inch, Jessica wriggles on her belly, worm-like, across the rough gravel path, past the greedy flames consuming the last of the shed. Her ankle feels the size of a football and each movement sends a thousand knives racing along the nerves in her legs and lower back. But she can hear something else now, something that gives her new hope and resolve. Sirens! Sirens are growing louder… thank God! And thank God she's almost out of harm's way too. A quick glance to her right tells her the shed's about to fall. One last push and she'll be clear of danger…

Somewhere behind her, a woman's screaming. A man's yelling something too, their combined voices melding with the billowing smoke. Jessica's screaming too. Screaming until her throat feels like it will burst. The struts must have fallen across her legs. The previous pain is dwarfed by the all-consuming agony of fire sweeping across her flesh. Jessica tries to beat the fire out with her hands, but it's useless. She fights with every ounce of strength she has left, clawing the ground, dragging herself along… and then she thinks the pain is easing. She thinks she sees Matt, but her brain might be playing tricks on her. 'Matt! Matt, is it you?' Yes, it's Matt. 'Yes… Thank God.' He's right there next to her. He's come to rescue her, and if he can't, at least they'll die together. Jessica reaches out her hand to him and smiles…

Chapter twenty-five

Nearly every male eye in the pub is gawping admiringly in Lavender's direction. One older man, obviously the worse for drink, is openly staring, a lascivious expression on his face. Lavender shudders, turns her face to the fire and takes a sip of wine. Why did she wear this damned dress? Having just shrugged off her coat, she wants to yank it from the back of her chair and cover up. She won't though. It would look odd. This thought makes her hide a smile. They think she's odd anyway, so what does it matter? Still, she'd feel so much more comfortable in her normal clothes.

There'd been no time to change after Jessica left, however, because Lavender had called Matt and they'd agreed to meet straight away. When she'd outlined his ex-colleague's visit and what she'd said, Matt was furious – called Jessica a few choice names. She'd told him to calm down and that she'd explain all when she saw him. Lavender can't stop thinking about the fact that he didn't flatly deny she wasn't his girlfriend, though. Shouldn't they have been his first words?

What will she say if he admits it – says him and Jessica are an item? There will not be much *to* say, will there? Matt and Lavender haven't sworn undying love for each other, they've not even done more than kiss, so she has no hold over him, does she? Why shouldn't he have a girlfriend? Then she takes a gulp of wine, shakes her head. Who is she kidding? If Matt had a girlfriend, he should never have kissed her and arranged to meet tonight, should he? It was wrong, and no amount of thinking it over is going to change that. If he says it's true, she'll just get up and walk out. Simple as that. Lavender looks into the flames and heaves a sigh.

It won't be simple at all, because Matt's already in her heart, her mind, her soul. She'll need a crowbar to lever him out.

Lavender glances at the clock above the fire. Matt should have been here ten minutes ago. He was the one who insisted they met immediately, and now he's late. She scrabbles in her handbag for her phone. No message from him either. Another five minutes and then she'll ring. After nearly ten, she scrolls through her contacts and punches 'Matt'. The way she's feeling now, that's exactly what she wants to do to him. The phone goes to voicemail. Damn. Where the hell is he?

Lavender almost finishes her glass and contemplates another. No. She wants a clear head when and if he does grace her with his presence. There's a huddle of people at the bar around Laurence Harris, the postman. They're all wearing grave expressions and a few women are oohing and aahing at something Laurence's saying, but Lavender can't catch it, as he's speaking in a low voice. Maggie Gwithian from the hairdressers sits down heavily on a bar stool and says, 'Oh my God! I wonder who it is?'

Lavender can't stand the suspense and goes to the bar, ostensibly to get another drink, but leans in as she approaches the little group.

'I don't know,' Laurence says. 'But the burnt-out car belongs to young Trevelyar. He's renting the cottage, so I'd guess it was him.'

At the mention of Matt's name, and burnt-out car, Lavender's heart leaps into her throat. She grabs Laurence's shoulder and he looks round at her in alarm. She doesn't explain, just blurts, 'Matt Trevelyar's car is burnt-out? Are you sure…? What the hell happened?'

Before Laurence can speak, Maggie Gwithian flaps her hand in front of her face, red-cheeked with excitement, gossip in her eyes. 'Laurence's just been past the cottage that Matt Trevelyar is renting, because he lives at the other end of the lane, you know? He wasn't going out tonight, but heard sirens and that, didn't you?' She looks at the postman and he nods solemnly. 'Anyway, he saw a huge commotion – police, fire engines, burnt-out car and a half-ruined cottage too. He managed to sneak up and take a peep just before they put a cordon across, didn't you, Laurie?'

Lavender leans against the bar. She feels faint... nauseous. 'The cottage was burnt too?' Her voice comes out as a whisper.

Laurence answers this time. 'Yeah. That's not all... They've found a body! They were just covering it over when I came through the snicket. Police weren't too pleased when they saw me, I can tell you! Asked me some questions and told me to bugger off, more or less. I said I lived along the lane and was just going for a walk when I saw all the commotion. There was no cordon when I came past.' He looks round the group, puffs his chest out.

'Chances are it's Trevelyar,' Maggie says, and fans her face again, this time with a beer mat. 'I know he's supposed to be a wrong 'un, but it makes me feel quite sick to think of it. Imagine, being burnt alive?'

A chill crawls from the pit of Lavender's stomach and spreads through her chest. No. No. NO! Someone's wine glass shatters all over the stone tiles at her feet. She looks at her beige boots spattered with blood. No, it's red wine – her hand is empty. She dropped the wine glass, and it had the dregs left in it...

The landlord rushes from behind the bar with a broom and Lavender somehow forces her numb legs towards her chair by the fire. Matt... Matt's house is burnt and so is his car. They've found a body... No wonder he's late. Lavender stifles a sob as she remembers she wanted to punch him a few minutes ago. She'll do anything now to see his face once more. She doesn't care if he has fifty girlfriends – *just be alive, Matt.* With trembling fingers, she takes out her phone and presses Matt's number again, but it goes to answerphone. Lavender grabs her coat from the chair so hard it topples on its side, and the group at the bar fall silent and look over at her, mouths agape.

'It can't be Matt,' she says to them, and tries to get her coat on... only the armholes appear to be missing, and the more she struggles with it, the more tangled up in the material her arms become. Her face flares red with anger, and she throws the coat to the floor. The little group look at her as if she has lost the plot. Which at the moment she has. Lavender bends to retrieve her coat and hurries to the door and out into the cold night air. All she cares about is finding out what happened to Matt.

The wind whips her hair across her eyes as she runs down the high street, the coat bundled up under her arm, tears coursing down her cheeks. Then she slows to a walk as thoughts of arriving at Matt's cottage swamp her brain. Lavender can't bear the thought of being shooed away by the police like an annoying fly. They won't tell her who the body is anyway, will they? She's not a relative. Not even a girlfriend. A gruesome image surfaces, so she tries to blink it away. But it won't go. It's a prone, twisted and blackened form – a charred, mangled… thing. A thing that once used to be human. It's being prodded by forensics. Poked, examined… They might not know who the body is for some time.

Lavender strangles a sob and sets off running again. If they won't tell her, then so be it. But she has to at least try… Then she stops again, abruptly. Someone's hurrying up the street ahead of her on the opposite side. It's dark at that end of the road but as they draw nearer to a street light, she can see it looks like… No. Her mind won't allow her to believe it… but please, God, let it be. The person's looking at their phone, holding it to their ear. Lavender's heart jolts as her phone goes off in her bag. She doesn't need to answer it, because she can see who it is clearly now as he crosses the road towards her.

'Matt! Matt, thank God!' Lavender leans against the window of a shop, sobs of relief loud in the empty street.

'Hey, hey, what's wrong?' Matt's arms go around her, hold her tight. 'Were you worried? Betty collared me in the shop, I went in to get some wine gums, because you said you loved them. Anyway, Betty was upset about her daughter. She's found out her son-in-law's been having it away with the babysitter. Chewed my ear off for ages. I couldn't leave her in floods of tears.'

'I tried to c-call you…' Lavender whispers and tries to calm her sobs.

'Yeah, sorry. Just realised my phone's been switched off. No idea how.'

Lavender wipes her eyes and looks into his. She holds his face between her two hands, kisses his lips and then rests her head on his shoulder. 'Oh, Matt. I thought you were dead... I couldn't bear it.'

Matt pulls away and looks at her intently, the turquoise of his eyes iridescent in the street light. 'Dead? I know I'm late, but...' He tries a laugh, but his face grows serious again when he sees Lavender's not amused.

The words she needs to say are on her tongue, but keep sliding back down her throat when she tries to free them. How do you tell someone their home's been on fire – car too – and worse, that a body's been found on the premises? Taking a deep breath, she blurts it all out and he raises a shaking hand to his mouth.

'Fuck...' He stares at her, shock etched into the contours of his face. 'You sure it was my house?'

'Yes – the postman told everyone in the pub. He won't have got it wrong as he only lives at the end of your lane.'

'It's unreal... I can't believe it.' Then Matt takes her hand and sets off at a brisk pace. 'Come on. There's only one way to find out.'

Chapter twenty-six

The stench of smoke hits them three roads away from Matt's cottage. It must have been some fire. Matt tightens his grip on Lavender's hand as she slows and stares into the darkness like a scared rabbit. 'I'm not sure I want to see. Might just go home and wait for you to tell me.'

Matt strokes her hair back from her face, places his hands on her shoulders. 'Okay. I'll walk you back first. You look a bit freaked out and–'

'No. I'll be fine. Go and find out what happened. Call me later or pop round, no matter how late.' Lavender places a quick kiss on his lips. 'I can't see me getting any sleep until I know.' Then she turns and hurries back the way they'd come. He wishes he could go too, but he knows he can't.

It's like walking onto a film set when he arrives a few minutes later. There's a fire engine, two police cars, a few more vehicles, an unmarked ambulance and about fifteen or so officials of various descriptions milling about, chatting, talking on phones and making notes. Behind the spotlights they've erected, he can see half a cottage and a roof. It's almost as if a giant has sliced the place in two with a jagged sword of fire. His car has a cordon around it and is barely recognisable. There's another car on a rescue truck, a tarpaulin loosely covering the majority of it. Matt doesn't recognise the little he can see, but he can tell it's not burnt.

As he's standing there, he hears his name being called from behind one of the police cars. It's PC David Cross, who's now hurrying towards him with a middle-aged woman he doesn't recognise close behind him. 'Mr Trevelyar,' Cross says. 'Matt... Come over here and have seat.' Cross takes his elbow and guides him over to the front seat of the police car. He nods to the woman standing on his right. 'This is DI Karen Price.'

DI Price inclines her head towards Matt, gives a brief smile and shoves her hand through her closely cropped red hair. 'As you can see, Matt… Can I call you Matt?'

He nods.

'There's been a fire at your home. I'm also sorry to say we've found a body.' She pushes her thick dark-rimmed glasses up to the bridge of her nose, tilts her head, studies his face. 'Can I get you some water?'

He shakes his head to water. 'Yes… I know. My friend heard people talking about it in the pub.'

DI Price rolls her eyes at Cross. 'Great. How the hell did they find out so quick?'

'Must have been that neighbour who rocked up before the cordon was put across.'

Price sighs. 'The postman… yeah. Bloody blabbermouth.' She looks back at Matt and takes a quick glance at Cross. 'Not only that… It's likely it was arson, according to the fire officer in charge. Until we've done a few more tests it won't be confirmed categorically, but the officer is fairly sure.'

Matt's jaw drops and he raises his hand to his mouth, but it trembles against his lips so he clasps his hands together in his lap. But the tremble spreads to his arms and legs. He thinks he can smell a whiff of petrol faintly on the air and nausea rises in his throat. His pulse is racing and he feels somehow outside his body. Someone has done this deliberately? Someone has burnt his house and someone has died.

'Matt, you okay?' Cross asks.

'No,' Matt manages after a few moments. 'Not really… Someone hates me enough to deliberately set my house on fire… Did they think I was in it?' He closes his eyes, thinks about the badger head, the vandalising of his car, the drugging and humiliation… 'They must have… *she* must have actually wanted to kill me.'

DI Price asks, 'She? Who do you mean?'

'Morvoren Penhallow, who else?' He looks at Cross, whose expression is unreadable.

'Ah, yes. PC Cross did fill me in about the previous events.'

A thought suddenly occurs to Matt. 'Is the body Morvoren's? Did she set the fire and then somehow get caught in it? Because if she did, I'm not bloody sorry.' He knows that sounds callous, but so what.

'No. The body isn't hers. It is a woman though,' DI Price says, and looks at Matt as if to gauge his reaction. 'I believe you knew her, too.'

He wants to yell at her to just bloody tell him, but he doesn't like the fact that her previous compassion has been replaced by a more suspicious demeanour. 'Really? Who is it?'

Price says, 'The body wasn't completely burnt, because the fire fighters got here and attended to her. Unfortunately, they were too late. We found a car at the end of the lane with a driving license in the glove compartment. We were able to identify her easily from that.'

Cross makes his lips into a grim line. 'Sorry to have to tell you, Matt, but it's Jessica Blake. I spoke to her briefly when I popped in to see your headteacher at the time of your last incident.'

Feelings of nausea intensify as he digests this news. Jessica is dead. Dead. What the hell was she doing here?

'Had you arranged to meet Ms Blake at your home?' Price asks.

'No. No, I've no idea why she was here,' Matt says, a tremor in his voice. Had she come here... started the fire because he'd rejected her? He realises DI Price is holding a bag up and asking him something else. 'Sorry, what?'

'We found this. Do you recognise it?'

Through the plastic evidence bag, Matt looks at the silver chain with a mermaid hanging from the clasp. Yes. He's seen this before, but where? Then it comes to him... *Shit. It's Lavender's!* He can't say that though, can he? Fuck. What the hell was Lavender doing here? But then she couldn't have been, because she was in the pub waiting for him… wasn't she? Aware he's taking too long to reply, he frowns and turns the corners of his lips down. 'Nope. Not seen it before. Probably Jessica's?'

'Hmm. Possibly. It was found in the victim's hand.' DI Price whisks the bag away. 'But we can't assume that, Mr Trevelyar.' She folds her arms, gives him a hard stare. 'Where were you coming back from just now? And what time did you leave?'

Lavender's bracelet was found in Jessica's hand? *What the hell? Keep calm, Matt.* He swallows and rubs his eyes, tries to remember what time he left. He tells them he went out straight after Lavender's call. So it must have been about five thirty. He tells them that and also about talking to Betty and meeting Lavender.'

'Okay. So this Betty will corroborate your story… Lavender too?'

Matt notices that PC Cross has his notepad out and is scribbling away. The penny drops… He's being questioned in connection with the bloody fire! His stomach flips. 'Why?' He shakes his head, incredulous. 'Do you suspect me?'

'We have to ask these questions, Mr Trevelyar. We also have to ask you to pop along there to our forensics guys.' She waves a hand in the direction of a white tent that's been erected. 'They'll want to have a look at you – your clothes too. You knew the victim, so…'

Matt notices she neglected to say they didn't suspect him. And what does that mean – 'you knew the victim'? He doesn't like where this is going at all. 'But can you do this without me having a solicitor?'

'You're just helping us with our inquiries. If you have nothing to hide, then there's no problem, is there? We can arrange a solicitor, but we'd have to take you to the station and–'

'No. I want to help.' Matt sighs and follows her to some people dressed in white coveralls. An hour later he's 'free to go'. Forensics have finished with him, and Betty and Lavender have corroborated his 'story'. Until they have more evidence, it looks like he won't be required again. They will, of course, want to speak to him at a later date and will keep him abreast of proceedings. 'Free to go', they'd said. Where he *will* go is a problem. Matt looks at the ruined cottage with dismay. Though the side housing his bedroom seems intact, smoke damage might have ruined his clothes. Therefore, he has what he's standing up in. There's no way they would let him look for extra clothes, toiletries, et cetera, as the house is deemed unsafe. But luckily, he has his phone and wallet, so can get a room in a hotel. There are at least two he knows of in the village. The police offered to help him find somewhere, but he just wanted to be rid of them. After tonight, he'll have to think again. And with a burnt-out car, he'll have to think about transport too.

Matt says goodbye to Price and Cross and with a head full of questions, sets off down the road. Could Morvoren actually have pulled a stunt like this? What was Jessica doing here – could she have set the fire, as had crossed his mind earlier? And what was Lavender's bracelet doing in her hand? Then he stops in his tracks. The CCTV at the side of the house that wasn't burnt might have picked up something if it hadn't been damaged. He runs back to the cottage just as Price and Cross are getting into their car. He tells them his idea.

'We didn't see a camera,' Price says.

'It's tiny and well hidden under the eaves,' Matt answers, pleased that he chose to spend the money on the latest type.

Cross gets out of the car. 'Excellent.' He makes for the side of the house. 'Let's hope it's intact and turns up something.'

As Matt sets off again, he remembers he's promised to tell Lavender what's happened. She'll be even more worried now the police have contacted her about his whereabouts. Matt shoves his hands into his pockets and wonders whether to phone or call round. He needs a place for the night, but he decides it's more important to forego a phone call and actually go and see Lavender first. Besides… he wants to see her face when he tells her about the mermaid bracelet. She can't possibly be involved, can she?

The wind blows the scent of smoke and ash into his face as he turns the corner towards the village, and a chill runs the length of his spine when he imagines what Jessica must have gone through.

Once more his mind is flooded with unanswered questions. What the hell was she doing at his house? And why did she have Lavender's bracelet in her hand? Matt tells himself off – no point in driving himself mad rehashing it all. Lavender will shed some light on it, perhaps. Did she have a fight with Jessica when she'd called round earlier? Did Jessica pull the bracelet off Lavender's wrist somehow?

Matt shakes his head and swallows down a mixture of nausea and anxiety. The village is quiet – just a few people walking to the pub, getting petrol and in the little supermarket at the end of the lane. He can see a line of shoppers at the checkout. People are talking, laughing, putting things into their baskets. Everything looks so normal, but how can it be, while his whole life is falling apart? It's surreal… like some terrifying nightmare. *Please God, let me wake up from it soon.*

Chapter twenty-seven

Lavender opens the door and Matt can tell straight away that she's had a drink. She gives him a quick hug and then he follows her to the kitchen and he clocks about a third of a bottle of red wine on the side, a glass almost empty on the table. 'Want a glass?' she asks, and picks up the bottle.

'I could murder one, but I need a clear head. Everything feels way out of control as it is.'

Lavender sighs and goes to refill her glass.

'Maybe you shouldn't have any more either.'

She frowns and tips a little in. 'This is my last one. I needed it after I spoke to the police.' Lavender goes into the living room and sits on the sofa, pats the cushion next to her. 'Why the hell were they asking me if I'd seen you tonight?'

Matt joins her on the sofa. 'Because the fire was arson – unconfirmed as yet, but the fire officer's more or less sure. Something about the fire pattern? Besides, I'm sure I could smell a faint whiff of petrol in the air. They were organising sniffer dogs too – but you don't need to be a rocket scientist.'

Lavender's eyes grow round and she grabs his arm. 'Who the hell would want to…' Her words run out and Matt imagines she's supplied her own answer.

'Yes, like you, I did think it was your lovely old granny.'

'When I saw her last, she was hell-bent on finishing you off… I never thought she'd actually try it though, not really.' Lavender stares into the fire, her bottom lip trembling.

'The thing is, it might not have been her.' Matt looks at Lavender, unsure of how to broach the subject of the dead body being Jessica's. Best to just tell her straight, and about the fact he slept with her last Saturday. In fact, he'll start there.

As he's telling her, Lavender gets up and tips the rest of the bottle into her glass. Tears are pouring silently down her face. 'Jessica was telling me the truth then... that she was your girlfriend?' Matt holds his hand up, shakes his head, but she ploughs on. 'Why the hell did you let me make a fool of myself the other–'

'Hey, give me a chance!' Matt reaches out a hand, but she folds her arms, fixes him with a hard stare. 'The next morning, I realised it was a huge mistake. I told her straight away that there was not going to be a next time... She was the one who practically forced herself on me, after all. I know it sounds trite, but it had been a long time since...' *Shit, this isn't going well.* 'Look, I know it's no excuse... but while Jessica and I were' – he feels a flush creep up his neck and looks away from Lavender's level gaze. 'While we were in bed, I pictured you. You were all I could think about, Lavender...'

'Right. That's supposed to make me feel better, is it?' Her voice is cold, sharp.

'No. But it's the truth.'

There's silence for a few moments and then she reaches for his hand. 'When I thought you were dead earlier, I told myself that I wouldn't care if you had fifty women on the go, just so long as I could see your face again. I'm prepared to forget it happened and move on if you want to. Jessica might not be though. She seems to have strong feelings for you – going to all the trouble of coming over here to tell me off and...' Her voice tails off when she notices Matt's grim expression. 'What is it?'

'It was Jessica. The body they found... it was hers.' Lavender gasps and covers her face with her hands. He gives her a moment and then tells her she was found next to his house. 'It's possible it wasn't Morvoren's doing at all. Jessica could have been the arsonist.' Even as Matt says this, he knows it doesn't feel right.

Lavender takes three big gulps of wine and sets the glass down on the coffee table. 'S-so you're telling me Jessica actually might have tried to kill you, because you rejected her? What, and she somehow succumbed to the smoke or something?'

'Possibly. It's a long shot, but why else would she be there?'

'Maybe she was going to tell you some cock and bull story about her meeting with me?' Lavender shrugged. 'Perhaps she knew I'd tell you that she came here and told me you were her boyfriend – told me to leave you alone. Jessica might have thought up a different story to spin you – so it would be my word against hers.'

Matt thinks this is possible, but he's girding his loins to broach the subject of the bracelet. The thought of it is a lead weight on his chest. 'We'll never know now, will we?'

'No, I guess not… I can hardly get my head around what you've told me. It's like walking through a nightmare.'

Matt nods. 'That's exactly what it's like… and there's more.'

'More?'

''Fraid so.' Matt shifts in his seat, looks at the rug in front of the fire. 'The police asked me if I recognised a bracelet that was found in Jessica's hand.' He pauses, glances back at Lavender. She's frowning, looks impatient for him to get on with it. 'I did recognise it, but I said I didn't.'

'Why would you do that?'

'Because it was a delicate little silver chain with a mermaid hanging from the clasp.'

Both of Lavender's hands shoot to her mouth, but can't prevent a moan of shock escaping her lips. 'That's mine.'

'I know, that's why I said I didn't recognise it.'

She stares at him, open-mouthed. 'Hang on. Do you think I had something to do with her death? And you didn't tell them the bracelet was mine to… what, protect me?'

He shrugs. 'It did cross my mind, but then I realised you were in the pub at the time of the fire. You told the police that you were, too, and they will check your story, ask witnesses if they've not done so already.'

'Oh, well, that's all right then!' Lavender jumps up, starts to pace the room. 'How the *hell* could you think I had anything to do with Jessica's death? What kind of a woman do you think I am?'

Matt jumps up too. 'Hey, calm down. What would you have thought if you were in my shoes? The police show you something that belongs to me and say it was on the victim's body? Come on, Lavender. Think about it!'

She stops pacing and heaves a sigh, looks into the fire. 'Yes, I suppose…'

'I didn't think it for long, you know. When I went over it in my mind later, I came up with a reason why she might have had it in her hand. When she came round to yours earlier, did you come to blows? Or did she grab your wrist, for example?'

Lavender shook her head. 'No. No, we never came to blows.' She walks back to the sofa, slumps down on it and covers her face with both hands. Then her shoulders start to shake, and Matt realises she's sobbing as if her heart will break.

He hurries over, puts his arms around her. 'Come on, love. We'll get to the bottom of it. There must be another explanation.' He can't think what the hell it could be right now, however.

'I don't n-need to get to the bottom of it, because I-I know!' A fresh bout of sobbing vibrates through his chest as she lays her head there. 'I wish I didn't know because it's t-too terrible to take in.'

Matt releases her and fetches a glass of water and a tissue from the kitchen. 'Here, drink this. Then take a deep breath and tell me what it is.'

Lavender does as he asks and then takes a deep, shuddering breath. 'It was my gran… no, I won't ever give her that title again. It was that bitch Morvoren's doing. We were right in the first place. She was the one behind the fire. I have no idea how Jessica ended up in the middle of it all, but Morvoren obviously wanted the finger pointed at me.' Lavender blows her nose. 'The last time I saw her, we argued, as you know. She grabbed my wrist and the next day I realised my bracelet had gone. I knew she'd never let me have it back… Ironic, as she was the one who gave it to me on my eighteenth birthday. She said it was because we have webbed fingers, and the old tales that webbed fingers on women meant they were related to mermaids way back.'

Matt slumped down next to her on the sofa. 'My God. Are you saying Morvoren burnt down my house, found Jessica was there and injured, possibly dying… so shoved your bracelet in her hand to make people think you did it all?'

Lavender gave a slow nod. 'Seems that way to me. How about you?'

Matt can hardly take it in. What kind of a person was Morvoren? Would she really stoop so low as to set her granddaughter up for murder? 'I honestly don't know, Lavender. We know she hates me and why. Also, because I'm back in the village and telling anyone who'll listen what an evil witch she is. But why would she try and do something so awful to you? I know you stood up to her after you found out she'd lied to you about me, told her you didn't want to see her again, but this…' He shakes his head. When he thinks of his own lovely gran, he can't conceive of such a terrible act.

'I think she must know about us… about the fact we are' – her face reddens – 'you know – close. No idea how. Probably spying. She hinted at it when we argued. It's her worse nightmare, isn't it? A Trevelyar and a granddaughter of a Penhallow reunited. The feud over.'

Matt nods. 'Yes. I think you might be right. But even so—'

Lavender holds up her finger, turns her mouth into a stiff line. 'Actually, no, it's much more personal than that. Her worst nightmare, and what she can't bear, is that the grandson of two people she despises most in all the world has won the heart of her granddaughter. That the granddaughter who, for years, she's nurtured, loved' – Lavender gives a humourless bark – 'well, supposedly loved, has rejected her in favour of you. It's Terry and Elowen all over again. Rejection and betrayal. For her, it's the ultimate insult.'

Matt sighs. 'When I was a kid my gran used to say I had a Cornish legacy. I'd been bequeathed the Cornish spirit and fire of my forebears and a bit of magic from Elowen. She said she knew I'd return here one day too, and I have. What a pity the Cornish legacy seems to be one of death and destruction in the end.'

'All because of the old bitch who calls herself my grandmother.'

Matt hates to see Lavender so distraught. Fury and sadness flit intermittently across her eyes as she stares into the fire. She's picking at the skin on the side of her thumb and he can only imagine the tangle of thoughts in her mind. He wants to make it all better, but his gut tells him it will take a long time to heal wounds like this. Matt remembers one positive thing she's just revealed to him. Something that makes him smile inside, despite the situation. He hesitates a while and then says, 'So, is it true what you said... you know, that I've won your heart?'

A frown furrows her brow as if she can't remember saying it. Then she shrugs. 'I guess it is. Not sure what future we have now though.'

Matt's not smiling inside now. 'Why not?'

'How can I be happy with someone who thinks I'm capable of murder?'

'I don't think that at all! I was confused when I saw the bracelet and was told where it was found. Anyone would be. To be honest, I thought you'd be relieved I didn't tell the police it belonged to you.' Matt's hurt, angry and resentful all at the same time. But most of all he's worried that he and Lavender's fledgling relationship is already dead in the water.

She's looking a bit sheepish now, puts her hand on his knee. 'I'm sorry. This whole thing is so hard to take in. I'm not thinking straight.'

He takes her hand, kisses the back of it. 'Of course you're not. And you must be emotionally exhausted. We both are. But the police will turn something up from the CCTV in a few days, no doubt, and we'll put our heads together in the morning.' Matt glances at the clock. 'And much as I don't want to leave you – I should get into the village and bag a room for the night.'

Lavender gives him a level stare. 'I have a spare room. You're welcome to it.'

Matt smiles. 'That would be brilliant. But can you imagine the wagging tongues if someone saw me leaving in the morning? Your gr… Morvoren would have heart failure.'

Lavender snorts. 'Yeah, and it couldn't happen to a nicer person.' Then she kisses him and gives him a shy smile. 'Why not share my bed – might as well? The tongue waggers will say you have anyway.'

'Look, there's nothing I would like more. But as I said, you're emotionally–'

'Just shut up and kiss me.'

Matt looks into her eyes and kisses her. Tomorrow's troubles can wait.

Chapter twenty-eight

If Morvoren had the strength to go and strangle that bloody cockerel over the back wall, she would. Not a wink of sleep all night, and now just as she's dropping off, she's being tormented by its incessant crowing. She heaves herself higher up the bed and tries to plump the pillows. Even this small action sets off the cough again that's plagued her for hours. Hawking into a tissue, she examines the blob of black phlegm. The black's to be expected after the smoke, but it looks like there's a bit of red in there too. That's been happening for weeks, but not quite as much as this.

Outside the window, the early morning light is filtering through the naked tree branches at the end of her garden. October is dying and so is she. Morvoren suspects she'll not see the leaves returning. A shame, as spring is her favourite time of year. But so be it. Lavender has betrayed her – what is there left to live for? Slumping against the pillows, she closes her eyes and takes a deep breath, which brings on a fresh bout of coughing. At least the young madam will be punished once they find her bracelet.

Morvoren will make an anonymous phone call about it all in a few days, once she's feeling a bit better. She'll say Lavender broke down and confessed to her dear old gran about the killing of Trevelyar and the manslaughter of Jessica Blake. She'd burnt down his house with him in it because he rejected her after stringing her along. Jessica Blake just happened to be there. She was distraught about that bit, and she'd left her bracelet at the scene of the crime, but Lavender had begged Morvoren not to say anything. Even though she adored her granddaughter, she decided she had to speak out – her conscience wouldn't allow her to keep silent any longer.

She thinks again about Jessica and her stomach rolls. Such a shock to see her coming out of the smoke like that yesterday. What the hell the schoolteacher was doing there, Morvoren had no idea. Maybe she and Trevelyar had a thing? Typical of him to have more than one woman on the go. This would be the perfect motive for Lavender, wouldn't it? Yes, Morvoren would say Lavender found out that Trevelyar was two-timing her, and so wreaked vengeance. Morvoren smiles. She'll change manslaughter to murder. Lavender Nancarrow murdered two people in cold blood because of betrayal. How fitting. Happy with the way things are slotting into place, at last she drifts off to sleep.

Someone's calling her name. No. *Go away...* She's tired. Morvoren pulls the pillow over her head, but then she hears someone hammering on the front door. Opening one eye, she sees the bedside clock flashing a digital 12.23am at her. No. That must mean she's been asleep five hours. It only feels like a few moments since she closed her–

'Morvoren! Mor! You okay? All your curtains are shut... Mor?'

'Bloody Annie,' Morvoren grumbles. What does she want? She tries to call down to her, but it starts her coughing, so she hauls herself up and slips her dressing gown on. All the while Annie continues to shout through the letter box. Because she feels so rough, Morvoren has to take the stairs even slower than normal, and when she arrives at the bottom, Annie's stopped. *If she's bloody gone after all that I'll...* Morvoren opens the door just in time to see Annie going through the gate.

'Oi! I'm here,' she wheezes.

Annie turns and hurries back. 'Oh, Mor. You look terrible, maid. Come on back inside.' She takes Morvoren's arm and guides her to the kitchen. 'You poorly?'

'No. I always stay in bed until past noon,' Morvoren snaps and starts coughing.

'Here, sit yourself down. I'll light a fire and make you some tea. Or soup? Soup's good for a cough.'

'Not sure it is. Besides, I'm not hungry – tea will do, thanks.'

Annie makes her comfortable on the sofa and tucks a blanket around Morvoren's legs. She's about to light a fire but Morvoren tells her to put the heating on instead.

'It's no trouble, Mor. There's kindling right there and–'

'Leave it, Annie. I can't be doing with the smoke with this cough. Make the tea and I'll tell you how I got it.'

Annie's eyes light up with excitement. 'I'll tell you a story about a fire! Someone's house burnt down last night. Wait 'til you hear whose it is!'

Morvoren smiles to herself as she listens to Annie humming while rattling about making tea in the kitchen. She can't wait to pop her little gossip bubble with a big story of her own. When Annie comes back in with two mugs and a packet of biscuits under her arm, Morvoren says gleefully, 'I bet I can tell you whose house burnt down.'

Annie pulls a face. 'Hmm. You always seem to know everything before I do. But I've no idea how, you being ill and in bloody bed.'

'I wasn't as ill yesterday.' Morvoren blows across the surface of her tea. Then she winks at Annie. 'In fact, I'd not felt so good in years.'

Annie settles herself in the armchair across from her old friend and raises an eyebrow. 'Bet you don't know about the body though, eh?'

Morvoren doesn't like the sound of this. Shouldn't she have said 'bodies'? 'I do, as a matter of fact… both of them.'

'Both of them?'

'Yes.'

'There's only one, as far as I've heard.' Annie purses her lips and looks a bit unsure.

'Well, you've not heard right, then. There were two bodies – Jessica Blake's and Matthew Trevelyar's.' Morvoren puts her mug down, folds her arms, gives Annie the hard stare.

'No. It's you who've heard wrong. As much as I know you'd wish he was, Mor, Trevelyar's not dead.' Annie crunches into a biscuit, triumph in her eyes at getting one over on Morvoren.

'He *has* to be.' Morvoren snatches her mug up, then bangs it down again on the coffee table.

'Well he's *not*.' Annie jabs a half-eaten biscuit at her. 'Betty told me this morning he'd had a bloody lucky escape. Last night he'd gone to meet your Lavender at the pub. On his way, he'd popped in for some sweets at the shop and they had a chat.'

No, no, no! Trevelyar's alive and Lavender was in the pub? That's buggered everything right up. Damn it all! Morvoren puts her hands over her face and tries to keep hold of her sanity. How could this be happening? She looks at Annie in bewilderment and then anger pulses through her veins. 'The jammy bastard must have gone out *just* before I set the fire. Must have been by the skin of his teeth – he's the luck of the devil that one!' The outburst sets her coughing so she grabs her mug, slopping tea on the carpet as she tries to take a drink.

Annie's mouth has fallen open and when Morvoren's coughing abates, she says, 'You started the fire? I can't believe it.'

'And I can't believe Trevelyar is alive.' Morvoren shakes her head. 'I mean, there he was in the window – I could see him washing up just a few minutes before I poured petrol all over everything.'

'You poured petrol over everything. I can't believe it.'

'Best way to torch a house.'

'You torched the house. I can't believe it.'

'What are you, a bloody parrot?' she fires at Annie.

Annie shakes her head and puts a trembling hand to her lips. 'I know how much you hate that man, Mor… but if anyone asked me if I thought you were capable of trying to murder him, I would have laughed in their face.'

'Really? Then you don't know me too well, do you?'

'No. No, I can't do.' Annie's voice is hushed, bewildered.

Morvoren wants to slap her. Annie knows what she's had to put up with over the years. 'Oh, come on. My ancestors suffered at their hands, don't forget. And I was betrayed in the worst way by Terry and that bitch Elowen. If Matt Trevelyar had died in that fire, the world would be better off.'

'And what about the schoolteacher? What had Jessica Blake ever done to you?'

Regret and guilt kick Morvoren in the gut. 'Nothing. That was a mistake and I'm sorry for it. But she just appeared from nowhere. She was wearing stupid high heels and must have tripped over. Hurt her leg.'

'Dear God, Morvoren. I can't take it all in.' Annie's eyes fill, and she covers her mouth as if trying to stop her words, but her voice escapes through her fingers. 'You've actually killed one person and wanted to kill another.'

'As I've just said – I'm sorry for the death of the teacher. It was an accident, okay?' Morvoren coughs again and spits into a tissue.'

Realisation dawns in Annie's eyes. 'You're coughing because of smoke damage… You don't have an infection at all.'

'Yes and no. I think I do have an underlying something or other, but the smoke's brought the cough out something awful.'

'Righteous punishment on you.' Annie's expression is not one Morvoren's seen before. She looks like she hates her, and Morvoren doesn't like it.

'Never knew you were religious, Annie.' Morvoren gives a wry smile.

'You don't care about what you've done at all, do you? You're just sitting there, poking fun at me.' Annie's voice is trembling with emotion.

'Hey, change the record. I told you the teacher was a mistake. Bad luck. I've had a run of bad luck, to be honest, because I was going to pin the whole thing on my mare of a granddaughter. That was until you told me she was in the pub, so of course she has a sodding alibi. Loads of people will be able to confirm it. I found Lavender's mermaid bracelet on the floor over there.' Morvoren inclines her head to the doorway. 'I grabbed her wrist the last time she visited. And this bracelet was "conveniently" left in the hand of the dying Miss Blake yesterday… Genius, if I do say so myself.'

Annie's aghast. 'Your own flesh and blood? I know you've had your differences and you say she's betrayed you – but how could you want to do such a terrible thing to her?' She heaves herself up and makes for the door, dabbing a tissue at the tears now pouring down her face. 'I'm going to tell the police what I know. There's no way I can live with this.'

Morvoren can hardly credit it. Annie's been her friend for nigh on seventy years and she thinks she's going to grass on her? *Well, she can fucking think again.* 'You'll do no such thing, Annie, or your precious Jamie will be looking at the inside of a prison before Christmas.'

Annie stops in the hallway, looks back at Morvoren, fear in every line of her face. 'W-Why? What do you mean?'

'Come back in here and sit down. You're giving me a crick in my neck.'

Annie comes back and perches on the chair arm. 'What's my Jamie got to do with it?'

Morvoren gives her a slow smile. She's enjoying this, having the upper hand after her plans have gone so badly wrong. 'Jamie got me the petrol. I managed to drag it there in my trolley, and was going to do it by myself, but the cannister was just too heavy to pour safely. I didn't want it all over me too, or I'd go up like a firework. So I called him and he came and helped.'

Annie's ashen. 'My Jamie... no, he wouldn't.' A sob escapes on the last word.

'Oh, he would, and he did. It's a good job too, because the smoke overwhelmed me at one point. He had to lift me from harm's way. Then he went and investigated Jessica Blake. She'd hurt her leg and was dragging herself along with her lower half afire, apparently. I didn't see her. Heard her screaming though. Gives me the creeps just thinking about it.'

Annie's shaking her head, sticking her chin out. 'Jamie might be a bit of a lad, but he would never do something like that!'

'A bit of a lad who's been betrayed by my granddaughter. It's amazing how love can turn so swiftly to hate, isn't it?' Morvoren treats Annie to a knowing smile. 'Once I'd told him that Lavender and Trevelyar have been at it like rabbits, he just wanted revenge. Got guts, that boy. Such a tragedy he and Lavender didn't get together. I gave him Lavender's bracelet and told him to put it in Jessica's hand. A pity it was all for nothing as Lavender has an alibi.' She holds up her forefinger and frowns. 'The weird thing was that Jessica apparently seemed to think Jamie was Trevelyar – called him Matt. Might have been her mind playing tricks as it closed down…'

Annie slumps in the chair and sobs as if her heart is breaking. Morvoren can't get any sense out of her at all, so gives up trying. She finishes her tea and contemplates a biscuit. But she decides against it, as the crumbs might make her cough. Looking up at Annie, she sees her staring vacantly into space, her face puffy and red, tears still silently coursing. Eventually, she says in a small, faraway voice, 'I've never felt so completely hopeless in all my life.'

Morvoren thinks she looks pathetic and wants to laugh. She just manages not to and says, 'Come on, old girl. Let's not fight and put this down to experience… My plans went wrong, and I'm sorry the schoolteacher got mixed up in it. Jamie did his best, and you should be proud of him. I can see you're not, mind.' A shrug. 'Obviously you won't be telling the police now… I need another sleep, I think, if I'm to shake this bloody cough. I've got a strong herbal remedy in the freezer which should help. It should be freshly picked stuff, but beggars, choosers and all that.'

Annie gets to her feet and gives Morvoren's face a disgusted sweep as she walks past. At the door, she says over her shoulder, 'Goodbye, Morvoren. I hope never to set eyes on you again.'

Morvoren jumps as the door slams behind her and sticks two fingers in the air. 'Up yours, Annie! Who bloody needs friends like you, anyway?' The defiance in her heart is absent from her voice, however. Her words spoken out loud, sound small and hollow and empty. An uncomfortable thought slithers to the forefront of her mind. Her life is like the words, isn't it? Small, hollow and empty.

Her husband's dead, her son and wife don't bother with her much, her oldest friend has deserted her and the one true hope, the one she was going to pass the torch of folklore and nature to… the one who she would live on through, has forsaken her. *And we all know whose fault it is, don't we?* Once she's fit enough, she'll make him pay. Trevelyar might have escaped death this time, but Morvoren *will* have her vengeance.

Chapter twenty-nine

Over the last twenty-four hours or so, Lavender's managed to compartmentalise her mind. It's been a struggle, but every time thoughts of Morvoren, the fire and the whole situation demand her attention, she forces them back into a strongbox, slams it shut and secures the padlock. It had been tough telling her parents about everything, but it had to be done because Mum was asking what had gone on between her and Morvoren. Morvoren wouldn't answer her questions, and Lavender had only divulged they'd had a big row and didn't want to say what it was about. After the fire, however, she needed to let them know the truth.

She'd told them about her part in Matt's downfall and about the fire. Mum had been horrified and sympathetic, but Dad was a bit distant. He told her he was always there for her, and he was sorry she'd been hurt, but Lavender did wonder if he totally believed what his mother was capable of. Dad wanted to go round and challenge Morvoren, but Lavender had sworn them to secrecy, impressed upon them they couldn't mention what they knew to Morvoren until investigations were over. God knows what she might do if she knew Lavender was accusing her, spreading it round the family.

Too much thinking and puzzling over death and destruction makes her despair as well. So today the only thoughts she's allowing to flourish are the ones about how happy Matt makes her. He's stayed in her house since the night of the fire – her bed too. Who would have thought it? There were times she wondered if it would ever happen. It has though, and she is over the moon, on cloud nine, head over heels and all the other little clichés in the world used to describe joy and happiness.

Lavender steps out of the shower, wipes steam from the mirror and smiles at her reflection. She knows it's daft, but as well as feeling different inside, she looks different too. Calmer, more in tune with who she is. This must be the power of love. Matt would probably run a mile if she dropped the 'L' word out loud. But he must have an idea. She's hinted at her feelings for him and she did say he'd won her heart the other day when they were talking about the fire and Morvoren. Matt had hinted at his feelings for her too on more than one occasion. No. She won't allow those thoughts. Bang. Slam. Click. The mirror has steamed over again, so she draws a little heart in it. Then, slipping on her dressing gown, she decides to cook a full English and take him breakfast in bed.

In the kitchen, she finds Matt at the table, his long hair wild and uncombed, his eyes red-rimmed and a thick dark shadow of stubble across his jaw. 'Hi, Matt. Thought you were still sleeping.' Lavender drops a kiss on his head and takes the frying pan off a hook on the wall.

'Chance would be a fine thing. I was just resting my eyes when I heard you get up and have a shower. Not slept a wink.'

This isn't what she wants to hear. She can feel the strongbox rattling at the back of her mind. 'Why's that?' Eggs, bacon, bread. She'd look in the fridge and the breadbin for those items, hum a cheerful tune and hopefully Matt would just say his insomnia was due to a stomach ache. Nothing at all to do with the thoughts in the strongbox.

'Because when I checked my phone late last night, I saw I had a text and a missed call from PC Cross asking me to come into the station today. Didn't look at my phone much yesterday as we were busy walking along the cliff path and doing other interesting things.' He gives her a cheeky smile.

No matter how much Lavender tries to disguise it with vigorous egg cracking and grill banging, the rattling grows louder and then the lid flies off the box. A dark swarm of worries strangles the happy, light feeling she's had since waking and brings her back from cloud nine to ground zero. 'They want to interview you again?'

'Possibly. Or they've found something on the CCTV? Or someone. Morvoren with any luck.'

'Hope so. Morvoren's not one for technology, so it wouldn't have crossed her mind to even be wary of being caught on camera.' Lavender turns the bacon and is a little surprised to realise all she feels for her grandmother is contempt. But then she supposes that the old woman's despicable actions have killed any affection that might be lurking in the recesses of her heart.

Matt nods. 'I'll text back and ask what time he wants me in. I need a shower and to make myself look presentable.'

As Lavender sets the plates down on the table and pours the tea, she knows she has to let the strongbox stay open. There's no going back to the pretence of the two of them living in their carefree happy bubble. The sooner they get to grips with the bad stuff, the sooner they can move on. 'I'll come to the station with you and tell them how you came to be found naked and drugged in your car.' She sighs. 'Well, our version anyway. Tell about the bracelet too.'

Through a mouthful of bacon, Matt says, 'To help them get more evidence on Morvoren?'

'Yes. And to clear your name. If by some chance they haven't got her on camera, I'm buggered if she's getting away with it. It had to be her, Matt. She's the only one who had my bracelet.'

He nods and wipes his mouth. 'Are you one hundred per cent on that one?'

'Absolutely.'

'It would be good if we could mention the bracelet, but I said I'd never seen it before.'

'That doesn't matter, because you might not have. I don't wear it all of the time. I'll tell them I lost it, where and how.'

Matt pushes his plate aside and takes a swig of tea. 'I just hope they don't try to suggest you had anything to do with it.'

'How could I have? I was in the pub at the time, with at least ten witnesses to prove it.'

'I know.' He places his hand over hers. 'But why can't all this be over? All I want is for me and you to carry on getting to know each other and be happy. Is that too much to ask?'

Lavender doesn't know. Her gut tells her they have a way to go before happy endings are on the horizon. She gives him what she hopes is an encouraging smile. 'It will all be over, Matt. Not sure when… but it'll have to be after Morvoren is dealt with, one way or another.'

***

They arrive at Truro Police Station a little after 2pm and are shown into an interview room. A young female officer explained PC Cross wouldn't be present, but DI Karen Price and a DC Steve Vincent would be along shortly, and asked if they wanted tea.

Nursing two cardboard cups of 'dishwater' as Matt calls it – he always makes her laugh – they hold each other's hands under the table to calm their nerves. Lavender remembers that when Matt contacted Cross about what time to come into the station, he'd asked if the CCTV had shown anything. Cross said it had, but wouldn't reveal what. Then the door opens and in walks Price and presumably DC Vincent. Price has a laptop under her arm.

She extends her hand to them both. 'Nice to meet you again, Matt. This is DC Steve Vincent. In murder investigations, it's usual to have CID personnel involved. PC Cross extends his good wishes, however.'

Vincent, a tall, dark-haired, brown-eyed officer in his thirties, shakes their hands.

'And this must be Miss Nancarrow,' Price says, giving a broad smile. 'Can I call you Lavender?'

Lavender feels like saying, no call me Gertrude. But says, 'Yes, that's my name.'

'Now, as you know, you're here for a voluntary interview, and we do want to tape it. To be clear, just because the tapes go on, you're not under arrest and you're free to leave at any time.' Both of them nod their understanding. And then Price turns to Lavender.

'Lavender, I understand you have something to tell us about Matt's incident of last month?'

Matt answers for her. 'Yes, but we'd like to hear what you have to say about the fire and the CCTV first, if that's okay?'

'Certainly.' Price starts up the laptop, folds her arms and sits opposite, next to Vincent.

Vincent smiles at Matt and says, 'Your story – that you were at the shop at the time of the fire with Betty Lawson – checks out was said the other day. Also, Betty can provide CCTV footage of you in the shop at the time, should we need it, which I can't see being necessary.'

'Glad to hear it. Though why I'd be a suspect at all is beyond me.'

'You knew the victim, Matt,' Price says. 'What was the nature of your relationship with Jessica Blake. Friends or…?'

Lavender doesn't like the way she leaves the question hanging and neither, apparently, does Matt, because he says, 'Yes, we were friends. Why is this important?'

'It's a murder investigation. We need as much information as we can get.'

Before she can stop herself, Lavender asks, 'Are you no nearer to finding out who the arsonist is?'

Price ignores her, directing her answer instead to Matt. 'We have one or two extra pieces of information since last we spoke, but nothing concrete yet.'

Lavender's heart plummets. Does this mean the CCTV hasn't caught Morvoren?

Vincent asks, 'Can you think of why Miss Blake would be at your place, Matt? Anything at all, no matter how inconsequential, could help us.'

Matt sighs. 'I might as well tell you. Jessica and I had a one-night stand just over a week ago. I can't see what difference it makes, but I want to be open about everything, given the circumstances.

Jessica was disappointed there'd be nothing further. But I have no idea why she was there at the cottage the other night. We hadn't arranged to meet… doesn't make sense. Unless she was the one who set the fire. A colleague once told me her marriage broke down because she was so jealous of her husband's female friends. Perhaps she was angry I'd rejected her, and she wanted revenge?'

'No. We're sure she didn't, which will become apparent from the CCTV… But as you were saying, Matt, you had arranged to meet Lavender?' Price says.

Matt nods.

'Did Jessica know? Could she have been there to try to persuade you to reconsider your relationship?'

'I can't see how she'd possibly know about me and Lavender. We have only recently become romantically involved.'

Lavender sees the slight rise of Price's eyebrow and decides to say her piece. 'What I have to say might help.'

Matt shoots her a frown, but she ignores him.

'Matt and I have been friends for a while, but my witch of a grandma, Morvoren Penhallow, tried to scupper it. Matt and I fell out because of what she'd done… but now we are, as he says, romantically involved.' She and Matt share a quick smile and they squeeze each other's hands under the table.

Price nods. 'Go on, please, Lavender.'

'Okay. Jessica came to my house the night of the fire, not long before I went out to meet Matt. She told me she was Matt's girlfriend and to come clean about what I'd done to him. I told her I'd not done anything, because I haven't. As I said, it was Morvoren. I also told her I didn't believe that Matt would ask his supposed girlfriend to do his dirty work for him. Perhaps that's why she went to the cottage – so she could talk to Matt about her visit to me, before I had the chance to.'

Price's eyes light up. She looks very interested now. 'I see. You think she might have wanted to tell Matt her story before you gave him your version?'

'I think it makes sense.'

'And what were you supposed to have done to him? According to Ms Blake?' Price asks. 'You say it was your grandmother, Morvoren?'

Matt says, 'Can we see the footage first please? It will make more sense to talk about Morvoren's part afterwards.'

Price nods and turns her attention to the laptop for a few moments. Then she turns it round to face Matt and Lavender, and both she and Vincent stand and move round so they can see the screen too. The picture is very difficult to decipher because it's obviously night and there's quite a bit of smoke. Then Jessica's there, feeling her way down the side of the house. She's coughing into a scarf and wobbling along on high heels. Lavender puts her hand over her mouth as bile rises in her throat. They are watching the last few minutes of a woman's life... it's unbearably sad. Then suddenly Jessica is no longer visible.

Lavender feels Matt tense by her side. He says, 'Where the hell did she go?'

Price says, 'She must have gone round the back of the house... She's gone for a few minutes. As you can see, the fire was well under way at the back of the house when she arrived, so she couldn't have started it.' Price runs the recording on and pauses. 'Here she is coming back now. I will warn you, it's not an easy watch, so if you'd rather not, I won't force you.'

Matt and Lavender agree to watch and the recording is started again. Jessica's dragging herself along the ground and her lower half is burning. Lavender covers her face and peeps through her fingers. Her heart's thudding in her chest and she feels like she's going to faint. There's no sound, but they can see Jessica's mouth is open in a scream and she's trying to beat the flames with her hands. Then she stops and renews her effort to escape. One of her legs is lifeless and the other is thrashing in pain. Moments later, she's screaming again – or is she saying something?'

Price pauses again and says, 'We've had a lip-reader in and she says there's no doubt she's calling for you, Matt. Asking for your help.'

Matt shakes his head and Lavender sees his bottom lip tremble. Then Price presses play, so Lavender squeezes Matt's leg and looks back to the screen. Jessica's not thrashing or trying to pull herself along now. She's talking again and, through the smoke, a hooded figure appears in front of her like some ghostly spectre in a play. Lavender looks more closely and can see it's a man of stocky build – broad shoulders in a long coat with his hood pulled up tightly. He's got his back to the camera, so they can't see his face. Even if he was facing the camera, it would be hard to see his features clearly because of the hood and the smoke.

Jessica tips her head back, looks up at the man who's crouching down in front of her. She says something. She's reaching out her hand to him and smiling. Smiling? This woman must be in unimaginable pain. Lavender wants to cry out, because dear God, that smile is so loving and beatific.

Price presses pause again. 'Apparently she said, "Matt! Matt, is it you? Yes… Thank God."'

Matt looks up at Price, aghast. 'It wasn't me! You know it wasn't.'

'Calm down, Matt,' Vincent says. 'Of course we know. But do you recognise the man, either of you?'

Matt shakes his head. 'No… but then it's so hard to make him out.'

Lavender purses her lips. 'No… but there's something… He looks faintly familiar.' She can't quite put her finger on what it is.

'I'll play the last little bit. See if anyone comes to mind,' Price says.

Jessica's eyes shut and the crouching figure pulls something out of his pocket with a gloved hand. He puts it in Jessica's and closes her fingers around it. Then the smoke rolls across once more. When it clears, he's gone.

Something about the way the figure holds his head when looking at Jessica pushes a memory button in Lavender's mind. Jamie… Jamie tends to put his head on one side when he's talking. Maybe he said something to Jessica, but of course his face isn't visible on camera. She turns to Price and Vincent. 'I think it's Jamie Penhale! And he just put my bracelet in her hand.'

'Your bracelet?' Vincent asks, looking at Price in surprise. 'And who's Jamie Penhale?'

Lavender thinks it's probably time to tell her story. 'He's a man I know who's been involved in persecuting Matt.' She nods at the laptop. 'Is that the end? Nobody else appears?'

'No, that's it. And you said your bracelet?' Price says, shutting the laptop and returning to her seat. Vincent follows suit.

Lavender sighs. 'Yes. Matt told me yesterday that a bracelet was found in Jessica's hand. He had no idea whose it was, but he said it had a mermaid on it. As soon as he said that, I knew it was mine. I'd lost it … or it had come off the last time I saw Morvoren. She grabbed my wrist at one point. Since then, I've been puzzling about what to do. I couldn't really believe it… but I have been slowly coming to terms with the fact that Morvoren has killed a person and tried to kill another… with Jamie's help, I know now, obviously.'

'Morvoren's your grandma?' Vincent says.

'Yes, unfortunately.' Then she tells them all about the feud, about Terry and Elowen, about all the lies she'd been fed about Matt by Morvoren, and their version of what happened the night Matt was drugged. Matt chips in now and again, but mainly leaves it to Lavender.

'Hang on, let me get this straight.' Price looks at the notes she's been making. 'You actually thought you were giving Matt a love potion? You really believe in that stuff?'

Lavender shrugs. 'I know it sounds pretty outlandish in this day and age, but Morvoren passed lots of herbal lore knowledge on to me. I've been used to picking plants and roots since I was about four years old. Making potions. I've used successful herbal remedies for colds, arthritis, heart problems, gut problems, depression, headaches, you name it. Love potions are just a normal part of life to me.'

'And love potions work?' Vincent asks, a twinkle of amusement in his eyes.

'If they're made right.' Lavender gives him a level stare.

'You also said that Morvoren substituted the love potion with a sleeping potion instead, unbeknownst to you,' Price says.

'Yes, that's correct. I would never have gone along with something like that. I told you – Morvoren tricked me into the whole thing. I was about to call an ambulance when he passed out, but then she came in and got Jamie to help her. She said that if I told anyone what they were doing she'd–'

'Tell the police it was you and they'd got a manufactured alibi… Yes, you explained that.' Price shoves her glasses further up the bridge of her nose and rests her chin on her interlinked fingers. 'No, what I don't understand is how you didn't pass out too. You were drinking the same wine the potion was in, presumably?'

Lavender had been expecting this and was glad she and Matt had planned their version so carefully a few weeks ago. 'No. I didn't, because only the intended recipient of the love potion should drink it.'

'But Matt…' Price looks at him quizzically. 'Didn't you notice Lavender wasn't drinking the wine on the table?'

'No.' Matt spreads his hands. 'Because Lavender went to the kitchen each time and came back with two full glasses. She was drinking normal red wine, I found out later. You know, when she'd come clean to me.'

'Which took you a good long while, Lavender,' Vincent says, furrowing his brow.

'I know. I wish I'd told him earlier, but as I said, I was afraid of getting blamed for everything and Morvoren had told me so many lies about Matt by then… especially the ones…' Lavender stops and swallows hard. She needs to explain about the teacher molesting her when she was a kid, but it feels so hard to muster the courage.

Matt puts his arm round her and she wishes he hadn't, because her eyes well up. He gives her shoulder a little squeeze and says, 'Don't worry, I'll tell them.' He looks at the two police officers and takes a breath. 'Lavender wants to say especially the lies Morvoren told her about me and my old school. She said I'd touched young girls inappropriately. This was calculated to have the maximum effect on her granddaughter, because this is what happened to Lavender when she was ten. A teacher at her school did it.'

Price's mouth drops open. 'What a terrible thing for a grandmother to do.'

'Indeed,' Matt says.

Lavender wipes her tears away with the heels of her hands and Price pushes a box of tissues across the desk. 'So, I hope you'll understand why it took a while to come clean, DC Vincent,' she says, plucking a tissue out.

Vincent looks much more sympathetic now. 'I do. And I'm very sorry you had to go through such an experience as a child. I have a daughter of my own...What happened to the teacher?'

'Prison. No idea if he's out now, but he won't be teaching.'

'No. Thank goodness,' DC Vincent says.

Matt says, 'I won't be pressing charges against Lavender, obviously. Can we just leave the matter there?'

Price shrugs. 'If that's what you want.'

'And you're convinced your grandmother was involved in the fire and Jessica Blake's death, even though we only saw a man on CCTV – this Jamie Penhale, according to you?' Vincent says.

Lavender nods. 'Totally. Even if she wasn't there, which I find hard to believe, she will have orchestrated it – given Jamie my bracelet to plant. All to pin everything on me because I dared to defy her. She'll see Matt and I as the ultimate betrayal.'

'She could well have been out the back garden waiting for Jamie,' Matt says. 'As you know, access is simple through a side lane and a rickety old gate. It's easy for anyone to slip in undetected, start a fire and then get out again.'

'But how could it be a set-up? We had no clue the bracelet was yours until you told us today,' Vincent says.

Lavender has puzzled over this herself. 'Perhaps she was going to tell you lot, but then discovered I was in the pub at the time and had loads of witnesses. I imagine she thought she was burning Matt alive in the cottage too. Must have been furious when she found he wasn't there.'

Price and Vincent talk quietly to each other for a few moments and then Price says, 'Thanks, both of you. The information you've given us has been extremely valuable. We have enough now to question both Mrs Penhallow and Mr Penhale. We'll let you know when there's more news.'

***

Outside the station, Lavender takes a deep breath of air. It's not as fresh as in the countryside, but it lightens her heart. The weight of their story is shed and, thank God, it looks like she and Matt are being taken seriously. Matt drops a kiss on her lips and leads her across the road to the car park in the court nearby. 'I don't know about you, Miss Nancarrow, but I could murder a pint. It's been a hell of a day.'

'I could murder one too. And let's hope that we'll soon see the back of hellish days.' As she gets behind the wheel, she makes a wish that hope is on their side.

Chapter thirty

Matt loads the washing machine and Lavender shows him how to operate it. Yesterday, after the interview, the police gave him some clothes of his that had been retrieved from the cottage, and now he needs to wash them to get rid of the stench of smoke. Lavender's debating about whether it's worth getting the clothes line out of the shed because the weather, unseasonably warm for the first day of November, shows signs of turning. Matt joins her at the kitchen door and looks out over the rolling Cornish countryside. Not far away, a huddle of grumpy clouds are arranging themselves across the blue sky, and in the distance, more dark rain-bearers are making their approach.

'Go and look out the front, over the sea, would you, Matt? The wind normally comes from that direction and if it's clear, I'm putting the clothes on the line. I know it's past noon, but if it stays fine, it should give them a good blow before the damp returns.'

Matt walks through the kitchen into the living room, a warm feeling in his chest. It's been a long time since he enjoyed simple pleasures like just being at home with someone he cares deeply for, talking about normal domestic tasks instead of murder and mayhem. He has a sense of being grounded... settled. Just as he's about to open the front door, his phone rings on the seat of the armchair. It's DI Karen Price.

'Afternoon, Matt. Just to update you about Morvoren Penhallow and Jamie Penhale.'

Matt sighs inwardly. More murder and mayhem. 'Okay, thanks. What's happened?'

'Not an awful lot with Morvoren. We called to see her today but there was nobody in. A neighbour said she'd been taken to hospital in the early hours. The hospital told us she's got suspected pneumonia, but they're doing more tests. They couldn't say more than that at present.'

Great. Matt's not sure whether Lavender will be upset about that, given the way things are between her and Morvoren at the moment. Still, a seventy-nine-year-old woman with pneumonia… She might never come out. 'Hmm. You obviously can't question her then… not until she's better.'

''Fraid not. And Mr Penhale agreed to an interview. He was charm itself – wanted to help, but couldn't because he had an alibi. At the time of the fire, he was in the bakery with his father, Bob. They were repairing a mixing machine until late that night. They needed it fixed for the following morning's bread dough. Bob, of course, supports this claim. When asked about the night you were drugged and stripped, Bob also supports his claim that he was playing cards with Morvoren, Jamie, and Jamie's grandma at the grandma's house. Jamie was horrified by Lavender's accusations and bewildered as to why she'd make something like that up, both about that night, and saying she recognised him on the night of the fire on the recording.'

The sinking feeling which had begun in Matt's gut when Price talked about the mixing machine grew heavier with every syllable uttered, until she'd finished speaking. Damn it. The lying bastards. When are we they going to get a break in all this? They'd have to wait until Morvoren pulled through – if she did. And then she'd have some airtight alibi, no doubt. Then a thought occurs to him. 'What about Jamie's grandma, Annie? Did she corroborate his story?'

'She wasn't at home and a neighbour said she'd gone away for a bit of a break. She couldn't or wouldn't tell us where.'

'Bollocks! This is a fucking nightmare.' Matt begins to pace the room as Lavender comes through, drying her hands on a tea towel. She mouths, *What's wrong?* He mouths back *police* and shakes his head.

'Don't despair, Matt. I know it sounds bleak, but something could turn up. We'll wait for Annie to come back and Morvoren to get better. The truth has a habit of getting out.'

Price's words are positive, but Matt can detect defeat behind them. She's just trying to give him a bit of hope, but right now, he can see Morvoren and Jamie walking away scot-free. They have no evidence on them after all. 'Right. Well, I hope so. Thanks for keeping me up to date. I'll let Lavender know.'

Matt ends the call and glances at Lavender. She says, 'You'll let me know what?'

He tells her and afterwards, she slumps down onto the sofa, head in hands.

He sits next to her, puts his arm round her. 'Come on. We'll get the truth eventually. Price says it has a habit of getting out.'

'You believe that as much as I do,' she says with a sigh.

'Morvoren might slip up… You said she was no good at lying to people's faces in a serious situation.'

'Yeah. But I might rethink that one. She lied to me pretty often about serious things.'

'But lying to the police is different, isn't it?'

'Yeah, I suppose.'

Matt thinks she looks completely beaten. Her ready smile is gone and the light in her eyes is dulled with worry. 'Are you concerned about Morvoren being in hospital?'

'No. If she dies, serves her right. She's killed Jessica and tried to kill you.'

Matt has no answer to that, except he worries she'll regret it in years to come. They were so close all through Lavender's life; it's such a shame for it to all go sour now. But he can totally identify with Lavender's sentiments. 'Funny your dad didn't tell you she was in hospital, isn't it?'

Lavender furrows her brows at this. 'Yes, it is. I phoned him when I saw her last to say I wanted no more to do with her ever… told him about her awful lies too. He was sympathetic, but it's his mother in the end. He must be worried about her.'

She gets up and searches for her phone. Matt helps her, but then she finds it down the back of the sofa and out of battery. When she plugs it in the kitchen there's three missed calls and four messages all from her dad. She says, 'I'm going to call him. Can I borrow yours while this is charging? I feel like getting some air.'

She takes Matt's mobile outside and sits on the wall overlooking the sea. Matt watches her chatting through the window. Her expression is grave and he wishes everything could be different. Once she's ended the call he goes outside. 'How are things?'

'Would you believe Morvoren had a terrible coughing fit when Dad went to visit her yesterday? He said he'd heard nothing like it.' Lavender gives him a wry look. 'I wonder where she got it?'

'You think it's smoke damage? But the police said suspected pneumonia.'

'I absolutely think it's from the smoke… but she also might have something more serious too. Dad said "suspected" pneumonia can cover a multitude of conditions. It might not be pneumonia at all. One of the doctors said it might be a severe chest infection, but until they've got test results back, they won't know. She's had a few chest X-rays and scans too, apparently.'

'Who called the ambulance?'

'Morvoren called Dad at 2am, coughing like a sixty-a-dayer and he went round there. Saw the state she was in and dialled 999.'

'Do you want to go and see her?'

Lavender snorts. 'I'd rather poke my eyes out with one of those clothes pegs.' She nods to the peg bag on top of the tea towel by the kitchen door. 'Talking of which, I'm going to put the washing line out. If it rains, it rains. I'm past caring.'

***

An hour later, Lavender decides to go to the supermarket and Matt remembers he must phone his gran about the recent events. He promised he'd keep her abreast of anything that happened when he visited her in London a few weeks ago. He grabs his mobile and settles himself on the window seat, looks out over the scrap of lawn to the lane and sea beyond. The weather has turned with the wind. It's not raining yet, but the waves have whipped themselves into a frenzy and seagulls are shooting past the window as if they've been fired from a cannon. Despite everything, he adores this place. Whatever happens, he knows he will make this village his home, come hell or high water. The luck he's having lately, he'll probably see both if he's not careful. *Right, phone Gran…*

'My poor boy. I'm so sorry you've had to suffer so much,' Gran says, a tremor in her voice. She's listened to the whole story, asked a few pertinent questions, tried to hold it together, but Matt worries she's on the edge now.

He can hear a rustling sound and then her blowing her nose. 'Don't cry, Gran. It will all work out eventually. The officer in charge said the truth always comes out in the end.' She'd actually said it had a *habit* of coming out, but his gran needs comforting words.

'Not always…' Gran sniffs. 'The old witch looks to have got away with it, now she's sick in hospital. She's been bloody sick for years. In her head!'

'Calm yourself, Gran. She'll get her comeuppance. Jamie too.' He's not sure he believes it – but what else can he say?

'People like them never get their comeuppance. They have to be made to pay. And bloody Annie – where the hell is she? Mind you, she'll be no use. Always was thick as thieves with Morvoren.'

'No point in getting beside yourself. I wish I'd not told you now.'

'You should have told me the day it happened. I'd have come down there and seen Penhallow. Can't bring myself to say her first name. God, I wish I'd never said you should go back to the village. It's brought you nothing but sadness and trouble.'

'Hey, you always said I have a Cornish legacy. You and granddad inspired it, encouraged my spirit and strong will. A bit of magic from you too, though Lavender's the potion-maker. One day, it will all work out as you'd meant it. We Trevelyars don't do defeat, remember?'

Gran sighs, and when she speaks again her voice is softer, calmer. 'I remember, my boy. And this Lavender… are you and she serious, like? Can you trust her, given who she is and what she did?'

'I think it's serious… Well it is on my part. We've not discussed it in detail, because of the shit that's been happening. And can I trust her? If you'd have asked a few weeks ago I would have said no. But when she explained why she'd done it – the way her grandmother used her, manipulated her – I totally understood.'

'Hmm. That woman is pure evil. My heart goes out to your Lavender. Poor maid's had a tough time… What with the bloody teacher when she was a kid and everything that must have been done to her over the years… then her gran turning on her. But I'm glad you two have managed to salvage some happiness out of the misery.'

'Thanks. I'm sure you two would get on like a house on fi…' Matt pauses when he realises what he nearly said. 'Anyway, I'd better ring Mum now, tell her too. She'll go bananas and demand I come home, I expect.'

'It might not be a bad idea. Just for a while. It'll give you some thinking time.'

'No. I'm not running away with my tail between my legs. Morvoren would love that… and besides, this is home now. I don't belong in London.'

Gran snorts. 'Me neither! That's something else I'll never forgive the old cow for – driving us out. Your granddad always says she didn't, and he'd have taken the job anyway. I'm not so sure to be honest. Still, no use pondering on what might have been. It's what we do now that matters. Once you're settled and you're sure you'll stay in Cornwall one hundred per cent, we'll move back. Move home. I expect your parents will do the same once they've retired and we can have a good few years all together in God's own county.' She gives a little chuckle. 'Might even be lucky enough to see the descendants of the feud united in matrimony – grandkids too!'

Matt bursts out laughing. 'I think you might be a bit ahead of yourself there! Give us a chance.'

Gran chuckles again. 'I know what I'm talking about. Something in my gut's telling me I'm right, and I'm a white witch, remember? Or so some say. And a damn sight better one than Morvoren. Lavender, on the other hand – hmm, she might give me a run for my money. The force is strong in that one, young Skywalker.'

Matt laughs again. 'You never fail to cheer me up, Gran. Even at one of the worst times in my life.'

'Oh, my boy. You have had a few of those in a short time, haven't you? Poor Beth will be happy for you, though. She'd give you her blessing, I know. She was one of the best.'

Matt's throat closes over when he thinks of his wife and how she suffered. Eventually he manages, 'Thanks, Gran. She was. I miss her every day.'

'Of course you do. Things will get brighter through, they always do. This time next year it will all be behind you. I'll let you go, but remember, any time, day–'

'Or night, you're there for me.'

'That's right. Always have been, always will be.'

Matt's goodbye is almost drowned out by the sound of rain drumming on the roof. Marvellous. He runs out the back and grapples with the clothes on the line. By the time he's back in the kitchen, he's soaked through and mud-splashed. More washing. Things can only get better. Can't they?

Chapter thirty-one

Lavender is hanging up Matt's ironed shirts in a space she's cleared at one side of her wardrobe. He was surprised when she ironed them, saying he could do it himself. But she wanted to. She's never really looked after someone else before, and she likes it. In the short time he's been staying, a natural division of labour has happened. It's not based on gender, just on the domestic tasks they each prefer. Lavender's always liked ironing – it feels therapeutic. Perhaps it's because she can see immediate progress: a crumpled bit of material turns into a crisp, smart shirt or dress. Matt prefers cooking and he's much better at it than she is. They have a bit of a tussle over vacuuming because neither is a fan, but slowly a routine is forming that's agreeable to both.

Shaking the duvet and plumping the pillows, she wishes life could be ironed out as easily as a shirt or dress. There's been no news from hospital yet and Annie is still AWOL. Dad said he'd phone as soon as he knew more about Morvoren, but it's been two days now. If he doesn't ring later today, she'll ring him. Matt's sorting out another car in Truro. The car insurance covered the fire, but there's always more red tape than anyone imagines in these situations. He'll be back for lunch in a hire car, and soon he'll look into getting a new car.

Matt also brought up the topic of looking for a place to live too. But Lavender changed the subject. She's been plucking up the courage to say he can stay with her as long as he needs to, but she hasn't managed it yet. What if he needs his own space? More importantly, what if he has no intention of living with her? It might put a real dampener on the relationship if moving in together is not part of his plan. Lavender picks up an empty water glass from the side table and goes down the stairs. Maybe she's rushing ahead too quickly. Living together might be part of his long-term plans, but not right now. She can understand that, because she wonders if she's jumping in too fast herself. Following her head instead of her heart might be an idea for a while.

As she's pondering, the doorbell rings and she runs to the door, water glass still in hand. Her dad's standing there, grim-faced, jaw set. 'Dad? You okay?'

Dad's shoulders start to shake and she bundles him inside, sits him on a kitchen chair, puts the kettle on. Is Morvoren dead? Lavender's not sure how she would feel about that if it were true. She looks at him as he's blowing his nose and waits.

'It's your gran… They reckon she's got lung cancer and heart problems.'

Not dead then. 'Right. What's the prognosis?'

Dad glares at her. His eyes, so similar to her own, flash deep violet and he shakes his head in bewilderment. 'Is that all you have to say? God, Lavender, you're so cold. After all those years you were so close – she worshipped you.'

She throws her arms up in exasperation. 'What do you expect? I've told you what she's done to me. To Matt!'

He folds his arms. 'What she's *supposed* to have done. You've no proof!' he yells over the roar of the kettle.

Lavender can't believe it. The kettle clicks off and she pours boiling water on a teabag, bangs the mug down on the kitchen table in front of him. 'Are you saying you think I'm a liar about the fire, the drugging of Matt? That I've made the whole thing up?'

'No…' He can't hold her gaze, takes a spoon and dunks the teabag. 'Just thought you might be mistaken.'

'Mistaken? I told you exactly what happened with Matt, not the version I gave to the police. I was there, took part – how can I be mistaken about it?'

'Exactly. So you can't just let Mum take all the blame. And the fire – you have no evidence whatsoever, do you? Got any milk?'

Lavender wants to pour the milk over his head. 'Yes, I *can* let her take all the fucking blame! Weren't you listening to the part where I told you she lied to me? Used me like some blunt instrument?'

'Don't curse at me, young lady!'

'You're lucky I don't slap you. Have you any idea at all what I went through growing up after that creature laid hands on me?' She's close to tears and hates that she is.

'No, Lavender. Because you didn't tell anyone, did you?'

'I couldn't. I was ashamed – thought I'd done something wrong. And Morvoren knew it. I told her, opened up to her… yet she used something that hurt me so badly to get me to wreak her filthy, disgusting revenge. Don't you see, Dad? She's obsessed. It's not about the feud, it's about Morvoren and her pride.' Lavender takes a breath, looks him in the eye. 'Everything is all about her… always was.'

He says nothing and stares at the table. Lavender takes more calming breaths and takes the milk from the fridge, shoves it along the table, but he doesn't move.

Then he says in a quiet voice, 'I'll grant you, Mum can be stubborn… vindictive even. I'm so sorry that she hurt you and played with your feelings, love. But as far as the fire's concerned, no.' He looks up. 'No. My mother would never go as far as that, no matter what the circumstances.'

'I wish I had your conviction.'

'Believe it. You've no proof, as I said. How do you know it wasn't Jamie all by himself? Takes a bit of swallowing, because he's a nice lad… but if you say you recognised him on that recording… or thought you did…' Dad ends on a shrug.

A shrug which speaks volumes. *He doesn't believe you, Lavender.* No point in trying to convince him, especially since he's had such bad news today. 'Let's not talk about it now, Dad. What did the hospital say the future was for Morvoren?'

Dad looks down into his mug. 'Can't even call her Gran, can you?' He sighs and continues, 'They said with chemo and or radiotherapy, she might have a few years. Without, she might have six months or a year. She's on intravenous antibiotics to clear a chest infection.' He shakes his head. 'Terrible cough she has. She's got angina too. Got meds of course… but when she's fit, she can come home.'

'Then she'll go back later for the other treatment?'

Dad's face crumples and he blows his nose again. 'She says she's not having it. Says she's got her own remedies, won't have their "poison" anywhere near her.'

Lavender isn't surprised. Morvoren has always despised and feared 'artificial' medicines, to an extent. And knowing her, she'll probably defy all odds, administer her own potions and get well. 'I see. Well, at her age I think I'd take my chances too. Chemo can make you really unwell.'

Dad furrows his brow. 'I did hope you could go and see her. Convince her to at least try the treatment. Your potions and stuff can work for minor ailments, but this is cancer.'

'You might be surprised at what our potions and "stuff" can do, Dad. And there's no way I'm going anywhere near her. Not after what she's done to me, to Matt and to poor Jessica.'

Exasperated, Dad exhales through his nose, scrapes his chair back across the stone flags, stomps to the door. Before he goes through it, he turns to Lavender. 'When did you get to be so cruel, so heartless?'

His words are a punch to the gut. Hasn't he listened to anything she's told him? Does he seriously believe she's mistaken? 'If I am cruel and heartless, I learned it from Morvoren Penhallow. And until you see that, I don't think we have anything more to say to each other.'

'Goodbye, Lavender. I agree. And don't bother trying to get around your mum, because she'll be appalled at your attitude when I tell her,' Dad snaps. Then he wrenches the door open and slams it behind him.

Lavender rests her head against it and closes her eyes. She's now effectively cut off from her family, such as it is. Her mum won't like it, but she'll do what Dad says. Her grandmother's evil knows no bounds. One thing's for sure, if Morvoren's going to die, Lavender wishes she'd bloody hurry up about it.

Chapter thirty-two

Thank God she's alone. Two weeks of poking, prodding, being woken in the middle of the night to have her blood pressure taken, or to be given drugs, is finally over. At last she's home in her lovely little cottage near the sea. Morvoren hated being away from it. Waking in the morning to the smell of disinfectant, other people's bodies, and overcooked food, instead of wet grass and salt air, had nearly driven her mad. But right now, she's waving her son Tony and daughter-in-law Katherine off from her door and she can't wish them away quick enough. Considering they didn't really have an awful lot to do with her day-to-day, when the chips were down, they rallied round. But then that's what families do, isn't it? Proper families.

In the kitchen, she puts the kettle on and drops a teabag in a mug. Simple everyday actions, but symbolic of her independence, her ability to function by herself. Morvoren's grateful for everything Tony and Katherine have done for her – shopping, cleaning, getting the house ready for her return – but now Morvoren just wants a bit of peace and quiet. Still, she'll have to put up with a nurse popping over now and then to check on her. Anything for a quiet life and to get away from that hellhole of a hospital.

Young Jamie needs to come over soon too. He needs to get picking. The sooner Morvoren gets some proper herbal medicine inside her, the better she'll feel. It might even see off this greedy tumour growing in her lung. Not long ago she thought she'd never see another spring – but this bastard of an illness has made her want to fight. Morvoren's never backed down from one, and she's not about to start now. Fighting gives her something to live for.

She takes the tea into the living room and eases herself into her old comfy armchair and smiles. That's better. Her backside must think it's Christmas – there were no proper cushions at the hospital. Then the smile turns into a grimace when she thinks of having to ask Jamie to help. Lavender should be the one doing the picking, shouldn't she? Morvoren wouldn't even have to tell her what to pick – she'd know instinctively. But she won't be doing it, will she? No. No, because she's dead to her now.

She takes a few sips of tea and ponders on the future. No Lavender, no Annie… John Parry has been avoiding her in the street since bloody Lavender collared him. The only people she can call on are Tony, Katherine and Jamie. A thought flits into her head and sends a chill down her arms. What if Jamie won't have anything to do with her either? Maybe he's had enough. He was furious enough to help her with the fire, mind, wasn't he? If he was prepared to burn a man to death, she doubts he'll just throw his hands up and want to forget about it. Deciding that there's no time like the present, she hauls herself up and dials his number.

An hour later there he is on the doorstep. He's a bunch of flowers in his hand and a box of chocolates under his arm. 'Mor, you old sweetheart, how the devil are you?' He steps forward and plants a kiss on her cheek.

'Oi, less of the old! I've been better, but getting there… and are those for me?' She takes the gifts and ushers him through. 'You're a good lad, Jamie. I just wish our Lavender realised what she was throwing away before she took up with Trevelyar.'

'Me too. But she's welcome to him. Can't hang around waiting for her forever. Don't suppose you know he's living at her cottage, do you, what with being in hospital and that?'

'Living together?' Morvoren stops filling a vase with water and looks at Jamie, open-mouthed.

'Yep. Moved in the night of the fire and he's been there ever since.'

'Bleedin' hell! She didn't let the grass grow, did she?' Turning her attention to arranging the flowers, Morvoren tries to gather herself and stop unwanted tears falling. This is a blow. She suspected Lavender and Trevelyar were sweethearts, but actually living together...

'You all right, Mor?' Jamie puts his hand on her shoulder.

She takes a deep breath and says brightly, 'I will be, lad.' Now, fill me in on what's been happening.'

While Morvoren makes tea and gets biscuits out of the cupboard, Jamie pulls a newspaper out of his back pocket and shakes it open on the table. 'The local paper did a two-page spread on the fire. Thought you might like a look. It made the national news too.'

Morvoren hands Jamie a mug and sits opposite him. There's a picture of the burnt-out cottage and car and the headline reads:

Arson Attack Turns Into Murder Inquiry

Morvoren scans the story, saying to Jamie as she reads, 'Oh... it goes on to say how the fire was set, that Jessica died and a bit about her age and family, then it says although people have been helping with police inquiries, the police have no leads at present. However, the inquiry is ongoing, and anyone with any information, no matter how small, should contact a DI Price – and then it gives the phone number.'

'Yeah, I read it a few weeks back, Mor.' Jamie smiles and tucks into a biscuit.

'Hmm? Oh yes, of course you did.' He must think she's dotty. The phone number catches her attention and prompts her to say, 'I wonder who they had helping with police inquiries? Do you know?'

Jamie's handsome face loses the smile. 'Yeah. Trevelyar and Lavender for two, Betty for another, and they dragged me in for an interview as well.'

Morvoren nearly chokes on her tea. 'You? But how did they know?'

'CCTV caught me putting that bloody bracelet into Jessica's hand. Couldn't prove anything mind, as my back was to the camera and I had my gloves on and my hood covering my face.'

Morvoren wonders if she's missing something. 'Well, if they couldn't make you out, how come they interviewed you?'

'Lavender told them she thought it was me, from my mannerisms or some crap. She told them she thought you were up to your eyes in it too, cos of the bracelet. She lost it at your house apparently.' He dunks a biscuit and stuffs all of it in his mouth at once, talks through it. 'She also told them about the night we stripped Trevelyar, put him in his car. Said you organised everything and I helped.'

'What? The little bitch!'

'Yep.'

'But how could she do that without implicating herself in it all?'

'She said you'd tricked her into it. She also told them we both said if she went to the police about it, we'd say it was all her fault.'

Morvoren put a hand to her mouth. 'What did you say?'

'I said you and me were playing cards with my gran and my dad. I said I knew nothing about no bracelet, said I was helping Dad fix a bread mixer in the

shop on the night of the fire. Dad backed it all up, so they had to drop it.' Jamie yawns and stretches. 'Oh, and Gran's gone on holiday, so they can't ask her. Mum's a bit worried, to be honest. Gran's phoned me a few times to say she's okay, but she apparently needs some time alone.' He pauses and stares off into the distance, starts to bite his nails. 'One of your neighbours told my dad that the police came around to question you too, but you were in hospital. They'll be back as soon as they know you're home, I expect.'

'And I have no alibi for the night of the fire, do I? Damn her!'

'No. But just say you were feeling ill and were in bed. That rings true cos of you being rushed to hospital. They have nothing on you, Mor, don't worry.'

She knows he's right. Nevertheless, her own flesh and blood has tried to turn her in to the police… in a bloody murder inquiry, when Lavender can't be a hundred per cent sure about her guilt, even taking the bracelet into account. The fact that Morvoren is in it up to her eyes is neither here nor there. The anger she'd felt towards Lavender before is nothing compared to the all-consuming hatred building in her chest now. Little mare thinks she's so clever. Well she'll have to think again. This betrayal has gone too far.

***

Upon coming over a field, picking basket in hand, Lavender spots Jamie's car outside Morvoren's house. She's still a way off and might not get a clear shot, but she instinctively reaches for her phone. She'll take a photo, and then ring Matt to discuss what to do next. The police might be interested in looking at it. Why is Jamie snooping round there when Morvoren is in hospital? Is he trying to plant some evidence? She wouldn't put it past him. About to dial Matt, she thinks better of it and decides to investigate further. By the time Matt gets here, she might have missed an opportunity.

A few minutes later, she's opposite the house behind a hedge. Setting her basket down, she peers around the end of the hedge, which adjoins a five-bar gate. Jamie's car's still there, so she takes another photo. Crouching low, and to the rapid thump of her heart, she hurries across the lane and flattens her back against the damp wall of the house. Looking this way and that, she sidles to the end and peeps round the back. Nothing. The little garden is silent, and the back door closed. She makes a similar examination of the other side of the house. Nothing. Where the heck is Jamie?

With her back still to the wall, she slips round so she's just under the kitchen window. The window's open a bit as it always is, come rain or shine. Odd. Dad must have forgotten to close it. Maybe Jamie's inside? He can hardly be anywhere else, can he? Lavender strains her ears for any movement or noise. Voices? Muted… but yes, she can hear a man talking. Now what? The last thing she wants to do is burst in on Jamie and a friend while they're up to no good. Because he must be up to no good, mustn't he? God knows what they'd do to her. If Jamie can watch a woman die in cold blood, he can do anything. Especially to someone who he sees as a betrayer.

Lavender is about to make her escape, but something won't let her. A little voice of courage drags her round to the back door and has her lifting the latch, silent as a thief in the night. She's come through this door thousands of times in the past and knows every creak of the floorboards. *Take your time, Lavender. Take it slow.* In the hallway she closes the door behind her and tiptoes forward. She can hear Jamie talking to someone in the kitchen a few steps away… The kitchen door is ajar, but she daren't creep up to that – too dangerous. Instead, she slips into the broom/coat cupboard next to it and hides amongst the coats, leaves the door open a crack, presses her ear to it.

'But how many of each do I pick? I've no bloody idea what I'm doing,' Jamie says with a laugh.

'Pick as many as you can get. There won't be lots around at this time of year, but if you find a good crop by some miracle, I can always freeze them.'

Inside the cupboard, Lavender covers her mouth. It's Morvoren! When did she get back?

Jamie's talking again. 'This book's pretty old and the drawings are faded. What if I get the wrong ones?'

'Don't you worry about it, lad. Do your best. I only wish I didn't have to ask you. If my bitch of a granddaughter had stayed loyal, I wouldn't have to.'

I'm the bitch? That's hilarious. Lavender takes a deep breath to calm her anger and an idea comes to her. Taking her phone from her pocket, she searches for record and presses play. It's not something she's done before, and she hopes she's done it right, because this might be just what the police need if Morvoren and Jamie start talking about the night of the fire. Holding the phone to the crack in the door, she listens again.

'You never know, Mor. Your Lavender might come to her senses and realise what she's done.'

A snort. 'And pigs might bloody fly. No. She's dead to me.'

'Talking of which,' Jamie gives a little laugh. 'Will it cure the cancer?'

'Get straight to the point, why don't you?' Morvoren laughs too. 'It might. It might not. But one thing is certain, nature's potion will make me feel better than all these chemicals they sent me home with.'

'I think it will take a lot to kill you off, Mor.'

'It will. And I'll need all my strength to get my revenge on Trevelyar. He probably thinks it's over. But if I'm checking out soon, he's coming with me. Lavender too, if she gets in the way.'

Lavender presses her hand over her mouth again to stop a gasp escaping. *Oh my God…. oh my God.* She hopes the phone's picking this up!

'Hmm. I'll draw the line at her. But if you need help like last time, just give me a call. Right, I'll get off and pick the plants or herbs or whatever the hell they are. Won't be long, hopefully.'

Lavender hears the kitchen door being pulled back over the stone flags and footsteps along the hall. She shrinks back from the crack in the door, huddles into the coats and crouches low.

'If you get stuck just give me a ring,' Morvoren says. Lavender can see her feet in pink fluffy carpet slippers and Jamie's boots. 'If you can't find any of them up in Lantwen's fields, try down by the river on the Old Oak side.'

'Right you are, Mor. See you later.'

There's a draft as he opens the door and a soft click as Morvoren shuts it behind him and goes back into the kitchen. Then there's a clattering of dishes and the sound of water running in the sink. Lavender can't decide whether to leave it a while longer before making her escape, or to go now. If she goes now, she might run the risk of bumping into Jamie if he's forgotten to ask something. If she waits, Morvoren might come to the cupboard. Unable to stand the thump of her racing heart in her ears and sweaty palms any longer, she eases the door open, slips into the hall and out the front door. Then she's in the lane, grabbing her basket from behind the hedge, and off like a hare across the fields.

Chapter thirty-three

Matt's on the computer looking at cars for sale when Lavender bursts in, golden hair tangled by the salt wind, face pink, eyes as wild as her hair and panting like she's run a marathon.

He gets up from the laptop and puts his arm around her. She's trembling but rummaging in her bag for something. 'Hey, what's up, Lavender?'

'I need my phone. Where the hell is it?' Tissues, a comb and a purse all end up on the floor, then she holds her phone up in triumph. 'Wait until you hear this!' She looks at him, eyes alight. He watches her fiddle with the mobile for a few seconds and then she curses. 'Shit! It hasn't recorded! It was on pause.'

'What were you trying to record?'

'Bloody Morvoren and Jamie.' She tells him the tale about overhearing Morvoren practically spelling out that she plans to kill him, and her too if she got in the way.

Matt's shocked at this but also concerned about how she knows. 'Hang on. You're telling me that you saw Jamie's car outside your grandmother's, so sneaked inside? Hid in a cupboard, even though you know what they're both capable of?' He's aware he's yelling, but my God, has she gone mad?

'Yes, but if this damned thing had recorded, it would all have been worth it!'

'No. You could have been hurt.' He steps forward, draws her into his arms. 'Please promise me you'll not do anything like that again.'

Her look is neither helpful nor friendly and she chucks the phone at the sofa cushions. 'I'm going to make some scones. I always think better when I'm baking,' she says over her shoulder as she goes to the kitchen.

Matt follows her and leans his weight against the doorjamb, folds his arms. 'You didn't promise me.'

Lavender pulls a flour cannister out of the cupboard and sighs. 'Okay, I promise I won't put myself in harm's way.' She runs the tap and washes her hands. 'But I won't promise that I won't try and record Morvoren's confession.'

He hands her a towel. 'Eh? How you gonna get her to confess? And how are you gonna get in the same room as her – she hates your guts, as you've just found out.'

Lavender sets a big mixing bowl on the table and tips flour onto a weighing scale. 'Well… when I was running back here, I had an idea. It might work, it might not. But I reckon if I pick her some herbs, make her some scones or cake and go round there in a few days, say I've made a mistake about you – that you're a bully or something… not decided what I'll say yet.' She weighs sugar and gets eggs and butter out of the fridge. 'And that I've seen the error of my ways and play to her ego, I reckon I could get her to talk. She likes to brag, and she'd be keen to tell me about the fire.'

Matt thinks this is a long shot. He can see Lavender is excited by her plan and has to think before he speaks. 'It might work… but won't she suspect you might be up to something?'

'No, because she doesn't do technology. She'll have no clue that phones record stuff.'

'Really?'

She shoots him a look and tosses her hair out of her eyes with a floured hand. 'Yes. Really.'

Matt sits at the end of the table, watches her work, her long nimble fingers rubbing butter into the flour. 'But doesn't she watch any crime dramas or–'

'No. She doesn't have a TV, says it addles her brain.'

'Okay, it could work… if she lets you in the house in the first place.'

'Yeah. I think she will. She'll be too curious not to.' Lavender beats eggs and tips them into the flour, sugar and butter. 'But as I say, I'll do it in a few days. Give her a chance to feel a bit better. Besides, I need to open the shop again before everyone thinks I've shut down for good. Not much passing trade this time of year, but there are one or two people. I need to feel normal. All this drama is "addling my brain" as Morvoren would say.'

Matt watches her work the mixture into dough on the floured table. 'Trouble is, in your conversation, she might talk about the drugging —that you were in the know all the time. Then you'd be in trouble when you give the recording to the police.'

'Hmm. I've thought the same. It is a risk, but if I'm lucky I can direct her to the night of the fire and just record that bit? Anyway, it's worth a shot.'

'Hope it's not a long one.' Matt receives an eye roll and a huff. He knows he's being negative, but he's still worried about her safety. 'Can I at least be nearby, in the field or something… in case Jamie comes round unexpectedly?'

A frown furrows her brow. 'No need, really. If she lets me in and he does come round while we're chatting, why should he turn nasty?'

'Hmm. Okay.' Matt feels a bit out of it. He wants to be there for her. 'I'll be in the car two lanes away. And I can teach you how to operate the bloody record function too – or it will all be for nothing.' He grins at her and receives a grumpy pout in return. But as she walks past to wash dough from her hands, she flicks some at his nose.

'Teach me how to operate the record function?' she says in a plummy voice. 'That'll teach you, Mr Teacher!'

He grabs her, spins her round, rubs his doughy nose on her cheek. Lavender shrieks with laughter and pretends to strangle him. Fun. This is what they've been missing over the past few weeks. Once the whole situation with Morvoren is sorted, he hopes they can settle down to just living their life, instead of lurching from one disaster to the other.

***

Lavender's stomach's pitching and tossing like a ship at sea. What seemed like a great idea a few days ago feels ill-thought-out and stupid now. At the end of Morvoren's lane, she stops and shifts the carrier bag with the cake tin into the other hand and shelters her picking basket from a fresh gust of sea air. The last thing she wants is the result of hours of foraging being blown across the countryside. It took her long enough to find everything at this time of year in the first place. Swallowing hard, she sets off at a fast pace before she can talk herself out of it. Once outside the front door, she sets the carrier at her feet and knocks. She notices the dark-green paintwork is fading and flaking in places. The whole house feels past its best, old, moribund... like Morvoren. She might be gone soon. Why did it all have to end up like this?

After the door is wrenched open, any sense of maudlin and regret in Lavender's heart are strangled at birth by the glare of unadulterated hatred in Morvoren's eyes. Morvoren's cursory look up and down lingers on the picking basket and carrier. 'What the *hell* do you want?'

'I've come to see how you are... brought you some pickings.' Lavender's glad her voice sounds regretful, sad, just as she intended.

Morvoren knits her bushy eyebrows together so deeply, her eyes are almost overshadowed by them. 'Don't make me laugh. You couldn't care less. You proved it when you betrayed me with that disgusting excuse for a man!'

Lavender lowers her eyes, sniffs. 'I know, and I'm so sorry. I made a terrible mistake. The worst.' She allows her eyes to drift upward, fix briefly on Morvoren's face and then away again. The expression of shock in the old woman's gaze, tinged with relief, is encouraging.

'What?' Morvoren rubs her arms as if she's chilly. 'You expect me to swallow that nonsense?'

Lavender does, and is convinced she's going to, given her manner. 'No. But I wish you'd let me explain, so we can at least try to mend our fences.'

A snort. 'You'll need some bloody big nails and a hammer to do that. In fact, no. No, you'll need a miracle.'

Lavender looks up and into Morvoren's suspicious gaze. This next sentence will make or break the deal. The words will stick in her throat… 'Please, Gran. I know what I have done is unforgivable, but I can't bear to think you're ill… that you might even, you know… without…' She covers her face with both hands and tries her hardest to muster tears. The well is dry until she pictures a life without Matt, Matt meeting an untimely death at the hands of Morvoren, and then her eyes fill.

It takes all her resolve not to flinch when she feels a cold papery hand pat her forearm. 'Come on. Come in and I'll hear you out.' Morvoren leads the way inside and over her shoulder says, 'It'd better be good though. There's something that don't feel right about this… not right at all.'

In the kitchen, Lavender sets the basket and carrier on the table and pulls a chair out. 'Is it okay if I sit down?'

Morvoren shrugs. 'Do what you like. I'll be sitting over here in my armchair by the fire. Can't do with uncomfortable chairs – had enough of those in the hospital.'

'I wanted to visit you, Gran, but I thought you might not want me there.'

'Huh! I know that's a lie because your dad says different. He's devastated by your attitude to your own flesh and blood. I mean, how could you have told the police I was to blame for the fire at his house because of your bracelet? I never had your bloody bracelet!'

Oh yes you bloody well did! If Lavender needs further convincing, which she doesn't, Morvoren's face is guilt personified. But she ignores it, says what she'd planned on saying. 'I know. I was still so angry then, but Matt has since shown his true colours and I really missed you over the past few days. Missed how we used to be… and I am so sorry for rejecting you.' Morvoren shakes her head, gives a wry smile. Maybe she's over-egging. It needs to be more realistic. 'But let's be fair. You did tell me a shitload of lies about him, so you're not blameless.'

The old woman glares at her, sticks her scrawny neck out, slaps her thigh. 'Ha! Didn't take you long to get rid of the sorry act, did it?' Then she gives a chesty cough and it turns into a coughing fit.

Lavender runs water into a glass and takes it over. Morvoren drinks half of it and heaves a sigh. Lavender says, 'I've brought some pickings – took me ages to find them. I'll make you a potion before I go. And I am sorry, it isn't an act. But if we're to mend fences, we have to be honest with each other.' She goes back and sits at the table. 'You told me some awful lies about Trevelyar so I'd help you do your dirty work. I mean, how could you tell me he was a kiddie fiddler? How could you – what with my history? Then the last time I was round here, you said you didn't care that you'd told me all those lies. Takes a bit of coming to terms with, to be honest.'

A shrug. 'Means to an end.' Then she gives her granddaughter side-eyes. 'I'll grant you, it was perhaps a bit mean.'

Great. *You're getting somewhere, Lavender, keep it up.* 'Hmm. Anyway, what really brought me up with a start, made me sorry I'd ever gone against you and trusted that man, was him admitting the other night he'd been having it away with bloody Jessica Blake.'

At this, Morvoren sits up in her seat, eyes round, mouth agape. 'I sodding knew it! That's what she was doing at his cottage that night.'

'Perhaps. But I reckon it was because she knew about me and was jealous. Trevelyar told me she'd found out he cheated on her with me. So she set the fire. It wasn't you at all. I must have dropped my bracelet at Matt's. She found it and was going to plant it nearby to implicate me. On the road leading to the cottage perhaps? Then she tripped or something... I don't know. The man I thought was Jamie must have picked it up, thinking it was hers, and gave it back to her. God *knows* what he was doing there. It's just a mystery, that bit – expect it always will be. But I'll tell you something. I wish Jessica would have succeeded in burning the cottage down with Matt in it, because he's a monster, Gran. A monster. He's a bully. He forced me into...'

'Forced you into what?' Morvoren says, her voice trembling.

'It's too humiliating to say. Unnatural things in the bedroom, if you get my meaning. Makes me feel sick to think of it.' Lavender pretends to cry again and reaches into her bag for a tissue, balances the phone on top of the packet and sets it to record.

'I knew he had a black heart!' Morvoren shrieks, and points her finger at Lavender dramatically. If the situation wasn't so serious, she'd laugh. 'And it was me that set the fire. I'd set it again in a flash if my body would let me.'

Yes! This information is beyond Lavender's wildest dreams. 'You did it, Gran? You set the cottage on fire?'

'I did,' she replies with a sickly grin. 'Jamie helped because this bag of bones my spirit is forced to live inside wasn't strong enough to lift and pour the petrol. But the filthy bastard Trevelyar wasn't even in, was he? No, he was off meeting you!' She wipes spittle from her lips. 'I was sad about Jessica Blake getting killed. Mind you, sounds like she was a deceiver too.'

'Bloody hell. I didn't think you had it in you, not really.' Lavender shakes her head and puts on a bewildered expression.

Morvoren preens. 'When I set out for retribution, I'll do whatever it takes. He wouldn't take the hint after the drugging and stripping. No, he came back for more. Well, he'll get more. I'll try again, and this time I'll succeed. Matthew Trevelyar will not make old bones. He's a stain on this village and needs scrubbing out. I pray I'll be given enough strength and time to do it.' She sighs and closes her eyes, leans her head back. 'Feeling pretty rough now though.'

Plucking out another tissue, Lavender switches off the recording. She's got everything she needs and as far as she can recall, nothing that was said implicated her. 'I'm with you there. Especially after what he's just done to me. And I'm not surprised you're feeling unwell with all that jollop they must have given you to take in hospital. I'll make you a nice potion with the pickings instead and then we can have tea and cake. I brought your favourite.'

Morvoren opens her eyes. 'If you don't mind, I'll leave the cake and tea. Might have a nap. But I'll have some later, thank you... And leave the pickings, I'll make my own potion. I know exactly what I need for this evil growing inside me.'

Lavender suspects she doesn't trust her. Not surprising really, given their relationship over the past month. No skin off Lavender's nose anyway. The sooner she's out of there, the better.

Chapter thirty-four

Well, well, well. What a turn up for the books. Lavender Nancarrow coming round here with apologies, cake and pickings. It's almost too good to be true. Morvoren yawns and gets out of the chair. She hopes it's the truth, but reserves her trust. She didn't get to be nearly eighty by just trusting people at face value, even if they were family. If her granddaughter's telling the truth about Trevelyar, which she suspects she is, he'll be dead before Morvoren is. Nobody does despicable things to one of her own and lives to tell the tale. There will be a way to end him, and soon. Morvoren just needs to think of the best method.

Lifting the lid from the tin, she looks at the three-layered chocolate cake. She pokes the chocolate icing with her finger and sniffs the blob on the end of it. Smells okay, but until she cuts it and examines it properly, she won't be eating any. Lavender could have put lethal pickings in it for all she knows. Talking of which… She looks over to the sink where Lavender has placed the mixture of herbs and plants in a vase. Running her fingers along the various stems, squeezing bulbs and stroking petals, Morvoren smiles. The dear girl must have been as far as St Ives for some of this stuff. All very useful. That hopeless lump Jamie brought back half this amount the other day, and most of it was a waste of space. She shouldn't be too hard on him, of course. He has no clue about the ways of nature.

Through the kitchen window, in the fading daylight, she watches a mountain of clouds gathering pace over the valley. The wind's got up and it's hurrying them along the sky as if they're late for a storm. Looks like rain won't be far behind. How she loves this place. Morvoren has a sudden desire to be out walking in the wind and damp fresh grass; to look over the wild ocean from the cliff edge and let her hair loose. A sigh of regret. Not yet a while though. Her strength needs building before she attempts to leave the house on her own. Thoughts of Trevelyar filter in then, and her hands grab the edge of the sink until her knuckles turn white. He might not have done any of those things she told Lavender about before, but it turns out he's just as evil as she expected. Trevelyar men are evil through and through. Always have been, always will be.

No point in getting beside herself. He'll get what he deserves by and by. Right. Now for the cake. She turns from the view and goes back to the table. Carefully, she slips her hand in the tin and lifts the cake out and onto a plate. A messy affair because of the icing and the layers. About to lick her fingers clean, she remembers her concerns about Lavender's intentions. Would she really poison her grandmother? Morvoren thinks not, but she can't afford to drop her guard. She cuts a slice and chops it into smaller pieces. Hmm, smells okay. There's a sense of disquiet in the pit of her belly, however. Something's telling her not to eat it. While the cake might be perfectly fine, she can't risk it… can she? A moment later, her gut wins and she tips the lot into the bin. Better to be safe than sorry.

Yawning again, she decides to make a cup of tea before having a nap or making the potion. No point in tiring herself out. Jamie said he was coming over about seven o'clock with some more pickings, such as he finds, and a glance at the clock tells her it's only five. She's a few hours yet. Looking forward to her nap, she runs water into the kettle and flicks it on while she tidies the kitchen a bit. As she's stirring her tea, the back door slams so hard she drops the teaspoon with a clatter. Bloody hell, that gave her quite a start. Lavender must have left it ajar, silly girl. Best go and make sure it's shut now.

In the corridor, Morvoren can see it's not shut, because the wind is opening and closing it for fun as if it's a naughty child.

The latch has got stuck up in the air somehow – it's a bit rusty. She'll have to get it sorted, maybe even get a new one in the spring; if she's still here, of course. About to close and lock the door, she hears an almighty crash come from the direction of the shed. Buggeration. What now? Grabbing a shawl from the peg and a stout walking stick, she goes out to investigate. The wind immediately grabs her long steely hair and wraps it around her eyes. She stops to wrest it free, twists it into a ponytail and stuffs it down under her shawl. Right, off she goes again. If it's a badger after her stored veg like it was last year, she'll give it a whack with this bloody stick. Varmints.

Back in the house, she takes off her shawl again and hangs it on the peg, noticing her flushed face in the hall mirror. Her breathing's laboured too – such a little trip has taken it out of her. And a trip for no reason either. No badger, fox or anything, just an old plant pot inexplicably smashed in two next to the shed. It was as if someone had chucked it down on the patio slabs. But why? No. It must have been the wind blowing it over from somewhere, that's all. Okay, now for that tea.

The smell coming from the bin as she chucks the tea bag inside makes her mouth water. Perhaps she was a bit too hasty dumping the cake. Lavender is a good girl at heart. Always has been. The necromancer Trevelyar just cast his spell for a while, but now her granddaughter's free of it. It takes more than a mortal man, demon-ridden or no, to quell the spirit of a Penhallow woman. A Penhallow woman who's won her spurs in the art of herbal lore. Learned at the knee of her grandmother. Morvoren's heart swells with pride at the thought. Her stomach grumbles at the scent of the cake too. Oh well. Nothing to be done about it now. She'll have the tea and then a nap. Cheese on toast after that, and then Jamie will be here.

Through the window, the rain clouds have melted into the night sky. They're evidenced by a patter of drops on the window though. Morvoren closes the curtains, puts the lamps on and stokes the fire. Everything looks so cosy and welcoming. God, she's glad to be home instead of in the hospital. At last, seated in the chair by the fire, she lifts the mug. With all this faffing about, it'll be lukewarm now, but she can't be bothered to make another. Morvoren takes a long drink and then bangs it down on the side table. What the hell! It's bitter as acid. She sniffs the tea. A faint tendril of a memory – of a picking – comes, but she can't grasp it. Then the cough starts.

Morvoren stumbles to the sink, gagging and coughing. Her airways feel as if they're closing over. She needs water, but her hands are trembling. She sees a glass of juice on the side she can't remember pouring, but grabs it, takes a big gulp… only this is worse than the tea! The liquid burns an agonising path through her gullet and she falls to the floor, clutching her throat. The name of the picking smashes into her consciousness like a wrecking ball. Wolfsbane! She's been poisoned with wolfsbane… Lavender. It had to be her! Oh God, how could she have been so stupid? The crash from the shed had been to tempt her out…

Oh God, Lavender, you sneaked back in and poisoned my tea and the juice. No wonder Morvoren couldn't remember pouring it.

Morvoren's losing feeling in her face, and her limbs are heavy. She's coughing but can't suck in enough air. Her heartbeat feels laboured… erratic… There's a pain in her chest. She doesn't want to die, not yet, not like this. She has so much more to do. Trevelyar needs to come with her…

She must have been on the floor for a long time because the microwave clock is showing a digital green 6.32pm. Jamie will be here soon. He'll save her…

In the next few moments, she thinks she must be hallucinating, because there's Terry again, a young man, fit and strong, and her heart leaps with passion. How she loved that man. Loves him still. Now, a scene of herself and Elowen running through a field of buttercups, bright with sunshine, daisy chains around their heads and wrists. She remembers it as if it were yesterday. They had such fun times in the days before the conniving bitch stole the love of her life.

As the scenes shut down and darkness enfolds her, she prays to God to spare her, promises she'll leave Trevelyar alone. Promises to be good… but unfortunately for Morvoren, God's not listening.

Chapter thirty-five

att leaves Lavender to sleep for a while longer. It's only just past half six, and she was pretty done in after the tension of visiting Morvoren yesterday evening. Thankfully, the recording worked this time, so they have the confession they need. Incredibly, Lavender managed to capture the relevant bit without implicating herself. She's so clever. After breakfast they are going to take it in to DI Price. Tiptoeing out of the room, he shrugs on his dressing gown and yanks his hair from where it's trapped between the gown and his back, over the collar. It's way past his shoulders now, but Lavender doesn't want him to cut it. Suits him she says.

The kettle and toaster on, Matt goes to the window to open the blinds and notices an envelope shoved under the back door. Lavender's name is scrawled across it in pencil and it's not sealed shut. Should he open it? It's not addressed to him, but he has a feeling it's not good news. Sliding a finger under the flap, he pulls out a scrap of note paper.

Called late last night but you didn't answer. I called four times! Came round earlier on my way to the police station just to deliver this note. If you are at all interested, your grandmother died yesterday evening. Jamie found her at seven when he popped round with her herbs. Police are involved as it looks like she's been poisoned. Ring me if you can be bothered.
Dad

Matt almost drops the letter, his hands are shaking so much. Poisoned. Who the fuck has poisoned Morvoren? Out loud, he says, 'Oh my God.'

'What are you oh my Godding about?' Lavender says as she comes downstairs, stretching and yawning.

Matt shoves the note in his pocket. What does he do now? He can't just spring it on her, can he? 'Er… I've put the toast on. Have a sit down, love.'

She frowns, ties the belt of her bath robe and sits at the table. 'What's going on? You look a bit shifty. Odd.'

Matt smiles and runs her a glass of water. Why, he has no idea – he's seen people do that on TV when they have a bombshell to drop. Or was it hot sweet tea? It might be tea. 'Want tea?' He turns and smiles again.

'Not until you tell me what the hell is wrong. Your smile looks like it's been painted on by a clown.'

Matt concedes defeat. He pulls the note out of his pocket and sits opposite. 'This note was pushed under the door.' He doesn't give it to her, just holds it up. It's Morvoren…' He sighs and hands it to her.

Lavender takes the note but doesn't unfold it. She looks at Matt. 'Is it bad?'

'Yes. I'm so sorry love. I'll get you that tea.'

'No. I don't want any,' she says in a small voice, and unfolds the note. 'Oh my God, Matt. Poisoned? What the hell?' She tosses the note on the table and covers her face with her hands.

He goes round the table and kneels by her chair, pulls her into his arms. 'It's nuts. And how do they know she's been poisoned already? It was only last night. They won't have had time to do a post-mortem will they?'

Into his shoulder, she mumbles, 'I don't know… This can't be happening. Cannot.' Then she jumps up and runs upstairs.

Matt starts after her. 'Hey, where are you going?'

'To get my phone. We put it in the safe, remember? Just to be extra sure because of the bloody recording.'

Matt does remember. After they'd listened to the recording last night, he'd suggested they find a safe place to keep it overnight, just in case something mad happened, like Jamie breaking in.

Lavender had a small safe where she kept the cash float from work – in the spare room cupboard. She'd locked the mobile away and that's why they hadn't heard the calls from her dad.

Moments later, she comes downstairs again, her face ashen, tears streaming down her face, phone pressed to her ear. 'Dad? Yes, I just got the note.' She sinks down on the sofa. 'I can't believe it.' She listens and then sighs. 'But are they sure she was poisoned? Couldn't it have been her illness? Because that seems the most logical to me… No, Dad, of course I'm not a doctor. Okay, calm down, I… Yes I can come down to the station to meet you. I was going to…' She shakes her head in despair at Matt. 'Oh, never mind, see you soon.'

'What were you about to say just then, but changed your mind?' Matt asks.

'I was about to say I was going to the station today anyway with the recording, but it all seems so pointless now. And so heartless given the circumstances. Besides, won't it look a bit suspect, me probably being the last person to have seen her alive?'

Matt releases a long breath and puts his head in his hands. She's right, but the truth must be told. Perhaps he's selfish, but he needs to clear his name and the confession certainly would do that. 'Suspect or not, you didn't do it, Lavender. We need to stick to the plan and turn the recording in.'

'But what about my dad? He'd never forgive me.'

'Maybe not. But at least he'd have solid proof that you were not to blame – that his own mother was an evil old witch who'd stop at nothing to get her revenge.'

'But don't you see, Matt? I was there not long before she died. They might try to say I poisoned her after I got the confession.'

'Hmm, what would be the point in that? You had the confession. Why kill her? You wanted her punished, and my name cleared.'

Lavender nods and ponders this for a few moments. Then she stands up. 'Yeah. Okay, phone DI Price and tell her we want to see her immediately. I'll give her the recording and tell her exactly what happened yesterday before they even have a chance to think about pulling me in for questioning. And we need to make a copy before we do. If the recording goes missing somehow, we're up shit creek.'

Matt takes her in his arms. 'Take a moment. Are you sure you're okay? It must be a huge shock and so sad that a woman who's been in your life for so long is now gone.'

Lavender looks into his eyes. 'It's a shock, yes. But I'm not sad. The old Gran had gone months ago…' She raises her eyebrows. 'If in fact there really was an old Gran. Maybe Morvoren has always been hateful deep down. If she'd lived, she'd have been put in prison probably, after the police got the recording. Might be the best thing all round that she's gone.'

'Might be. But you're allowed to be sad, despite everything she did to you, did to me. Remember what she was like when you were little. Everyone has some good in them somewhere – hang on to the happy memories.'

Lavender brushes away tears and takes his hand. 'Yeah. Come on, let's get this over with. The sooner we do, the sooner we can get on with our lives.'

***

Lavender wishes she'd never come. Wishes she'd thrown the recording in the sea and left well alone. DI Price and DC Vincent listened to the recording, but then questioned her for two hours. Then they asked Matt in and are now questioning him too. Price and Vincent asked her to wait outside the interview room, as they want to have a further 'chat' after they've finished with Matt. Dad popped in and practically accused her of murder after she explained to him that she was at Morvoren's and about the recording. Even if he does eventually believe her, Lavender can't see that they'll ever be the same again.

She sips a cup of water and rehashes the whole sorry mess again. Morvoren came into contact with poison – almost certainly ingested. The doctor who was called out to certify her death was alerted by the blister burns on her lips and a rash on her neck. He said the poison might have triggered a heart attack or stroke, but a post-mortem would be the way forward. In Morvoren's kitchen and living room, half a cup of tea and some fruit juice had been discovered. These were analysed and significant quantities of plant-based poisons were found in them. DI Price had read out their Latin names to Lavender and she knew immediately they were referring to wolfsbane and foxglove. Why the hell would she take those? They were two of the most deadly plants to be found anywhere. It didn't make sense. Surely, Morvoren knew what they were – her brain wasn't that addled…So she must have been poisoned by someone. But that didn't make sense either. Morvoren would have done her best to fight back if someone forced her to drink.

Just then, the door opens and Matt comes out. He has no time to say anything as Lavender is called back in to the interview room immediately. She sits back at the table and the tape is switched on. Once again, the police officers stress she can leave at any time, which right now is exactly what she feels like doing.

'Right, Lavender, this won't take long. It seems like we're not coming up with an awful lot. Matt can't really shed any more light. He corroborates your story and is as baffled as you as to why your grandmother died from poison.' Price scratches her head and does the shoving-the-glasses-up-the-bridge-of-the-nose thing she always does. 'Once again, can you think of anyone who would want to poison Morvoren?'

'As I said before, no. Although, as you know, she wasn't my favourite person, nor Matt's, but we wouldn't poison her. And I've been thinking while I've been outside. My grandmother would have put up a huge fight if someone had forced her to drink it. She might have smelt it, and the taste of it would have been incredibly bitter. In the struggle, her face would have been blistered too, as the liquid was spilt. Did she have facial burns?'

Vincent says, 'Not as far as we're aware.'

'But couldn't it have been a mistake? You said she was going to make a potion for her ailments after you'd gone,' Price asks.

'No way. Anyone who practices herbal lore knows about the dangers from day one. It's one of the first things I learned as a child. Morvoren would never mix up such deadly plants. And where would she get them from? I saw none when I was there… You can find foxglove at this time of year, but it will be few and far between – unless she'd frozen them? That's possible. She might have been planning to bump Matt off with them. Check the freezer.'

'Are you being serious?' Vincent asks.

Lavender shrugs, 'Yes. You heard the tape. But you didn't see her face when she said she'd try to kill Matt again. Pure hatred. It made me shudder.'

'So now you're saying she could have mixed them up? Taken something from the freezer which she thought would help her illness and picked the wrong one?' Price asks.

Lavender ponders on this. 'It is possible I suppose, because the frozen batch might not be as recognisable as the fresh. But even so… it is a very long shot. Surely she would have labelled it carefully.'

Price nods. 'I'll get someone to take a look at the freezer's contents.'

'Still feels far-fetched to me,' Lavender says, almost to herself as she thinks aloud. 'If I had to guess, I'd say that she decided to take her own life. Why, I have no idea, because she seemed pretty pleased with herself when I left. Perhaps she'd just realised what she'd done and wanted control of when and how she went. Doubtful though.'

'It's a possibility. And as you say, Lavender, if someone had tried to physically poison her, she'd have struggled,' Vincent says.

Price finishes her notes and sits back in her seat. 'Okay, I think we're done for now. We'll know exactly how your grandmother died when we get the post-mortem results. It'll take a while, so we'll let you know when we know.'

'What about evidence from the recording? My grandmother has escaped prosecution, but she did say Jamie helped her. Will you arrest him?'

'We'll look into it again. But he has an alibi, and we only have the word of your grandmother. You kind of recognised him but you couldn't say it was Jamie one hundred per cent. She's no longer with us, so... not sure the Crown Prosecution Service would want to run with it.'

'What, so he just gets away with attempted murder and the manslaughter of Jessica Blake?'

'As I said, I'll look into it, have a word with my superior officer and see what we can do.'

Lavender can tell by the tone in Price's voice she is just placating her. Damn it. Morvoren decided to top herself, so she's got away without suffering humiliation and being vilified by everyone she knows. The easy way out, some say. And Jamie Penhale gets off scot-free. So unfair.

Matt's waiting outside. She tells him what's happened and he's furious too. Then he says, 'We did everything we could. I think it would do us both good to get away for a few days. Fancy a trip to London? We'll do all the touristy things and perhaps visit my family before coming home. What do you say?'

Lavender says, 'I think that would be perfect. Right now, I want to be as far away from all this as possible.'

Chapter thirty-six

London is everything Lavender dreamt it would be. Her first time in the capital has been amazing and in four days, they'd managed to get all the main sights on their list seen. Matt took more photos of her looking enthralled, excited and amazed than he did of the tourist attractions themselves.

Outside the hotel, she helps Matt load the suitcases in the car. They are due to visit Matt's parents for dinner later and his grandparents will be there too. Lavender is thrilled Matt thinks so much of her that he wants her to meet his folks, but her stomach is churning on a sea of nerves. What if they don't like her? She's just a young Cornish girl from a small village – what does she have in common with them? Okay, his grandparents are from that village, but they'd been away for many years.

Lavender looks at her hands and splays her fingers. Not for the first time she wishes she'd been born without the extra skin between them. She mentions this to Matt and he says he wouldn't have her any other way. Mostly she never thinks about it – just when she meets new people. He also says not to worry about meeting his folks because they would love her. Lavender smiles, she knows he's just trying to reassure her, but she feels a bit better about the visit now.

On the drive to Hackney, a text comes through from her dad to say that the post-mortem results came through quicker than they expected. Morvoren died of a heart attack due to the ingested poisons. Nothing was found in the freezer. Lavender knew that was a long shot and she also knows both plants slow down the heart rate and can bring on paralysis and heart failure. Morvoren would have suffered and death wouldn't have been immediate.

Even though Lavender feels sorry for her, as she would any person who'd had a tough passing, she feels mostly distant and cold about Morvoren. It's to be expected given the circumstances. And all those years they were so close. But had they been? Was it all really about Lavender being under her thumb? Scared to go against her? Had she confused love with fear? Whatever the answer, she was under her control enough to believe all the nonsense about Matt. If she hadn't been, they'd be in a better place now. But it's no use going over the past. What's done is done.

Johnny and Maria, Matt's parents, are so welcoming, Lavender wonders why she was nervous. They're down to earth, funny and warm and she feels likes she's known them for years. His grandparents aren't here yet, but she's less worried about meeting them – they're Cornish after all. And if truth be known, she's excited about meeting Elowen in particular – she's the woman who incited the wrath of Morvoren and got away with it. Must be quite a character. She's on her second glass of wine and hoovering up the nibbles when they arrive. Terry's an older version of Johnny and Matt, and still handsome. She can see why Morvoren fell for him. Elowen comes in behind and makes a beeline straight for her.

'Lavender! My God, maid, you're beautiful!' Elowen says, and pulls Lavender into a hug. Then she holds her at arm's length and scrutinises her face. Lavender does the same and is amazed at how the woman's eyes are so like Matt's. Maria's are too, but Elowen's have notes of the ocean on a sunny day in their depths. Her hair is styled into a no-nonsense dark bob, shot through with streaks of white. A trim figure too. Matt said she was seventy-seven the other day, but she looks a lot younger.

'Thank you. You're not so bad yourself,' Lavender says with a smile, and allows herself to be led into a large conservatory which overlooks a long rambling garden.

'That's it now, Matt.' Terry chuckles and slaps his grandson on the shoulder. 'Two Cornish women having a chat – we won't see them for the rest of the evening!'

Elowen sits on a big blue leather sofa and pats the seat next to her. 'I can't tell you how pleased I am to meet you at last. I've heard lots about you – my boy is quite smitten I think.' She gives Lavender a wink.

'Oh, I hope so.' Lavender laughs and feels her cheeks heat up. 'I'm pleased to meet you as well. I've heard quite a lot about you over the years too.' Lavender laughs again and then wonders if it was the right thing to say because the conversation will automatically turn to Morvoren, won't it? Matt told Elowen she'd died over the phone the other day. Not the happiest of topics.

A few clouds scud across Elowen's blue eyes and she sighs. 'I'm sure you have. Me and Morvoren had a dodgy history, as I'm sure you know… and I won't pretend I'm sorry she's no longer with us either. Hope you're not offended.' She puts a hand on Lavender's.

How refreshingly honest. Lavender smiles. 'I'm not offended because I feel the same.' She goes to pat the other woman's hand and notices a dressing on her thumb. 'Oh, you hurt yourself?'

Elowen looks at her thumb. 'Burnt it on the cooker. It's not too bad. Anyway, tell me about yourself. I hear you're a champion picker! Can't tell you how much I miss the Cornish countryside. In fact I might have a bit of a surprise to spring on you lot after dinner.'

***

Johnny puts down his knife and fork and stares at his mother. 'Bloody, hell, Ma. Moving to Cornwall…That's a bit of a shock.'

Terry nods. 'It was to me too, when she came back from her jaunt to that yoga retreat and said she'd made her mind up about going back home. I thought she'd gone a bit gaga at first, didn't I, El?' He gives his wife a wink. 'I said, "What do you mean? You are home, love." Didn't I?'

Elowen smiles. 'You did. Being at the retreat made me think about my life… what I really wanted. And you soon came round to my way of thinking, I noticed.'

Terry pushes his plate away and rubs his tummy. 'Arr. That's because I've a hankering for windswept beaches and rolling hills. We always said we'd return to our beloved Cornwall one day.'

Matt raises his glass. 'Well I for one can't tell you how happy this news makes me. Here's to a swift homecoming!'

They all clink glasses and repeat the toast. Lavender's pleased too, but notices Maria and Johnny aren't as thrilled as everyone else.

Johnny takes a big glug of his wine and says in a voice full of emotion, 'I know it's what you both want – but we're gonna miss you, aren't we, Maria? First Matt, now you two old sods.'

Elowen says, 'And we'll miss you two. Nothing stopping you following in our footsteps, is there? We've talked about it in the past.'

'Just our jobs. I know we talked about it, but talking and doing are a bit different,' Maria says, and pulls a face at her husband. He nods and sighs.

Terry says, 'You're a shop assistant, Maria, and you're an electrician, Johnny. They have those types of jobs in Cornwall, you know.'

'Yes, it's so easy, isn't it? Just sell a house, buy another and get a job – move nearly three hundred miles,' Johnny says.

'Didn't say it was easy, lad. Things that's easy aren't generally worth having.'

After dinner, Lavender, Matt and Elowen are having coffee in the living room. They'd offered to help with the dishes and been refused. The others are clearing things away in the kitchen and talking about the logistics of a move to Cornwall. Lavender asks Elowen where they plan to move and if they have any properties in mind.

'Nothing specific in mind yet. But we are definitely moving back to St Agnes. We've been looking on Rightmove and there seems to be some lovely properties to choose from. House prices here are ridiculous, so we'll be able to buy a lot for our money back home.'

Matt nods. 'I need to think along the buying lines soon. As you know I rented until I decided St Agnes was a place I'd want to stay. Which it is, despite all the crap that's happened since I moved there. Bloody arson, murder and mayhem. Who'd have thought it? I'm effectively homeless. Or I would be if it wasn't for this lovely lady.' He inclines his head to Lavender and smiles.

'And we all know why so much crap has happened to you, don't we?' Lavender says, feeling partly to blame. She can feel Elowen's eyes on her and it makes her uncomfortable. 'I'm sorry Morvoren was able to trick me so easily.'

Matt shakes his head. 'Don't you dare blame yourself. Morvoren used you. Used Jamie too – though he didn't need much encouragement by all accounts. Not sure he's the sharpest tool in the box, either. Bastard looks like he's going to get away with it through lack of evidence.'

'Let's hope not. And Matt's right. Morvoren was always a manipulative… person.' Lavender could tell Elowen wanted to use another word, but perhaps thought it disrespectful. 'She was clever, spiteful and cruel. Nothing you could have done would have prevented it. You mustn't feel responsible.'

'Thanks, Elowen. I can tell you knew her well,' Lavender says, with a lump in her throat.

'I did.' Elowen sips her coffee and makes herself more comfortable on the sofa. 'We were the best of friends as girls. Such a damn shame it all ended like it did. And a shame she decided to end her life in that painful way. God knows what she was doing drinking a potion like that… because suicide's the only conclusion I can come to.'

Lavender sits forward, eager to hear more. 'Me too. The police tried to suggest she was poisoned by someone!'

Elowen's eyes grow wide. 'There's no way that would happen. Morvoren would have put up a fight once she tasted the tea. But why put it in her tea *and* in the cranberry juice? It's as if she wanted a choice of drink. Maybe the potion mixed with juice wasn't as bitter?' She shrugs. 'Anyway, we'll never know now.'

***

224

On the way home the next day in the car, something's bugging Lavender and she can't shake it. It's an idea that's been buzzing around ever since their conversation with Elowen last night, but it's too ludicrous for words. And she saw something too. Something she wishes she could unsee. In the end, she can bear it no longer and says to Matt, 'When you phoned Elowen to tell her Morvoren was dead, did you say which drink the poison was found in?'

Matt frowns. 'Er, yeah. I said tea and fruit juice. Why?'

Lavender feels a chilly finger trace its way down her spine. In a trembling voice barely louder than a whisper, she says, 'Yes, that's what we were told. Tea and fruit juice. Price and Vincent just said fruit juice.'

Matt checks his mirrors and indicates into the outside lane. 'Right... not sure where you're going with this.'

'Because last night Elowen said it was cranberry juice...'

Matt frowns again and comes out of the fast lane. 'Was it cranberry, then?'

'Matt, pull into the services ahead. I've got a theory that's not safe for you to hear while driving at seventy-odd miles an hour.' He sighs and does as she asks.

***

In the services, Matt's raking his fingers through his hair so hard Lavender's worried he's going to pull it out by the roots. 'But this is bloody ridiculous!' he says, glaring across the table at her. 'You're sat there suggesting that my gran killed yours. What, because she knew what kind of fruit juice the poison was in?'

'But how could she have guessed? It's not like saying orange juice or Ribena, is it?'

Matt opens his hands in exasperation. 'No, I guess not – but it's not *that* uncommon, is it?'

'No. But–'

'And if the police didn't tell us what type of fruit juice it was, how do you know it *was* cranberry juice? Gran might like cranberry juice herself and just said it by mistake.'

Lavender swallows hard. She hates hurting him like this, but he has to know. 'Because Morvoren only ever drank cranberry juice these past few years. She said anything else gave her heartburn. Your gran couldn't have known that. She also has a dressing on her thumb which she says was a burn from a cooker... but...'

Matt covers his face with his hands and says through his fingers, 'But what?'

'But later, as we were about to leave and she stretched her arms up to hug you, I noticed her sleeve ride up above the dressing. There was a fading rash, Matt. It looked a lot like skin does if you brush it against wolfsbane.'

Matt's hands fall away from his face. 'And there's no other explanation for it then? It has to be a wolfsbane rash?'

'No. It could be perfectly innocent. But I think—'

'I think you think too much. I don't want to hear any more, Lavender. My gran would never do something like this, no matter what Morvoren had done. Besides, how could she have got her to drink the stuff? You and gran both said it had to be suicide because of that.'

Lavender has no answers there. 'I don't know. Perhaps we never will... and Matt. If it does ever come to light that it was Elowen, I wouldn't blame her. She's a good woman and would do anything to protect her own. Especially her "beautiful boy".'

Matt shakes his head in bewilderment and stares out of the window at the traffic.

Chapter thirty-seven

'Matt! Matt! You'll never guess what!' Lavender yells, as she runs outside the cottage to where Matt's balancing on a ladder, busy putting up Christmas lights.

'Um... the end of the world is nigh and we're all going to hell in a handcart?'

'No, but Jamie Penhale is!'

Matt looks down at her and the wind whips his hair across his eyes. 'Eh?' He pulls it free. 'What do you mean?'

'DI Price just phoned. She tried to phone you, but you obviously didn't hear up there in the wind. Jamie Penhallow has been arrested and has confessed to his part in the fire and the night you were drugged. He's trying to implicate me, too, but they're having none of it.'

Matt comes down the ladder. 'That's fantastic!' he says, his eyes shining. 'But how come they arrested him? Did new evidence come to light?'

'Not to do with our case, no.' Lavender can hardly contain herself, but she wants to make her announcement even more dramatic than it already is. 'Oh, Matt. You'll never believe it, but he murdered Annie! He murdered his grandmother.'

Matt drops the bundle of Christmas lights. 'What?! Why?'

'Come inside and I'll tell you.'

Inside, in front of the fire, they drink brandy and eat mince pies while Lavender explains that poor Annie's little holiday away had been only as far as a hole in the ground in her own back garden. The neighbour who'd told the police she'd gone away on holiday heard it from Jamie. She hadn't seen Annie herself. It was the same neighbour, a Mrs Fairchild, who'd let her dog off the leash a few days ago, and it had scooted down the side of Annie's house and started to dig furiously at a patch of lawn.

Mrs Fairchild tried to pull the dog away, but it kept running back. On closer inspection, she could see the turf looked loose, and the ground disturbed. Something didn't feel right, so she allowed the dog to keep working away until he'd uncovered a hand sticking out of the soil. She then phoned the police and later, in questioning, she'd explained that Jamie was the one who told her his gran had gone away.

They'd arrested him, and he said he'd nothing to do with it. But apparently his dad had later co me forward and said he suspected Jamie of killing his mother-in-law. He'd been acting weird for days and kept saying odd things. His dad retracted his alibi for the fire and everything else.

'Bloody hell!' Matt says, knocking back the brandy and pouring another.

'I know,' Lavender says, holding out her own glass for a refill. 'Apparently, Jamie then confessed he'd killed Annie because she was going to tell the police about him when he'd popped round to her house to see her one day. Morvoren had apparently told Annie that Jamie helped her set the fire and placed my bracelet in Jessica's hand. She was appalled at what he'd done and ashamed of him. She was also going to retract the alibi for the night you were drugged. He tried to convince her not to, but she wouldn't listen. So, in a fury, Jamie pushed her and she fell, cracking her head on the edge of the kitchen table. Death was instant. Then he buried her in the back garden.'

Matt shook his head. 'Not the sharpest tool in the box, as I said the other day.'

'Nope. But this all this is fantastic! Apart from poor Annie of course.'

'Why?'

She looks at him, bewildered. 'Because it means your name is cleared for the night you were drugged! He's admitted it was him and Morvoren. You can hold your head up in the village now. You might even get your job back if there's still a vacancy.'

Matt covers his mouth as if he's just realised. 'My God. Yes! My head was too full of all this to even think straight. Hallelujah!'

She laughs, and they embrace and he plants brandy kisses all over her face. Then they sit back in companionable silence. Lavender sips her brandy and looks into the flames. The whole thing is still sinking in.

After a few minutes Matt says, 'I had a call earlier too. Not sure you'll want to hear from who though.'

Lavender's heart sinks. What now? 'Just tell me.'

'Gran. She and Granddad are coming down for Christmas. Mum and Dad are coming too, but a bit later. They've all booked into a hotel. They'll use the time to look at a few properties… and see us of course. Not sure you'll want to see Gran?'

Lavender's heart stops sinking. 'Of course I do. As I said, if she was to blame for Morvoren's death, I won't think any less of her. Morvoren tried to kill you and was going to try again – she got what she deserved.'

***

With Christmas dinner over, everyone retires to the hotel lounge to let their food go down and have coffee. Terry's already in a comfy chair nodding off, hands clasped over his extended tummy. Elowen's showing Maria and Johnny the details of a lovely house overlooking the sea, and Matt is pondering on an extension to the cottage. He keeps whipping out a little sketch pad and showing Lavender the details and rough drawings he's made. A promise to leave the DIY alone on Christmas Day is well on the way to being broken, she thinks. It's nice that he's so excited about it though.

A few days ago, she mentioned that he didn't seem to be in a hurry to look for a house, unlike his grandparents. He'd taken it the wrong way at first, thinking she wanted him out. Lavender had soon put him right, and told him she was happy to have him living with her as long as he liked. Forever, hopefully. He'd then flushed with relief and said he'd been plucking up the courage to ask if he could do exactly that. Then they'd talked long into the night about Matt investing his money from the sale of his London flat and extending and modernising her little cottage. It needed a few structural tweaks, and a new bathroom and kitchen wouldn't go amiss.

The hotel looks out over the bay and Lavender goes to stand at the huge picture window, watching the white caps ride the tops of the waves. It's one of those sunny, clear winter days, but bitter sharp with cold. She wants to be out on the beach wrapped in the new red woollen coat that Matt bought her for Christmas, striding across the sand, letting the wind make streamers of her hair. She goes over to the sofa where Matt's sitting and scoops up her coat.

'Just popping down to the beach for a walk. I expect you have plans to look through?' She smiles and drops a kiss on his forehead.

He looks up at her and smiles back. 'Am I that transparent?'

'You are, my dear, and I love you just the way you are.' They'd started saying the 'L' word to each other quite often lately. It still felt strange – but good strange.

'Love you too, Lavender Blue.'

She rolls her eyes and shrugs her coat on. As she's walking to the door, Elowen calls her over, asks what she's doing. 'Just going for a walk on the beach. It's a lovely day for it.' Lavender buttons up her coat and pulls gloves out of her pocket.

'Do you know, I was thinking the same. Can I join you?'

'That would be lovely,' Lavender says. And it will. She has an affinity with Elowen – must be the picking history they share. They link arms and head for the beach.

Half an hour later, the wind has put roses in their cheeks and made bird's nests of their hair. The two of them decide to sit on a huge flat rock at the end of the beach and watch a few hardy surfers take to the ocean.

Elowen shudders. 'How they can go in the Atlantic on such an arctic day, I don't know. It's a wonder they can feel their vitals afterwards.'

Lavender laughs. 'You wouldn't get me in there for quids.'

'Me neither.'

Lavender takes a glance at Elowen and then away. Suddenly it's become really important for her to know the truth about how Morvoren met her end. The more Lavender's thought about it over the past few weeks, the more she's convinced Elowen had a hand in it. But how can she broach it? Tentatively, she says, 'It's such a relief that Jamie Penhale has confessed. Matt and I can look to the future with real hope now.'

Elowen links her arm through Lavender's. 'It is a relief. And I'm so happy you two are making a serious go of things. The descendants of Kenver Penhallow and Jory Trevelyar are now united in love. At last the Trevelyar–Penhallow feud is dead and buried.'

Before she can stop herself, Lavender says, 'Yes, like Morvoren. She'll be spinning in her grave.'

Elowen looks quickly at Lavender and then back at the ocean. 'She will. I didn't think it would be appropriate for me to attend the funeral. Sorry, Lavender.'

'Don't apologise. I went, but I didn't want to. It was a tiny affair – she wasn't well liked, as you know. Dad apologised, but it won't be the same between us now.'

'It could have all have been so different.'

'It could.' Lavender sighs and wonders how to proceed. *Nothing for it – jump right in.* 'I expect you'll think I'm heartless, but if someone did somehow organise her death, I wouldn't blame them. She was going to try to kill Matt, after all.'

Elowen stops and stares at Lavender intently. 'I wouldn't blame them, either.'

'But I don't get how anyone could have forced her to drink the potion… so it must have been suicide?'

Looking away at a surfer bouncing along the waves again, Elowen says, 'Not necessarily. I could see a scenario whereby Morvoren might have made her tea and then went outside to get something... perhaps she was distracted by a noise out there?'

Lavender looks at the surfer too, her heart thumping in her chest. 'Okay... then what?'

'Whoever had the potion might have then sneaked inside and mixed it in her tea – put some in a glass of juice, too, for good measure, and sneaked out again,' Elowen says to the sea.

'But how could that person have known Morvoren wouldn't smell the potion, or take a sip and spit it straight out again?' Lavender can hardly speak as her breath catches in her throat.

'That person couldn't know. They probably just hoped for the best. Morvoren wouldn't be expecting the tea she'd just made with her own hands to be laced with anything, would she? Perhaps she took a big drink and then realised too late. Perhaps she drank the juice to hopefully flush it out. Who knows?'

Lavender takes a deep breath and tries to calm herself. Has Elowen just told her she was actually the person with the potion? One last push. 'Funny how you knew the juice was cranberry...'

Elowen smiles at the ocean. 'Hmm. Matt asked me about that the other week when he phoned. He told me you were puzzled as to how I knew. I told him I had no idea... just came to me. People always did say I was a witch – had a sixth sense, knew stuff others didn't.' Then she looks Lavender directly in the eye. 'I think you have drawn your own conclusion, haven't you?'

Lavender nods. 'Yes,' she says in a small voice.

'Then I think your conclusions are right. Might be as well not to speak of it again though, my dear.'

Lavender nods again. 'Your secret's safe with me.'

Elowen stands and brushes sand from her trousers. 'Okay, these old bones are getting stiff with cold. Let's go back for a hot toddy... And I'm looking forward to the spring. We'll be living here by then hopefully. You and me can go picking together. Won't that be fun?'

'It will be wonderful.' Lavender stands and feels her heart lighten. 'We can have competitions to see who can make the best potions…'

'No contest, young'un. It will be me.' Elowen sets off up the beach, laughing.

'We'll see about that!' Lavender runs after her and links arms with her again. As the sun sinks lower in the sky, Lavender notices their shadows are lengthening and overlapping as they walk. She smiles and leads the way into the hotel.

The End

Acknowledgements

Thanks as always to the entire wonderful Bloodhound team. A special thanks to Heather for reading and deciding very quickly that The Feud was a winner. Thanks also to fellow Bloodhound writer and big friend, Trish Dixon for reading an early version and for her general craziness and unfailing support. Also to Betsy, Fred and Sumaira for their tireless work behind the scenes.

And last but certainly not least, a huge thanks to my husband and wider family. Without you all your incredible support there would be no book.

Lightning Source UK Ltd.
Milton Keynes UK
UKHW010638220419
341406UK00001B/26/P

9 781912 986200